WHITEHORN'S
WINDMILL

or, The Unusual Events Once upon a Time in the Land of Paudruvė

OTHER TITLES IN THE SERIES

On the cover: "Windmill" by Piet Mondrian, 1917

WHITEHORN'S
WINDMILL

or
The Unusual Events
Once upon a Time
in the Land of Paudruvė

Kazys Boruta

Translated and with an afterword by
Elizabeth Novickas

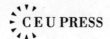

CEU PRESS

Central European University Press

Budapest • New York

English translation copyright © Elizabeth Novickas, 2010
First published in Lithuanian as *Baltaragio Malūnas* in 1945

Published in 2010 by

Central European University Press
An imprint of the
Central European University Share Company
Nádor utca 11, H-1051 Budapest, Hungary
Tel: +36-1-327-3138 or 327-3000
Fax: +36-1-327-3183
E-mail: ceupress@ceu.hu
Website: www.ceupress.com

400 West 59th Street, New York NY 10019, USA
Tel: +1-212-547-6932
Fax: +1-646-557-2416
E-mail: mgreenwald@sorosny.org

This publication is financed by the "Books from Lithuania" from the resources
of the Foundation of Culture Support of the Republic of Lithuania.

BOOKS
FROM
LITHUANIA

ISBN 978-963-9776-71-5
ISSN 1418-0162

Library of Congress Cataloging-in-Publication Data

Boruta, Kazys, 1905-1965.
  [Baltaragio malunas. English]
  Whitehorn's windmill, or, The unusual events once upon a time in the land of
Paudruve / Kazys Boruta ; translated and with an afterword by Elizabeth Novickas.
      p. cm. -- (CEU Press classics, ISSN 1418-0162)
  First published in Lithuanian as Baltaragio malunas in 1945.
  ISBN 978-9639776715 (pbk.)
  1. Millers--Fiction. 2. Fathers and daughters--Fiction. 3. Mate selection--Fiction.
4. Lithuania--Social life and customs--Fiction. I. Novickas, Elizabeth. II. Title. III.
Title: Whitehorn's windmill. IV. Title: Unusual events once upon a time in the land
of Paudruve. V. Series.

  PG8721.B6B313 2010
  891'.9233--dc22

                                        2010010419

Printed in Hungary by
Akadémiai Nyomda, Martonvásár

Contents

I

Whitehorn's windmill stood atop a steep bluff of Lake Udruvė. From time immemorial it had waved its huge wings as though it wanted to lift itself up and fly away from the precipice.

Lower down, at the foot of the hill, sprawled the clear waters of Lake Udruvė, which branched between the surrounding pine-covered hills and the valleys cloaked in the duckweed of the bogs. Whitehorn's mill was on the highest shore, and its wings, flashing from afar through the blue pine treetops, would turn at the slightest breeze wafting from the lake.

The waters of Lake Udruvė constantly lapped at the crumbling slope of the hill where the mill stood, as though intending to wash it away together with the windmill. Nevertheless, Whitehorn's fathers' fathers had lived out their days there; the lake constantly lapped at the shore and the mill stood on the precipice as it had always stood, its wings spun and hummed constantly. The humming of the mill blended with the murmur of the lake into a single, intoxicating sound, which enchanted with its mysteriousness.

Perhaps it was this sound that had bewitched the last miller of Paudruvė, Whitey Whitehorn, who lived alone in the mill with his only daughter Jurga. The old widower so loved his only child that he wouldn't let her out of his sight day or night. Sometimes he would beam as if some unusual good fortune shone upon him; sometimes he would be so sad and anxious that the wreath of gray hairs around his bare head would grow even whiter. What the old miller thought about, or how he felt, no one knew, unless perhaps they sensed that his beautiful daughter was all his joy, his worry, and his life.

But the daughter gave little thought to what made her father brighten or turn gray when he looked at her. To her, life was one gay, youthful lark, and her every step echoed with the laughter of her eighteen carefree years. She was the merriest girl in the entire village of Paudruvė, who with her ringing laugh and gay alluring glances had driven more than one suitor out of his mind, and promised to do the same to many more. She was a real mischief-maker, the widower's only child, and spoiled; she made a joke of everything and was the first to laugh.

Many wanted to steal that laugh of hers for a lifetime, but nothing came of it, despite untold efforts to seduce her. The gay, carefree Jurga would slip loose from love's every entanglement and simply laugh all the merrier. One after the other, suitors with their matchmakers journeyed to Whitehorn's mill, but they would never succeed in getting there. They would barely reach the serpentine shoreline of Lake Udruvė when somehow, and without themselves understanding what had happened, they would go astray, even though Whitehorn's mill could be seen a mile off.

It was some sort of an unsolvable mystery that stumped even the cleverest, and no one could understand what, in the end, was blocking the matchmakers' path to Whitehorn's daughter. On even the clearest afternoon a fog, which would turn the brightest day into the darkest night, would suddenly rise from the lake, or the horses themselves, spooked at who knows what, would turn from the straight road onto some side track and drive off only heaven knows where, or else the bridges over the inlets of the lake—and there wasn't just one, but seven of them—would suddenly disappear, or something else would happen, so that the matchmakers, instead of arriving at Whitehorn's mill, found themselves on the opposite side of Lake Udruvė, or worse yet, right next to the mill in Paudruvė's oozy bogs, where they would struggle until dawn without finding a way out. Only at daybreak would they realize that they were stomping around in the mire at the foot of the hill, and return home cursing and empty-handed.

And so, ever since the time one landowner's son lost his horses in Paudruvė's bogs and nearly met his own end, along with his matchmaker, defending themselves from assorted apparitions that hounded them and led them astray all night long, luring them into the muck of the quagmire—and then another proud old bachelor with his matchmaker drove off the steep bluff straight into Lake Udruvė, smashing up the wagon and breaking the neck of the best matchmaker in the district, who shortly afterwards surrendered his last deceitful breath to God—after that no one, not even the boldest, dared to go calling on Whitehorn's daughter with a matchmaker.

3

No one really knew what was going on. Gossip got around that Whitehorn's beautiful daughter kept company with the witches of Lake Udruvė, and that the devil himself had taken her under his wing. Others even ventured to name the devil: none other than Pinčukas, the devil of Paudruvė's bogs—well known to everybody and Whitehorn's nearest neighbor. Still others, unwilling to believe such talk, maintained that Whitehorn himself was to blame, in that loving his only daughter to such an extreme, and being himself a sorcerer (talk that he had some sort of dealings with devils and other spirits had been going about for some time), he had cast all sorts of spells and traps so that the suitors and their matchmakers never arrived to snatch his daughter away.

No one knew how things really were. Jurga would merely laugh when she heard talk of that sort, and old Whitehorn was as silent as the tomb. If someone persisted in asking him about the suitors and their matchmakers' misfortunes, Whitehorn simply shrugged his shoulders.

"They were probably too drunk to find their way," he would sometimes answer. "The mill is on the hill—you can see it from a long way off, even from the other side of the lake. So how can you get lost? People drive to the mill every day, and no one gets lost."

This was true. You could drive to the mill day or night and never get lost, but with a matchmaker don't even try—you'd surely break your neck. No one could fathom why this was so. Whitehorn himself had an idea, but there was nothing he could do. In the meantime, his daughter grew more beautiful by the day, and although

4

she sometimes expected matchmakers with suitors, she waited for them in vain. Then Jurga's merry eyes unconsciously grew somber and the laughter died on her lips. Seeing this, her father shut himself up in the mill more and more often, pondering something, but not coming up with any solution, merely getting grayer. He knew what was going on and why the matchmakers couldn't get to the mill, and if at first he didn't take it seriously and was even pleased, now, when he sometimes noticed his daughter's sadness, his conscience gnawed at him, but he was as silent as the grave.

And then that sanctimonious old maid, Uršulė Muddy from Švendubrė's almshouse—who had lived at Whitehorn's mill for years and had had some peculiar things happen to her there—went and opened her big mouth. Before no one had wanted to believe her; but now, with these unfathomable things happening, many people were inclined to believe even an old biddy like her.

II

That sanctimonious old biddy Uršulė—that shriveled and sour little woman, eternally dissatisfied and mean as a hornet—returned home to the mill one morning at dawn covered with muck from Paudruvė Bog, and then, scolding all the while, fled Whitehorn's house, where she'd been the housekeeper for many years, and moved into Švendubrė's Almshouse for Pious Ladies, so as to be safe from any more frightful incidents.

She blamed Whitehorn, claiming that he, the old sorcerer, wanted her, a maid sworn to chastity, to make a match with none other than the devil himself, who had long since lived in Paudruvė's bogs and went by the name of Pinčukas.

There was no way to know what had really happened, and Uršulė herself wasn't telling the whole truth, since in fact she didn't understand it all herself, or if she did, then her old maid's modesty wouldn't let her say. It was just that one day, when her patience with knocking about the old miller's house had simply run out (she had, in fact, lost her hopes of marrying Whitehorn and becoming a real miller's wife, something she had been dreaming about fruitlessly for a long time), a sin occurred—the terrible words had unintentionally sprung from her lips, that she would take the devil himself, just so she wouldn't have to waste any more time at Whitehorn's house, where her youth had withered away in vain.

When he heard these words uttered in frustration, Whitehorn was pleased for some reason, and even thoroughly cheered up, which was a rare thing for him.

"Very well," he said, "I can arrange it. Our neighbor Pinčukas is moping away in the bogs without a wife."

Shocked, Uršulė crossed herself and then made the sign of the cross over Whitehorn.

"Begone!" she said. "Don't you know I've made a vow to live in chastity?"

Then Whitehorn laughed and merrily declared:

"That's nothing," he said. "Vows are vows, but when you lay your eyes on a suitor with a matchmaker, you'll forget all about them."

6

Uršulė got angry and said nothing more to White-horn, but Whitehorn didn't even notice the absence of her chatter; he merely went on about his business. He walked about mysteriously, with a cunning smile, as though he was getting ready to deceive someone and the very thought of it cheered him.

The treachery wasn't long in coming. The next Saturday evening, at sunset, matchmaker's bells began ringing. Those bells always went straight to Uršulė's heart, and now she stopped in the middle of the yard, watching to see which farmstead the matchmaker would pull into. It never even occurred to her to think of herself; instead she thought of all the richest and prettiest brides in Paudruvė, but look—the matchmaker went right up to the mill, as if to turn in there.

"Did they get lost?" This thought cheered Uršulė because she was perpetually furious with the matchmakers, since they had never once arrived with a suitor for her.

At that very moment, while Uršulė stood gaping in surprise and rejoicing that the matchmakers had lost their way, the bay steeds flew into the yard and a gilded carriage stopped by the rue garden.

"What's this now?" Uršulė grew faint.

Out of the carriage stepped a serious gentleman with a gray beard and a young gentleman with a smart little hat. Both of them bowed to Uršulė, and the older one asked:

"Is this, by any chance, Squire Whitehorn's renowned estate?"

"Oh, no, sir," said Uršulė, more dead than alive, "It's just plain Whitehorn, and it's not an estate, it's a mill."

"Just what we're looking for," said the graybeard, and bowed even lower. "Will you take in some travel-weary visitors?"

"You're very welcome," answered Whitehorn, who had appeared from the mill. "We've been waiting for our honored guests for quite some time."

Whitehorn then led these unusual visitors to the parlor, while Uršulė hid in the pantry, terribly ill at ease. Could this be her long-awaited prince, arrived at last?

In the meantime, the gray-bearded matchmaker, barely setting foot into the parlor, without even taking a seat, began his oration standing by the door.

"I've driven along the lakes, past the bogs, and I found a little rooster," he said. "The little rooster crows and fusses, he's looking for a speckled hen... perhaps we will find her here?"

"Just exactly so," answered Whitehorn, and he led Uršulė out of the pantry. "Isn't this the one you're looking for?"

"The very one," answered the pleased matchmaker, while the suitor crowed with joy like a rooster and spun around in a circle.

At that point Uršulė blushed as red as a poppy and couldn't utter a word. She glanced out of the corner of her eye—the suitor was unspeakably handsome. Her heart throbbed and she could barely stand on her feet; things seemed to spin in front of her eyes.

The couple was seated at the table, upon which immediately appeared the appropriate bottle decorated with a green sprig of rue. Of what happened afterwards in the parlor, Uršulė herself would never remember;

some madness came over her and she completely lost her head. Now she knows perfectly well that it was all a plot put together by that old sorcerer Whitehorn and his friend, Pinčukas of Paudruvė Bog, to make her break her vow of chastity.

However, at the time Uršulė, utterly stunned, didn't understand a thing, and she only remembers she drank sweet mead with the long-bearded matchmaker (just where had that one come from?), and her heart melted at the suitor's loving words. She was so happy, happier than she had ever been in her life (truly she must have been bewitched!), and she hasn't the slightest idea of how long all this lasted. It was only later that she re-membered, like a dream, how she had left the parlor dizzy with happiness, the gray-bearded matchmaker leading her by one arm, the suitor by the other, and he so handsome, so loving, that you couldn't have imagined it even in your dreams. Behind them followed that shameless Whitehorn—a distant relative, but worse than an enemy!—smiling treacherously and looking pleased about something, but as far as Uršulė was concerned he might as well not even have been there. But while she was leaving, she noticed the suitor gave him some sort of paper, which he cheerfully tucked into his jacket. That was probably when he sold her virginity, while she, poor thing, didn't have a clue.

So the stunned Uršulė was planted in the gilded car-riage; next to her on the right sat the graybeard, and on the left—the gallant suitor. The bay steeds could hardly stand still by the porch; their ears twitched and their eyes flashed lightning. The matchmaker said:

"We're off for the banns!"

"Best of luck!" Whitehorn wished them.

The bay steeds leapt from the spot like dragons, the ground thundered, and the carriage flew off as if caught up in a whirlwind. Frightened and excited, Uršulė didn't even have time to shed a tear for her maidenhood, since everything happened so quickly.

It was Uršulė's good fortune that in her fright she managed to cross herself. At once lightning flashed across the heavens in a cross, and suddenly everything vanished. Neither the carriage nor the matchmaker with the suitor remained, as if they had never been, and the startled Uršulė found she was in the middle of Pinčukas' swamp, having fallen out of a feeding-trough and sunk up to her armpits in duckweed. Not only that, but something was pulling her hard by the legs, intending to submerge her entirely.

It was then that Uršulė understood to whom Whitehorn had wanted to betroth her, and she began shouting for the intercession of all the saints, and particularly the Innocent Maiden of Švendubrė, to whom she had made her vows and who sheltered innocent maidens and guarded their chastity. But because Švendubrė was too far away, or perhaps because it was a dark, stormy night, only a hellish cackling answered Uršulė's cry, and with her very own eyes she saw the devil of Paudruvė's quagmire, Pinčukas.

"Scream, or don't scream," he said, showing up as suddenly as an apparition, "It will come to nothing. You were promised to me a long time ago and you're going to be mine."

Pinčukas made a move to lovingly hug his betrothed and kiss her, but Uršulė angrily shoved him away.

"What do you mean, I'm yours?" she said, seriously incensed. "Who could have promised me to you?"

"Whoever promised kept his word, and you stop shoving!" answered Pinčukas, who, as if bullying or teasing, impudently tugged at Uršulė's full, pleated skirt.

This was inexcusable impudence on Pinčukas' part, for which he was justifiably punished. The indignant Uršulė suddenly turned around and gave him such a smack on the cheek that Pinčukas fell to his knees, hooked his horns on her skirt, and pulled it over his head. Frightened, Pinčukas wanted to get out from beneath that pleated skirt as fast as possible, but in his haste, as could be expected, he managed to entangle himself even further in the pleats, and tumbled down at Uršulė's feet.

Then Uršulė, without pausing for a moment even though she was left without her outermost pleated skirt (fortunately, she was wearing nine of them), and dreadfully infuriated, lit into Pinčukas so, that he whined and whimpered, but he couldn't escape from under that skirt. Perhaps Uršulė would have completely trampled Pinčukas to death, except that he, having no other choice, tore through the pleats of the skirt and dove for the bottom of the quagmire, pulling Uršulė down after him.

Finally, almost drowning in the murky swamp, Uršulė seized a juniper bush with her left hand and with her right hauled the muddy Pinčukas out of the duckweed. She wanted to get her hands on him again, but he broke free and started tearing about, squealing and whining but

11

still not backing off. Then Uršulė, with her last strength, crawled out of the swamp, took the rosary with scapulars off her neck and started to flail Pinčukas with them, letting the blows fall where they might—on his eyes, on his horns, on his flanks, on the backs of his knees. He writhed as if on hot coals, and ran about the swamp as if his pants were on fire, but the aroused Uršulė was never more than a step behind. She followed stumbling through the bog, blessing him with her rosary and doing the honors by every means possible, so that at last the poor little devil couldn't take it any more, swore and said:

"Nine poxes on you, you witch! I don't want you anymore. Begone with you!"

"I'll begone you!" Uršulė fumed, and grabbed Pinčukas by the horns.

Uršulė wanted to throw the torn pleated skirt over his head again, wind her rosary around his neck and drag him back to Whitehorn, so he could see, shameless creature that he was, what sort of a suitor he had wanted to fix her up with. But then the roosters in the village began to crow. Pinčukas shook himself and disappeared as if he had never been. Uršulė was left with nothing but some piece of bark in her hand, like from a juniper root, and her torn skirt remained where it was, snagged on a bush. What could you do with it, defiled and shredded as it was by a devil? Uršulė, spitting, slung the piece of bark away, too.

Afterwards Uršulė floundered through Paudruvė's bogs until dawn, terribly vexed and unable to extricate herself. It was only as daylight broke, as furious as a witch and completely covered in mud, her remaining

skirts pulled up to her knees, that she returned to
Whitehorn's mill.

It was Whitehorn's good fortune that he heard the
sanctimonious old biddy coming home fuming from the
bog (he might not have, if not for Pinčukas' running
back in fright earlier), so he managed to hide himself in
the mill and bolt the door shut from inside just in time.
He might have felt her fury as well, no less than Pinčukas, or perhaps even more so—because of her withered
youth and the horrible mockery.

When Uršulė returned—since she was unable to
barge into the mill and vent her frustration on that malicious creature's head—she just stormed through the
yard cursing with all her might, and then, as if coming to
her senses, she ran into the cottage, wrapped her clothes
into a bundle, and tore off at a run, down the slope, in
the direction of Švendubrė. As she ran, she kept turning
back to shake her clenched left fist threateningly in the
direction of the mill, while with the similarly clenched
right one she crossed herself, and all the while a stream
of maledictions flowed.

"The old biddy's gone completely off her rocker,"
thought Whitehorn, watching the receding Uršulė from
the little window at the top of the mill. "It looks like
even the devil couldn't manage to get his hands on her."

III

After that unfortunate incident, Uršulė, who had run off
to Švendubrė, started spreading far-fetched rumors

about Whitehorn, which no one wanted to believe. They were simply too strange.

Perhaps only the pastor of Švendubrė, Boniface Bobbin, would have listened seriously to Uršulė's story. It was just his luck, to get a parish set in the middle of marshes, lakes, and forests, and plagued by devils, and he was always on the verge of launching an all-out war on spells and superstitions. But one delay led to still another, until at last he grew old, and, like an old woman, came to believe in their invincible power himself. He might have been the only one who could have properly heard Uršulė out and duly evaluated her adventure, but, most unfortunately, he had spent the previous night playing cards with the neighborhood's down-at-the-heels gentry and he badly wanted some sleep, so he wasn't in the mood for Uršulė's stories.

It was an early spring morning when Uršulė ran straight from Whitehorn's mill to the parsonage with her terrible news. The sun's rays pierced the grimy windows, flies buzzed about, and in the corner a spider spun his web. Cards lay scattered about on the table, and the pastor, asleep in an armchair, snored so loudly that even the windows rattled.

"The Lord be praised…" said Uršulė, opening the door, but all that answered her was the pastor's snoring.

Startled, Uršulė wanted to flee, but suddenly she took hold of herself: after all where could she go, poor thing, after such a misfortune? So she set her bundle by the door and crept closer. The pastor was snoring with his mouth wide open, and the flies buzzed about his mouth, as if tempted to fly into his gurgling throat but afraid of vanishing there. Uršulė waved her hand, shooing off the flies, and the pastor stopped snoring and looked about blinking.

Uršulė brightened up, kissed the pastor's hand, and started telling him all about her ancient injuries and insults and the strange incident at Whitehorn's mill.

"I've heard about that mill of Whitehorn's," the pastor yawned, cutting Uršulė's story short. "Apparently, it's a rallying-place for devils."

"Most certainly," confirmed Uršulė.

"Maybe that was why he wanted to marry you off?" The drowsy pastor looked at Uršulė and nodded his head sadly. "Yes, maybe he wanted to make a family alliance."

"Why, of course," Uršulė brightened up and her eyes got as big as dinner plates. "That must be the answer."

Suddenly it was all as plain as the nose on her face, and Uršulė got it into her head to tell the pastor her story all over again from the beginning, but behold—his nose drooped and he fell asleep. Uršulė's jaw dropped and she stopped talking, and the pastor started snoring again.

Uršulė stood there by the snoring pastor for a good half-hour, not knowing what to do. She was just dying to tell him the whole story, but she was afraid to wake him. At last the snoring pastor, in the soundness of his sleep, nearly swallowed his tongue, and it seemed to Uršulė as if he wanted to say something more. She quickly bent over and kissed his hand.

"What did you say, Father dear?" she asked.

The pastor opened his eyes again, and, seeing a little woman bending over him, thought it was one of those biddies from the almshouse come to bother him, so he knit his brow sternly and said:

"What are you doing here? Go back to the almshouse and rot."

Uršulė got completely flustered and didn't know what to say. So she picked up her little bundle and was already on her way out the door when the pastor, as if remembering something, stopped her.

"Wait a minute, wasn't it something about Whitehorn you wanted to tell me?"

"Oh yes, indeed, Father," said Uršulė, brightening up as she stopped in the doorway. "About that very devils' sorcerer."

"Well, what was it you were going to tell me?" the pastor inquired.

"Well, it was like this!" Uršulė set down her little bundle by the door, walked over to the pastor, kissed both his hands, and started her story all over again. The pastor listened, and listened, and then he got sleepy again.

"Very well," he said, "I see. You can go now. I will think about what should be done."

"But where will I go, Father dear?" Uršulė was dismayed.

"What do you mean?" The pastor was bewildered. "Home, of course."

"I can't go back to that sorcerer."

"Oh, I see!" the pastor caught on. "Well, like I said, go to the almshouse."

Uršulė thanked him and went out, and the pastor fell asleep again, completely forgetting not only the odd incident that had occurred in his parish, but even Uršulė herself.

From that time on, Uršulė settled into the almshouse amidst the biddies, all of them as mean as hornets in the fall, and had neither the time nor the opportunity to remind the pastor about herself. It became Uršulė's lot to spend all her time fighting tooth and nail. You see, Uršulė, although no milksop, found herself among a tough crowd, so there was always someone to lock horns with. And Uršulė wouldn't have been Uršulė, if she didn't win. After a while, the biddies went to complain to the pastor about the devil's bride (that's how they nicknamed poor Uršulė, erroneously, but the nickname stuck to the end), because there was no living in the almshouse with her there.

"What devil's bride?" the pastor was baffled.

"Oh, you know, the one that Whitehorn wanted to marry off to the devil, but couldn't."

The pastor had completely forgotten about the unusual incident in his parish that Uršulė could never finish telling him about because he kept falling asleep. Now the other biddies told him. But they were telling it thirdhand, and got it all confused.

"Very well," said the pastor to the biddies. "I'll investigate this matter."

He promised, but then he forgot. Doesn't a pastor have enough to worry about?

Once, however, when he noticed an excessively zealous biddy down on her knees and couldn't remember where he had seen her before, he stopped her and asked:

17

"Wait a minute, what was it I wanted to ask you?"

Caught by surprise, it occurred to Uršulė that the other biddies had been complaining about her, but she collected herself and answered:

"Wasn't it about Whitehorn, Father dear?"

"Yes, yes, about Whitehorn," remembered the pastor. "What's going on with him now?"

"I don't know, Father dear," answered Uršulė, and piously lowered her eyes, as she had already learnt a great deal of a sanctimonious biddy's modesty.

"Well, it needs to be looked into," said the pastor, and went off displeased that he had spoken to that biddy.

This hint of the pastor's planted Uršulė back in the saddle. The squabbling and bickering in the almshouse had long since grown old. At this point the other biddies would tremble if Uršulė, without even opening her mouth, so much as flashed her eyes. And she had already gone around all the corners of the church dozens of times on her knees. She needed to think up something, and now the old wound had been opened again. She started questioning people, gathering all sorts of rumors and gossip about Whitehorn, but for a long time she couldn't get any news about either Whitehorn or his mill. Sometimes people just laughed at her—perhaps she missed Pinčukas and was planning to go back to him? Uršulė would just cross herself, and then pile on a furious scolding. But then one day she heard how Whitehorn's mill spun without wind.

"This is surely some new sort of spell," Uršulė grasped at once, and went to work.

The first quiet day, when there wasn't the slightest breeze, right after morning prayers, Uršulė ran out to check if it really was the way people said.

She didn't have far to run. From the first knoll, still some distance away, she saw that Whitehorn's mill was turning its sails, even though it was completely quiet and not a leaf stirred on the trees. No doubt remained. So she breathlessly ran straight to the pastor.

"Father dear," she said, bursting in, "Whitehorn's mill is turning."

"Well, what of it, if it's turning?" the pastor was perplexed.

"But without any wind, Father dear," Uršulė explained.

"What do you mean, it's turning without any wind?" the pastor asked in surprise.

"Just exactly so, it's turning without any wind." Uršulė wanted to demonstrate how the mill was turning with her skirt, but all she succeeded in doing was raising the dust. "That sorcerer has thought up some new spells again."

"This will have to be investigated," the pastor agreed. "If you hear anything new, let me know."

But even though Uršulė exerted herself to the utmost, she didn't hear anything new. The mill simply spun without wind, and that was that. Who could make sense of it? The pastor, even though he wanted to get to the bottom of it, had too much to do. Besides the church and the farm, there were the cards, there was this and there was that, and the pastor forgot that there was such an extraordinary miller living in his parish.

19

It was only later, when the matchmakers started driving out to call on Whitehorn's daughter and just couldn't get to the mill, that Uršulė, as spry a little woman as she was, couldn't keep up with gathering up all the rumors and running to the pastor with them. At first the pastor listened, was astonished, promised to think about it and to investigate the matter; but later, suddenly and for no apparent reason, he got exasperated, stomped his foot so hard the floor shook, and pronounced:

"Begone from me, you and your Whitehorn! I don't want to hear anything more about him."

For the second time, the disheartened Uršulė left the parsonage and didn't know what to do. And the rumors about Whitehorn's mill were spreading thick and fast. The end of the world was surely coming, but what could Uršulė, all by herself, do about it?

IV

Uršulė was perfectly well aware that these were Whitehorn's and his friend Pinčukas' insidious doings, but what she couldn't understand was, why the new spells? Finally, it came to her, and she smacked herself on the forehead:

"What a fool I am, even if I am an old biddy. It's no wonder the pastor got angry with me. What else could it be—that accursed Whitehorn, since he couldn't pass me off onto Pinčukas, promised him his daughter, and now the devil's the one who's turning the mill without wind. There's nothing else it could be. My vow of chastity saved me, but she, poor thing, is doomed to eternal damnation. And how is it that didn't I catch on at once?" Uršulė wondered to herself. She reported the wicked deeds and crafty intentions of Whitehorn and Pinčukas to everyone. But it wasn't clear to anyone, including Uršulė herself, whether she was pleased or angry about it. Both pleasure and anger took hold of her the moment she guessed Whitehorn and Pinčukas' plot.

Uršulė had hated Jurga from the very beginning. She would pour all of her old maid's bile on her whenever Whitehorn wasn't around.

On that account, the old widower wouldn't have been left in her debt, even if he had married her off to the devil himself. Uršulė knew very well why it was that Whitehorn hated her, and how he could evict her from his house in such an ungracious fashion.

As a result, Uršulė was therefore extremely pleased when she found out that her detested stepdaughter (that was what Uršulė sometimes called Jurga) was to be doomed.

"That's just what she deserves," she said to herself more than once, regretting that she had spread the secret about so much. "The devil was the mother's match-maker; the devil will snatch the daughter, too."

But in the end Uršulė's conscience began to gnaw at her. She wanted to confess her mortal hatred to the pastor, but he wouldn't let her get anywhere near him. Because poor Bobbin had failed to think up a solution (despite the fact that he had done more than his share of slumbering), he was so annoyed with Uršulė's White-horn that he said:

"Let him and that Uršulė sink into the earth, as long as they don't plague me about it."

But Uršulė's aroused conscience gave her no peace. It seemed to her that her entire life had been one terrible sin (after all, she hated Jurga just because her mother had stood in the way of her marrying White-horn), and she resolved to redeem her mortal sin with some noble deed. That Uršulė wasn't such a bad-hearted little woman, in spite of everything.

Thus resolved, the next Sunday Uršulė stood in the narthex with the old ladies, and as Jurga was leaving—a truly shameless girl, throwing glances and mocking the boys before she had even gotten out of church—she tugged at Jurga's skirt and whispered:

"Daughter dear, I have to talk to you."

Jurga looked over her shoulder quizzically and said out loud:

"And what do I have to talk to you about, Auntie? Pinčukas is waiting for your loving words and never gets any, and I can do without them."

Uršulė got riled at hearing such insolent words, but, remembering her mortal sin, she calmed herself down again. She dragged Jurga off by force to a sheltered spot by the church tower, and there she laid out the full horror of what was to happen to Jurga if she didn't heed her. At first Jurga listened impatiently, and then, choking with laughter, she declared seriously:

"So what do I have to do, Auntie, to avoid damnation?"

Then every wrinkle on Uršulė's face beamed, just at the thought that she had already redeemed her enormous sin and saved Jurga.

"My dear girl, make an oath of chastity," said Uršulė cheerfully. "Promise yourself to Joseph, the purest of the pure, only then can you be saved."

"And go to the almshouse," added Jurga, bursting with barely repressed laughter.

"You could go to the almshouse, too," Uršulė agreed soberly, but Jurga couldn't restrain herself and laughed out loud.

"I can't, Auntie," she answered. "I like the boys so much that my heart skips whenever I see a handsome one. I wouldn't last a single day in the almshouse. You can say what you like, Auntie, but the almshouse is not for me."

Uršulė sighed then; she saw that nothing would come of it, but all the same she hadn't completely lost hope, so she said reproachfully:

"You'll be sorry, daughter dear, only then it will be too late. Your father will marry you off to Pinčukas, and then you'll be eternally damned."

It seemed as if Jurga had gotten frightened, or as if she had caught on. She stopped laughing and sobered up, but there was an impish gleam in her eyes.

"Could that really happen, Auntie?" she asked.

"You know yourself that he wanted to marry me off to that devil!" Uršulė bobbed her head sadly, like a worn-out horse.

"Have you seen this Pinčukas?" Jurga asked, again seriously.

"Of course. I rode together with him in a carriage for the banns," Uršulė answered somberly.

"But you didn't get there?"

"No, I didn't get there," sighed Uršulė. "My vow of chastity saved me."

"Now I understand, Auntie," Jurga went along with her in all seriousness, "who it is in the Paudruvė bogs sighing so sadly every evening that it makes you want to cry. So, it's him, poor thing, waiting and waiting for you all this time, and here you never show up. You should be sorry for him Auntie, and marry him instead of being such a stubborn goat. After all, one way or another, you are his betrothed."

"What are you saying, daughter dear?" said Uršulė, who didn't understand whether Jurga was speaking seriously or laughing in her face.

"The same nonsense as you," said Jurga, and went off roaring with laughter.

Uršulė sighed; she wanted to rebuke her again, but instead with an angry, reproachful look in her eyes she watched Jurga go off without saying anything more, even though her tongue was itching terribly.

"Damned for eternity," she said to herself in frustration, and pulled out her rosary to calm herself.

She went back to church counting her beads, no longer thinking about Jurga but rather about whether she had redeemed her mortal sin or not. At last she soothed herself with the thought that she had more than made up for all of her life's sinful hatred (how could she be at fault if that piece of fluff wouldn't listen?), and started her repentance by saying the rosary. But she was interrupted even while doing repentance, because Jurga's lively laughter drifted all the way into church from the churchyard. Jurga was poking fun at the old biddy and teasing the young men.

"That's the real devil's bride, not me!" Uršulė thought dolefully, saying her rosary and completely forgetting that she was sinning again.

V

At that time, seven miles from the land of Paudruvė, in the village of Manywish, lived Jurgis Girdvainis, a daring and proud young man, who couldn't manage to find himself a girl, even though he and his matchmaker, the herdsman Anupras Hearall of the same village, had driven for seven miles around with his best dapple-gray steeds.

Those dapple-gray steeds were left to him by his dying father, who had ordered him to guard them like the apple of his eye, declaring that as long as those stallions were dappled, his life would be charmed. The son kept his father's order sacred, and those dapple-gray steeds were his pride and joy. It was just that Girdvainis was young and knew no moderation. On account of those dapple-grays he neglected the entire farm, his father had left as full as a grain-bin, for if he went out for a ride with the dapple-grays, he was gone with the birds—be the roads good or bad, he took flight.

Girdvainis started driving around with his dapple-grays searching for a girl, one who wouldn't be afraid to spend her life riding around with whirlwind horses like his. He traveled around all fall paying calls on the neighboring maidens, even as far as seven miles away, but he didn't find any that suited him. The problem was Girdvainis' own overdeveloped pride and his unspeakable smartness.

Girdvainis would harness up his dapple-grays, who could hardly stand still, not to his beautifully painted carriage, but to a mud-splattered dung-cart; for a matchmaker he didn't take a talkative farmer, but the shabby village herdsman Anupras Hearall, who was blind in one eye and deaf in one ear; he didn't dress up in his Sunday clothes, but instead in a sheepskin turned inside-out, so that strange girls wouldn't pester him; he would tie a chain around his waist, so as to ward off spells, step into his clogs, and throwing Anupras into the cart, Lord help us, with his pair of dapple-grays he would tear out of there and fly like the wind, through the highways or the byways, depending upon where the girl who had caught his eye was. If it was summer, then the suitor with his matchmaker would leave nothing but columns of dust behind on the road, or if it was fall, then mud would be splattered to the skies.

That was how Girdvainis went about scouring the entire neighborhood for a girl but not finding one of his own, because all of the potential brides started laughing and scaring each other over such a smart suitor. Girdvainis himself paid no attention to this, and did as he saw fit, saying:

"With horses like these, even if I have to go to the ends of the earth, I'll find my girl."

26

Unfortunately, he still hadn't found a girl, one who would be tempted by such a suitor and his horses. Moreover, the fathers-in-laws weren't tempted, since it seemed to them that Girdvainis' life was like a barrel without staves, one that would never be full.

Who's to say how it really was with those staves. If they were already burst, all of those staves that serious farmers used to prop up their lives, then Girdvainis not only didn't rely on them, but with those dapple-grays of his seemed to want to dash them to the four winds. That was why he needed a girl with whom he could fly like the wind, without touching the ground.

But where was he to find such a girl? They were all serious daughters of good farmers. So, hearing that there was an unusual daughter of the miller Whitehorn in the land of Paudruvė, whom no one could succeed in visiting with a matchmaker, on the very next Sunday he drove his dapple-grays to Švendubrė to look around and make inquiries about what sort of girl this was and what was going on there.

The young maids and swains of Švendubrė instantly recognized Girdvainis because of his dapple-gray steeds that stopped by the churchyard, neighing. The girls, sniggering, scurried off to the side, so that the queer suitor wouldn't speak to them and there wouldn't be any talk of it later. The young men crowded around Girdvainis' dapple-grays and couldn't admire them enough.

More than one enviously said aloud:

"There's some horses for you!" and thought to himself, "With horses like that, you could drive to Whitehorn's daughter, no matter what witchcraft there might be."

Jurga, too, immediately heard about the unusual suitor who had arrived in Švendubrė, as soon as she left Uršulė by the church tower and went off laughing. A few of the girls, fleeing from the churchyard, sniggered at Jurga:

"Your man has arrived!"

"What man?" Jurga didn't understand.

"You know—the one with the dapple-gray horses, wearing his sheepskin inside out."

"Well, maybe he is mine. What do you know about it?" Jurga said testily, since the girls dared to make fun of her.

"Where is he?"

"That one, don't you see, standing there," pointing a finger at Girdvainis standing by the churchyard's oak and looking around at the crowd.

Jurga went straight over to Girdvainis. She had heard a great deal about his dapple-gray steeds, the dung-cart, the inside-out sheepskin, and the deaf matchmaker that he drove around frightening the maidens with. Now Jurga stood in Girdvainis' way just as he, looking for her, intended to walk through the churchyard.

"You've been to call on all the girls," she said, looking him straight in the eye, "but you haven't been to see me. Am I too ordinary of a girl for you, or is it that you're afraid of the gossip that the road to my house is bewitched?"

Girdvainis immediately recognized that this was the one he was looking for, because he had never before seen a girl so beautiful and so bold. Exactly what he needed.

"You're no ordinary girl," Girdvainis answered her directly, "and I'm not afraid of gossip. With my dapple-grays I can break all of the spells in your path."

"Then break them," Jurga answered, and her eyes smiled. "If you break them, then maybe I'll marry you."

"It's all the same, marry me or not," said Girdvainis, remembering his pride, "but next Saturday I'll be there with my matchmaker Anupras."

At that moment, seeing Girdvainis talking to Jurga, a crowd of young men and ladies gathered around, while still others ran through the churchyard, leaving Girdvainis' steeds behind.

When Girdvainis promised to come calling with his matchmaker, the girls giggled into their hands and the boys laughed out loud.

"Birds of a feather flock together," someone opined.

Jurga, completely forgetting that there was a crowd gathered about watching her, looked at Girdvainis admiringly, straight in the eye, and blushing all over, declared:

"I'll be waiting. Don't forget."

Having said this, she walked away with her eyes down but her head up, as pretty as a princess.

But her heart skipped a beat with a sense of foreboding. It seemed he was a proclaimed suitor, the kind that haunted a girl's dreams. Was he the promised one?

Hardly believing it, Jurga glanced back over her shoulder, and her eyes met Girdvainis' burning glance. She quickly turned around and went off feeling terribly unsettled.

That glance over the shoulder completely did Girdvainis in.

"There's a girl for you!" he said to himself, faint with joy and completely unable to tear his eyes away from her slender waist and graceful walk, waiting for her to look back again.

However, Jurga didn't turn back, and she quickly vanished from sight. Girdvainis wandered fruitlessly through the feast day crowd, searching with his burning eyes, hoping to see her once more. But she was nowhere to be found. She and her father had gone straight home.

So Girdvainis, too, without delay, turned his dapple-grays around and drove off with so much joy in his heart that it seemed even his dapple-grays couldn't carry him fast enough, though they flew by leaps and bounds.

But was Girdvainis' euphoria premature?

VI

The rumors spreading about Whitey Whitehorn and his mill weren't entirely groundless. This was not simply the ravings of the sanctimonious biddy Uršulė or the inventions of drunken suitors and their matchmakers. Whitehorn himself wasn't without blame; the road to his daughter Jurga was difficult because he himself hadn't had an easy time of it, making Marcelė Alburn, the most beautiful girl in Paudruvė, his wife. Where there's smoke, there's fire.

It all boiled down to the fact that Whitehorn, from very early on, was too attached to his mill, and because of it he had forgotten not just himself, but all the rest of God's creation.

Even as a child Whitehorn couldn't get enough of listening to the humming of the mill's wings when the waters of Lake Udruvė joined in. It was as if that humming had bewitched Whitehorn. Half grown, he spent his days and nights at the mill. He didn't want to know or even hear about other work.

He was happiest when the wind would rise up and turn the mill's wings. Then he would joyfully knock about his mill, never tiring, only fearing the wind might die down. Even then he began to dream—wasn't there some way to turn the mill without wind? He particularly pondered this when the wind died down, and he would spend entire days sitting on the mill's threshold, watching the waters of Lake Udruvė to see if the surface hadn't started rippling from a slight breeze. And of course he had adjusted the mill wings so the slightest puff from the direction of the lake would catch them. Other than the humming of the mill, nothing else captivated Whitehorn in his youth; for him there was no other kind of life.

And so it was that Whitehorn, with the mill humming, never noticed his youth pass by, his parents dying, his brothers and sisters leaving home. He was left alone with the aging biddy Uršulė, a distant Whitehorn relative, who grew old unmarried and seemed destined to remain forever as an occupant of Whitehorn's house. But fate would have it otherwise.

With Whitehorn's family scattered, Uršulė took on all the household cares, since Whitehorn didn't bother at all about these matters, as if they didn't exist. It was the mill alone that filled his head.

"That mill has addled your brains," Uršulė would sometimes say, giving Whitehorn a reproachful look. "You don't see anything else but your mill, as if there's nothing else in the world."

"But I don't need anything else," Whitehorn would answer, without even looking at Uršulė.

Uršulė would give him a dirty look, and, turning back to the stove, she would bang the pots about even harder. Sometimes Whitehorn would look up to see what was she banging about for, or sometimes he would go out to the mill without even glancing in her direction.

At other times, Uršulė would start complaining that it was too much work for her, looking after the house, that he never helped out, and that she couldn't be two people at once.

Whitehorn, surprised and perplexed, would shrug his shoulders.

"Why not? Split yourself, and there'll be two of you."

Uršulė, thinking he just didn't understand a thing (after all people considered him a fool on account of that mill), would hint that people sometimes talked nonsense about this or that, and blushing from her ears to the top of her head, she would say that it wasn't right for a young man to live with a girl under one roof, and who knows what people might think up. Whitehorn would act as if he hadn't heard a word of what she'd said, even though Uršulė not only blushed, but would try to throw affectionate glances at him as well. And when she had annoyed him enough with her sweetness, Whitehorn would cut back boorishly:

"What do you want? Are we really living under one roof? I'm in the mill—you're in the cottage or the pig-pen."

Then the angry Uršulė would start spitting like a cat, threatening to throw him over, to leave home entirely, let him hang himself on that mill of his, or whatever else he should think up.

Whitehorn, quite calmly, sometimes even cheerfully, would answer:

"Then what are you still waiting for? Go on. It'll just be more peaceful by myself."

Uršulė, by now seriously peeved, would start packing up her things, but then, while still packing, she'd unpack, and then she would sigh deeply and calm herself down:

"Now how can I leave him all by himself? I'll wait a bit, maybe he'll come to his senses."

However, Uršulė's hopes were in vain. Returning from the mill, Whitehorn wouldn't be in the least bit happy to find Uršulė still stirring about the house; he would just be surprised, or even angry:

"So, you haven't left yet?" he would rebuke her.

"To hold your tongue is to love God," Uršulė would sigh, and for a few days she would be quieter.

"If only God would give you that much sense," Whitehorn would wish her, "then we really could live in peace."

This wish of Whitehorn's, or maybe the years that stooped the already shriveled old maid even more, must have helped, for Uršulė became more and more God-fearing every day. Earlier she had tried every conceivable method, even spells, with which she hoped, in spite of it all, to seduce Whitehorn, but when even that didn't help, with her last hope gone and in regret for her sins, she made her vows of chastity to the Innocent Maiden of Švendubrė and started going to church more and more often, sometimes even wasting the entire day there, thereby cheering Whitehorn in no small measure.

"You see, maybe she'll come to her senses for once," he'd say to himself, even though the more God-fearing Uršulė got, the meaner she got. All the same, Whitehorn didn't lose hope that the old maid's meanness and fury would some day come to an end. But in this Whitehorn was mistaken.

In the meantime, the days slipped by, year after year went by, and Whitehorn, battling with the sanctimonious old biddy with the mill humming on, didn't even notice that he was getting old himself. His large forehead grew even larger, and so much flour dust fell into the crown of hair at his temples that even the pure waters of Lake Udruvė couldn't wash it out.

VII

Whitehorn could quite contentedly have grown old in this way, left alone with his humming mill and the grumbling old biddy. However, one spring day, as a soft wind blew, the snow began melting, and the cheerful brooks started foaming and raising the ice as they gathered into Lake Udruvė, the Alburns' young mischiefmaker Marcelė, from the other side of the lake, came over to the mill.

"Those men of ours drove off into the woods, they said the road might run off," Marcelė laughed rather than spoke, "so I drove straight across the lake to the mill. Let the road run. I'm not going to chase after it."

She herself laughed just like those spring brooks babbling on their way to Lake Udruvė. That laughter was soon ringing throughout the entire mill and bewitched the aging Whitehorn, even though Marcelė didn't intend to at all. It was her first visit to the mill, and it pleased her so much that she hopped about like a little bird over all the mill's floors, chattering and laughing, pulling the miller by his graying hairs, and begging him to let her take a ride on the mill's sails.

"I'd sure see a long way off!" Her laugh sounded like silver bells, and her merry eyes were already following the sails.

"That's not a girl, that's a little bird," thought Whitehorn, unable to get enough of her merry chatter, which began to drown out even the mill's humming and the burble of the awakening lake.

He didn't realize himself how, listening to that chattering, he started moving about more nimbly, as though he had gotten a few decades younger. He ground up Marcelė's grain quickly, loaded it into her sleigh, and when Marcelė got in ready to drive off, Whitehorn for some reason was terribly sorry.

"When will you come again?" he asked, wanting to delay Marcelė.

"When the road runs off," Marcelė answered as she drove off, and, glancing back at him, she laughed mischievously.

That laugh, or the glance backwards, completely sent the aging bachelor out of his head. Wherever he went, whatever he did, Marcelė was constantly in front of his eyes; he heard her musical laugh and saw her alluring smile everywhere. The mill, the spring fields, the lake were full of laughter. That laugh and that smile persecuted Whitehorn wherever he went, and sometimes it even seemed as if that merry, carefree laughter of youth was mocking his balding head, graying temples, and empty, lonely bachelorhood. And the longer it went on, the more lonely Whitehorn felt, because he realized he had spent his youth in vain and there was no catching up with it now, not even on the wings of the wind.

An uneasy spring passed in this way. The waters of Lake Udruvė quieted down, everything turned green, and a layer of mist covered the banks of the lake and the surrounding hills and mounds, which, as the legend says, a giant dumped between the lakes while scraping out his clogs. But Whitehorn still couldn't forget either that laugh, which still sounded everywhere he turned, or that smile, which had bewitched him.

That laugh wasn't drowned out by a calm summer, which, like a dreamy fairy tale, shimmered blue in the lakes and green in the pinewoods. That smile's charm wasn't even broken by the warm starry nights drowning in the pure waters of Lake Udruvė. Whitehorn's heart was full of that laughter, and he went about as quiet as a shadow, listening to it, enjoying it, but sometimes so heartbroken that he couldn't settle down anywhere.

And in the fall, when the matchmakers' bells started ringing on the other side of the lake, Whitehorn's composure was completely shattered. At night he couldn't fall asleep; during the day he couldn't wake up; he forgot even his mill, which now stood with its wings folded up like a ghost, even though it was prime time for milling grain.

The miller, although he was sometimes scolded by the farmers for delaying the milling (which had never happened before), would spend his days sitting on the mill's threshold and watching, his eyes locked on the other side of the lake. And in the evenings, when the matchmakers' bells would start ringing as they turned into the Alburns' farmyard, Whitehorn couldn't stand it even on the mill's threshold, and, getting up, he would run from the mill to the lake, from the lake to the mill, as if he wanted to drown himself or something.

Sometimes, completely losing control of himself, he would let the millstones run wild, so that their grinding would drown out the matchmakers' bells. The mill would howl in a cacophony of voices, raising a horrible shuddering, but all the same, it wouldn't stop those matchmakers' bells from ringing in Whitehorn's ears. The bells and the laughter that had persecuted him since early spring all melted into the mill's hum, and he wouldn't know what to do. Then, stopping the mill, Whitehorn would tear out his graying hair and curse his bachelorhood.

To drive to the Alburns' farm himself with a matchmaker, even though the temptation had arisen on more than one occasion, Whitehorn didn't even dare consider. Who on earth would let his daughter marry a crazy old bachelor miller, not to mention that the daughter herself would run from such an ancient suitor? The entire neighborhood would be guffawing over it; there would be nowhere to hide. In his anguish, Whitehorn no longer knew whether it would be better to hang himself from the mill's wings or drown himself in Lake Udruvė. The only thing that was clear to him was that he couldn't go on living like this, if he were to go on living at all.

Seeing this, the old maid Uršulė sincerely started to worry about Whitehorn, stopped scolding him and threatening to leave, and sometimes she even wiped a tear from the corner of her eye with her scarf and asked him in concern:

"What's the matter with you, Whitey dear? Maybe you're sick, is something hurting you? Tell me, it will be easier for you, I've got all sorts of herbs here, I'll boil some up… Maybe it will help…"

"Oh, get away…" Annoyed, Whitehorn would brush off Uršulė's worries and go shut himself up in the mill.

But even shut up in the mill he didn't know what to do with himself. Day after day, he was as silent as the grave, stupefied by his heartbreak, and every day feeling more and more as though he was getting ready to crawl beneath the turf still alive.

Now Uršulė got seriously worried that the mill had really addled Whitehorn's wits and his brains, and she started running to the neighbors, seeking medicine and help, but where are you going to find medicine or help for an illness like that?

It was Whitehorn's bad luck that it wasn't just Uršulė who was concerned for him, but also one neighbor whom no one had a good word for.

That was Pinčukas.

VIII

On the other side of the bluff from Whitehorn's mill stood Paudruvė's bogs, where Lake Udruvė ended amidst the duckweed and Bygodit's Creek began, linking Lake Udruvė with Gloomspot and other lakes.

Although the bogs were not very large, they were marshy and impassable, overgrown with scrub brush and berry patches, where all kinds of berries ripened in the fall and attracted berry-pickers from the entire area. But it was dangerous to gather berries there.

The bogs were treacherous, even in the places where small meadows would grow, waving atop the surface as if the meadow were swimming on top of the water. Sometimes, standing atop a raised clump, you'd crash through into the quagmire, and you'd be lucky if you managed to grab hold of some shrub in time to save yourself, otherwise—you'd be buried alive. The marsh would pull you down to the bottom and leave no sign of where you'd fallen through.

In those bogs, it was said, lived this miserable little devil, Pinčukas by name. Everyone blamed him for whatever misfortune befell humans or animals in the swamp. But that wasn't fair. Pinčukas was such a sorry devil, and so lazy besides, that he didn't do anything, good or bad, to anyone. He was such a good-for-nothing that he wasn't interested in anything, not even himself; he merely slumbered endlessly, listening to the hum of Whitehorn's mill.

People would have completely forgotten about him if the women or shepherd boys didn't from time to time run into him dozing in the swamp. The women, of course, would get frightened, even if he was nothing more than a drowsy devil, so they would run off; while the bolder shepherd boys wouldn't just wake Pinčukas up: they would drive him through the bogs from one den to another. Then the angry Pinčukas would crawl into some more out-of-the-way swamp and doze day and night. When he got bored with dozing, he would sometimes daydream that maybe it wouldn't be so bad if he had a wife. In any case, it would be cozier with two. But where was he to get one? No fairy or witch would go for such a miserable little devil, and what ordinary woman could be seduced into coming to the bogs? So, Pinčukas had to be content with just his fantasies.

If it hadn't been for those fantasies, Pinčukas' life would have been terribly boring. So boring, that a human in his shoes would go and hang himself, but for a devil, and such a sorry one at that, even that sort of life was all right. He grew accustomed to his dreams and to the constant humming of Whitehorn's mill, which he listened to while he was slumbering, and it was enough for him. If there was no wife, well, then he'd do without. So there wasn't much for Pinčukas to worry about, except that sometimes, while listening to the humming of Whitehorn's mill, he would get concerned.

"What is he grinding up over there?" he'd think, but then he would nod off again. "Big deal, so the mill is grinding. Let it grind."

And so Pinčukas never got around to going to see what it was that Whitehorn's mill was grinding. And maybe he would never have gone there, and even now he'd still be vegetating in Paudruvė's bogs. But how can people recognize their own bad luck, if even the devil himself isn't aware of his?

Pinčukas was so accustomed to the humming of the mill, that sometimes, when the mill stopped, he would become uneasy—there was simply something missing—and he would start getting anxious. So when Whitehorn, charmed by Marcelė's laughter, more and more often forgot the mill and quieted its constant humming, Pin-čukas found it extremely boring and eventually terribly nerve-wracking.

"Why isn't it grinding?" Pinčukas became more and more worried, because without the humming of the mill he could neither doze nor dream of a wife.

At last one evening, finding it unbearable, he got up out of his moss-covered den, fixed himself up decently behind a bush so as to be fit to be seen in human company, and went to pay a call on Whitehorn. He found him sitting on the threshold of the mill and looking at the other side of the lake.

"Good evening, neighbor," said Pinčukas in greeting, and stopped in front of him.

Whitehorn was so deep in his misery that he didn't even notice someone had come by. It was only when he heard a voice that he raised his eyes, thinking some neighbor had come by again to scold him that he was too long about grinding the grain, but behold—in front of him stands this itsy-bitsy, silly little gentleman, like a German, with a little hat on his head, and what's more, a rooster feather stuck into it.

"Where did this one come from?" wondered White-horn and thought to himself, "Maybe he's come to buy the mill?"

So once more he looked the strange visitor over from head to toe. "Looks just like a buyer!" he thought, and then, to avoid wasting his breath, he said right off:

"No, I'm not selling the mill."

"I've absolutely no need for your mill," said Pinčukas, shrugging his shoulders indifferently. "Only its hum. Why aren't you grinding?"

"I have absolutely no interest in grinding," White-horn grumbled, wanting to shake off this annoying presence as soon as possible, and he again turned towards the other side of the lake.

"Then what are you interested in?" Pinčukas leaned on his walking stick, preparing for a long talk.

Whitehorn didn't answer; he just stood up from the threshold's millstone where he had been sitting. On the other side of the lake the matchmaker's bells rang out, or maybe he just imagined they did.

Pinčukas also straightened up and looked in that direction.

"I see," he said. "You wouldn't by any chance want to get married?"

"How did you know that?" said Whitehorn, astonished, and turned towards his visitor.

"What's there not to know?" Pinčukas shrugged his shoulders. "I've been thinking myself that it's about time to get married. But I can wait a while still, if only the mill would keep humming."

Whitehorn looked at the little gentleman, wondering what he wanted, and saw that he wasn't quite like other people—he had only one hole in his nose.

"Who on earth are you?" Whitehorn asked, shocked, knowing the answer and fearing that which he knew.

"Don't you recognize me?" said Pinčukas, also shocked. "I'm your neighbor. I live in the bogs right at the bottom of this hill. Pinčukas."

The little gentleman took off his tiny hat and bowed. Whitehorn saw two little horns sticking out of his forehead and now there was no doubt left.

"You're really one of those?" Whitehorn asked, still not believing it.

"As you see," Pinčukas grinned. "And, like a neighbor, I can help."

"What on earth could you help me with?" Whitehorn was even more astonished.

"Why, to marry the one you want," answered Pinčukas, quite seriously.

"Then help me!" Whitehorn blurted out without thinking.

"But what will you give me in return?" asked Pinčukas, tilting his head smartly.

"Whatever you want. Take the mill at least, and I'll throw the old maid Uršulė in, too," Whitehorn answered, not giving it much thought.

"That I don't need," Pinčukas shook his head. Then he thought about it for a bit and added, "If you'll give me what you don't have, but will have when you get married, then I'll help you."

43

"With pleasure," Whitehorn agreed, not imagining anything bad of it.

"Very well," answered Pinčukas, and pulled some paper out of his sleeve. "We'll sign a contract."

"What do we need a contract for?" Whitehorn questioned. "We'll agree like neighbors."

"Neighbors are neighbors," interjected Pinčukas. "So that we won't forget what we've agreed to, we'll sign."

"Why is that necessary?" said Whitehorn, still doubtful. "A neighbor's word is dearer than gold."

"Words are words," Pinčukas disagreed. "But what's written an ax won't sunder!" He pulled the feather out of his little hat, set the paper on his knee and wrote up the contract, then thrust the quill at Whitehorn. "Prick your little finger and sign it."

Whitehorn still had doubts about whether to take the pen, but at that moment the matchmaker's bells rang out from the other side of the lake. Shuddering, Whitehorn took the quill that Pinčukas was thrusting at him, poked it in his finger, and signed.

"I'll come back in twelve years to take what belongs to me according to the contract," declared the satisfied Pinčukas, sticking the feather back in his little hat and the paper in his breast pocket. "So, don't waste any time, harness the horse, take a matchmaker along, and go pay a call on the one you want. The wedding will be in three weeks."

Having said this, Pinčukas, who had just been there, disappeared, leaving the astonished Whitehorn alone in the middle of the yard.

"Perhaps I've been dreaming?" he asked himself and rubbed his eyes.

On the other side of the lake the matchmaker's bells rang. But they were heading back. No luck, apparently.

IX

Whether it was a dream in broad daylight or some spirit's materialization, Whitehorn himself couldn't very well say, but that very evening he harnessed the horse and drove over to the village of Paudruvė to pay a call on his closest neighbor—the blacksmith Juozapas Blackpool, an honest and sensible person—and asked him to be his matchmaker and drive over with him to call on the Alburns' Marcelė.

"Brother, have you lost your head?" Blackpool scolded him. "A girl like that marrying an old geezer like you? We'll just bring shame down on our heads, and nothing more."

"So be it," said Whitehorn, not giving in. "For your help, I'll do your milling for free for the rest of your days."

"You can mill to your heart's content, but nothing will come of it," said Blackpool, trying to shake him off.

But Whitehorn begged so persistently that the man eventually relented.

"If you want it that badly," he said, "then confound you: we'll drive over and come home with nothing. Big deal!"

But at that moment, from behind the stove, out jumped Blackpool's apprentice boy Jurgutis, who pumped the bellows at the forge and knew how to cheerfully blow

45

his nose the span of a fathom through just one nostril. For this reason he considered himself a fine fellow and was dying to go out with a matchmaker. He was eternally pestering his master to just once take him somewhere to pay a call on some marriageable girl. So now, while Blackpool and Whitehorn were discussing matchmaking, he stood by the forge as if he were rooted there, listening closely and even forgetting to blow his nose. But when Blackpool gave in to Whitehorn and agreed to be his matchmaker, Jurgutis blew a span and chimed in:

"Take me, too," he proposed. "After all, you promised to be my matchmaker and take me somewhere a long time ago. If the Alburns' Marcelė won't marry Whitehorn, then maybe she'll marry me."

"Now how am I supposed to go calling on one girl with two suitors?" Blackpool laughed. "Maybe I'll go with you later to pay a call on Whitehorn's Uršulė?"

"It's all the same to me," Jurgutis agreed. "To the Alburns' Marcelė or to Whitehorn's Uršulė, just so long as you take me out matchmaking at least once."

When Jurgutis jumped out from behind the stove so suddenly, Whitehorn got somewhat flustered and sobered up. Maybe he was acting like a fool himself, like some young whippersnapper? However, Blackpool ran out of patience and finally made up his mind:

"Has the devil gotten into both of you?" he yelled. "First one, then the other wants a matchmaker… All right!… Go on, go tie the bell to Whitehorn's horse," he ordered Jurgutis. "First I'll take Whitehorn to Marcelė, then you to Uršulė… maybe I'll get someone fixed up… confound you both…"

"Oh, how wonderful that'll be!" Jurgutis once more blew his nose a span through one nostril and ran out, skipping and dancing, to tie the bell to Whitehorn's horse.

It was already dark when Blackpool and Whitehorn drove out together to the Alburns' farm, ringing the matchmaker's bell along the lakeshore, and everything turned out fine. At first the bride's parents weren't in the least interested in accepting such an elderly suitor and his matchmaker, but then Marcelė herself, for some reason, set her heart on the match, forgetting all of her maidenly modesty.

"I won't marry anyone else," she said, "only Whitehorn. At least he'll give me a ride on the mill's wings."

At last her parents gave in.

"Go on," said her father, "if you fancy miller's swill so badly. But you, my dear son-in-law, now don't get angry, but there won't be any dowry. Take her, if you want her, as she is."

"There's nothing else I want; just Marcelė and her laughter," Whitehorn answered, unable to believe his luck.

"Well, that's something you'll get in full measure," the father agreed, "it won't be much of a loss for us."

The two sides quickly came to an agreement. In joy, Marcelė burst into laughter and went so far as to confess:

"Then it wasn't in vain that I counted nine little stars for nine nights, asking who will be mine. Here on the tenth night he shows up. He's the one for me."

The parents couldn't care less whether the stars helped or not. The cottage was full of growing girls— who could they marry them off to, and how could they provide them with dowries? The parents had pricked and prodded Marcelė more than once to take one or another of the suitors who came calling with their matchmakers, just to make room for the next one in line, but Marcelė, not knowing why herself, for some reason shook them all off and didn't want to marry. So now she surprised everyone to no small degree, most of all Whitehorn himself, when she agreed to marry him.

"Well, now all that's left is to marry off Uršulė to my boy Jurgutis," said Blackpool cheerfully, pleased by the unexpectedly successful match. "But two new brides in one house is too many, and I don't need a daughter-in-law in the smithy yet. What would the old lady say? She'd drive the newlyweds out with a broom."

That was the only worry tainting the otherwise successful match. Whitehorn simply had no idea of how to shake off Uršulė. And even Blackpool couldn't think of anything reasonable, even though Jurgutis, like a thorn in his side, wouldn't give up:

"When, oh, when are we going match-making to Whitehorn's Uršulė?" he would ask every day.

"Wait," the blacksmith said, nearly at the end of his patience. "We'll see how it turns out for Whitehorn. You're still young and you can wait."

The disgruntled Jurgutis blew his nose a fathom through first one nostril, then the other, and pumped the bellows so hard that sparks spurted from the forge and flew up to the ceiling through the vent. What else can you do when you have to wait?

When Uršulė learned about the match, she slammed the doors in anger and, green with envy, threw dirty looks at Whitehorn. She mulled and pondered how this could have happened, that a mere slip of a girl, by coming once to visit the mill, had turned Whitehorn's head, while she, having put all her heart in it, dedicated her life to it, fearing neither scandal nor sin (more than once she had cast spells just so Whitehorn would look her way), but nothing had helped and it had all gone for naught. Her long years of love turned into hate for Whitehorn and rancor for his bride.

Week after week the banns were called in the Švendubrė church for Whitehorn and Marcelė, and there was nothing to be done. Perhaps she could have complained to the pastor, but what could he have done? After all, she had made her vow of chastity a long time ago, seeking revenge on Whitehorn, and he hadn't paid any attention. And now he avoided meeting her; he knocked around by himself, shut up in the mill, and waited for his wedding.

Uršulė would have rather seen the end of the world than the day a new mistress came to the mill. The mere thought of it was unbearable. She considered going wherever her feet might lead her, but she just couldn't tear herself away from the place where she had put so much of her heart and hopes. However, as soon as Whitehorn drove off to the ceremony, she came completely undone by heartache, and nearly went out of her mind. Running to the village cemetery, she filled her apron full of sand and scattered it on the road where the newlyweds had driven away, so that their road would be blocked by troubles and they couldn't come home. Then she took the ashes out of the hearth, so that it wouldn't burn for the new bride and warm her, scattered them on the threshold, so that she couldn't step over it, or if she did—she would leave only in a coffin... When she had finished all of her ritual spells and curses so that nothing would turn out well for the newlyweds, Uršulė clambered on top of the fences and sobbed in an unnatural voice.

A lot of people saw Uršulė running around as if she had lost her head, clambering onto the fences and sobbing, but no one was very surprised the old biddy was being such a fool, since everyone knew about her love for Whitehorn and felt the old maid's disappointment. But alas, no one understood that there was something more going on with Uršulė and that someone needed to take her off the fence and pacify her with an ashberry switch. But, at last, when she heard the newlyweds driving home, Uršulė herself came to her senses: she nearly tumbled off the fence, quickly grabbed her bundle and, with her scarf pulled down over her eyes, took off running to the foot of the hill.

On the road up the hill the merrymakers were driving like mad, and in the first wagon sat Whitehorn, his arms around Marcelė in her white wimple decorated with rue. But Uršulė through her tears didn't see the newlyweds' happiness, and in turn no one noticed her. Driving by they merely raised a cloud of dust from the same sand she had sprinkled there. Maybe that was why her witchcraft and curses went for naught and came down on her own head. At least for the time being nothing bad happened, and no one missed Uršulė, except that after the wedding Jurgutis again pestered the blacksmith about when he would take him match-making.

"How are we going to do that," the blacksmith answered, "when Uršulė cursed Whitehorn's mill and ran
away?... You'll have to wait."

"Wait and wait..." mumbled the discontented Jurgutis, and blew his nose a fathom through one nostril,
since there was nothing else left to do.

X

Whitehorn brought his new bride home to his cottage
as if he had brought home his lost youth. The wedding
went on for three days; the entire village of Paudruvė
gleefully shouted about the mill's hill. The mill itself
stood with its wings raised, as if intending to rise up
and fly from joy or set to dancing with all the merrymakers.

And it was impossible to recognize Whitehorn himself, who had turned livelier and younger so suddenly.
He danced all the wedding rounds like a real bridegroom,
despite his gray head, never letting Marcelė, his unexpected good fortune, out of his sight, as she seemed to
him like a dream that could vanish at any moment, leaving behind a terrible disappointment.

But Marcelė's laughter, like a silver bell, rang out everywhere, even above the din of the wedding. She spun
herself around Whitehorn like a hop-vine opening all of
its blossoms. She flew with him through the yard and
the mill, now holding hands, now breaking free again
and luring him to follow, so that Whitehorn's heart in its
joy hardly stayed in his chest.

Marcelė rejoiced as if she had found herself in the charmed kingdom of her dreams. Hadn't the mill across the lake on the hill with its spinning wings fascinated her since childhood? Now here she was as a young bride and mistress-to-be. Whitehorn didn't look like an aging bachelor to her; he looked just like the king in a fairy tale. Now both the fairy tale and the king himself belonged to her. So what was there not to rejoice in, if her heart itself rang like a silver bell?

"You are my little moon with silver edges," Marcelė would laugh, stroking Whitehorn's gray head, "and I'm your little morning star... our whole life will be like a fairy tale..."

"Oh, you, my little fairy-tale princess!" Whitehorn caressed his young wife, still unable to believe his luck and hardly able to speak from the joy that filled his heart and the entire surroundings—the cliff, the mill, the lake, and the glimmering tops of the pines—to overflowing.

The wedding roared noisily on the hilltop, and Whitehorn came to believe in the fairy tale of his heart, impatiently waiting until he would be alone with his happiness and no one would get in the way of him enjoying it. At last all of the guests dispersed, wishing the newlyweds much success and a long life. The matchmaker Blackpool, although he was roasted for making a crooked match, managed to make it through alive, and, presenting the young bride with the traditional gift of twelve-thread towels, winked merrily while taking leave of Whitehorn:

"Now, look here, don't forget your promise," he said. "For a match like this, I expect you to grind for me for free, not just for the rest of your life, but the rest of mine as well, and I intend to live for a long time. So see to it that you produce some heirs."

"All right," agreed Whitehorn, "I'll grind for you for free, for long as you and I live and throughout the ages, as long as the mill's wings turn on the bluff and your smithy rumbles at the foot of it."

Taking leave of the neighbors and Blackpool, their matchmaker and godfather-to-be, the newlyweds were left at home alone with one another and their longings, which floated like clouds in a clear evening sky.

Early in the morning after the wedding, with the mill humming, Marcelė awoke in a strange room, unable to grasp whether she was dreaming or if it was really so—her dream had come true. The first rays of the sun shone into the cottage and Marcelė, happy and cheerful, ran to the window, as if she wanted to convince herself she had begun her new life. Sure enough, the mill's wings spun above the precipice and the mill hummed, Lake Udruvė sprawled in the distance, and beyond a bend her moss-covered childhood home glimmered.

For a second Marcelė felt a pang of longing in her heart for home. Had she really left it forever? With an uneasy glance, she turned back into the cottage that was to become her new home. Only now did she notice how overgrown it was with cobwebs, and full of strangers' dust and dirt.

Quickly opening the windows and the door, she grabbed a broom and soon all the corners were rolling with clouds of dust that swirled outside. After she had swept the dirt floor and scattered sand and rush over it, she opened her dowry chest and started covering all the furniture and accoutrements with brightly patterned linens, so the gloomy cottage suddenly looked as bright and new as a bride.

When she had finished cleaning up, Marcelė ran to the stove and lit a fire for the first time. It started smoking; the fire was slow to catch, but here, too, the new broom helped out, and soon a little fire merrily flared up in the stove. With breakfast warming, Marcelė ran out to the mill with the broom.

Whitehorn, spotting her running over from the top window, met her on the stairs and wanted to hug her, but she escaped and ran upstairs.

"What are you going to do here, my little bird?" wondered Whitehorn, following behind her.

"You'll see," answered Marcelė as she ran, on the way opening all the mill's bolts and windows, waving the broom about and sweeping all the dust and dirt downstairs.

Whitehorn was buried in a cloud of dust and fled his mill sneezing, and behind him came Marcelė, laughing and sweeping all of the mill's spider webs and accumulated dust balls down the stairs. With the mill swept, Marcelė threw the broom aside and took off running down the precipice to the lake.

"Now catch me, if you can!" she shouted to the stunned Whitehorn.

Dust was coming out of every crack of the mill, but the wings spun and blew the dust away, and Whitehorn, coming to his senses, rushed to follow Marcelė flying down the bluff. But by the time he got there, Marcelė had already undressed, plunged into the clear water, and swum far out into the lake.

That was how the newlyweds' first day began. Whitehorn caught up with his bride by the water lilies, of which she had gathered her arms full. Cheerful and happy, they returned from the lake holding hands. Whitehorn out of joy would have carried his happiness up the hill, but Marcelė broke away and ran up the hill by herself, roaring with laughter.

They met in the yard by a blooming apple tree, which covered them with its boughs. Marcelė's bubbling laughter drowned out the hum of the mill. And when Whitehorn went into the cottage, he hardly recognized it—it looked so new and pretty that it was a sight for sore eyes.

"Oh, you, the light of my life!" said Whitehorn, hugging Marcelė again. "You've brought your youthful joy into my dreary cottage."

Marcelė, laughing, slipped away from Whitehorn's grasp, and the next moment was bringing steaming bowls to the table.

"Sit down to breakfast and stop staring. You'll be charmed," she laughed.

And it was a charmed Whitehorn who sat down at the table and cut into a new loaf of bread, still unable to take his eyes off Marcelė, and smiling a smile as pure and joyful as never before in his life.

"Eat, it's fresh!" Marcelė merrily tapped Whitehorn, who was still staring, on his forehead with a spoon.

Whitehorn laughed, and for the first time spooned breakfast porridge from the same bowl as his wife. Joy overflowed in the house. And the sunlight in the cottage adorned with the young bride's colorful linens grew ever brighter.

XI

But Whitehorn's happiness was as fleeting as a midsummer night's dream. A year went by like a single day, and he still hadn't gotten over his joy. He constantly looked at Marcelė as if he couldn't believe his luck or get enough of looking at her. The foolish old bachelor, winning such a beautiful and cheerful wife, had simply lost his head. He was afraid to let a word go by unheard, a smile—unseen. He followed his Marcelė everywhere, never more than a step behind.

Marcelė could have gotten annoyed by this love of Whitehorn's, but she knew how to turn everything into laughter. She flew like a little bird from the cottage to the mill, from the mill to the lakeshore. Whitehorn, even in his renewed state, couldn't keep up with her, and she would laugh so hard that tears would come to her eyes.

The house, the mill, the slope, and the lakeshore were full of her cheerful laughter, and Whitehorn was so happy he even feared his own happiness, as if sensing some misfortune to come. Marcelė, however, paid no attention; everything cheered her and made her heart sing. She didn't in the least feel like a married woman who ought to be serious; she was still the same carefree, mischievous girl who wanted to take a ride on the mill's wings.

One time—this was a year later, in the fall, when the cranes were flying—Marcelė ran out on the porch and saw a line of cranes flying over the lake. The plaintive cry of the cranes suddenly tugged at Marcelė's heart, and she ran out to the precipice of the lake with her arms outstretched, wanting to see them once more flying out of sight, or to fly off into the blue with them herself.

But then a wing of the mill flashed by. Marcelė herself didn't know how she got caught up on the wing, but she started rising to the top as if she had remembered her old dream to swing on the mill's wings.

It was a good thing that Whitehorn, hearing the cranes' cry, glanced through the window and saw Marcelė rising on the sail of the mill. He nearly died of fright, and had a terrible premonition.

"Marcelė, what are you doing?" he cried in an unnatural voice, and rushed to stop the mill.

The mill came creaking to a halt, and Marcelė jumped down from the wing and laughed.

"That wasn't nice," she said, "that you stopped the mill. I wanted to go up, up, up and fly with the cranes. I was so happy."

But suddenly the smile disappeared from her face; she turned pale all over and staggered.

"For some reason things are spinning," she said, clutched at her heart, and collapsed in Whitehorn's arms.

"What's the matter, my little bird?" said the frightened Whitehorn, taking her into his embrace.

Marcelė shook all over like an aspen leaf.

"I don't know," answered the pale Marcelė. "It's as if the vein of happiness in my heart has broken."

"Oh, you little naughty creature of mine," said Whitehorn, looking at Marcelė's closed eyes with reproach and love. "Why on earth did you need to go riding on the mill's wings?"

Marcelė didn't answer; she just pressed herself up closer to Whitehorn. She was carrying a new life under her heart.

Whitehorn carried Marcelė back into the cottage in his arms and laid her down. From that day on, her cheerfulness disappeared, as if the vein of happiness in her heart really had broken and silenced the bells of laughter.

The autumn clouds crept by the mill's wings, the wind whistled, and the weather turned foul. It was the time for grinding grain, but more and more frequently the mill stood frozen like a ghost on the precipice. The farmers who came to the mill and found it motionless went into the cottage, sensing misfortune. There they found Whitehorn with his head in his hands, sitting by his wife's bed.

"Why are you tormenting yourself?" they said, understanding his grief at once. "That's the way it's always been and always will be, without pain there is no pleasure… grind the grain, brew some beer, and wait for the christening."

Whitehorn, looking at the farmers with silent reproach and at his pale wife with affection, would get up and go out to the mill. But after pouring the grain into the millstones, he would return again and sit by the bed, stroking Marcelė's head and looking into her eyes that smiled sadly, in spite of the pain, with a mother's pure hope.

But then Marcelė started writhing in unbearable pain, and Whitehorn, not knowing what to do except tear his hair out in grief, changed places by the birthing bed with the midwife sent by the neighbors.

"What is it, sweetheart?" the midwife leaned over the birthing bed, smiling with all of the wrinkles on her face and worrying: "Maybe it's a bit too early? But just bear it, bear it, after the pain you'll have a bundle of joy…"

The midwife started preparing for the newborn, and then turned to the distressed Whitehorn, who was still at loose ends.

"There's nothing here for you to do," said the midwife to him forgivingly. "Better go out to your mill."

Whitehorn, glancing beseechingly at the midwife, knelt one more time by Marcelė's bed and met her I-can-bear-anything glance, along with a smile that shone through the pain. Then a hope glimmered in Whitehorn's heart that everything would end well, and Marcelė's pain and grief would multiply both their happiness.

With that hope, Whitehorn went out to the mill, even though he felt oppressed by his worries and torn by a sense of foreboding. He set the mill's wings turning so they would count the slow minutes faster, and listening to the hum of the millstones, he gazed out the topmost window, waiting and fretting terribly.

Little by little, the first snowflakes fell through the mill's slowly turning wings and glistened in bright little sparkles. The heavens were gloomy and dark, without any glow. Through the mist of snow, the lake at the foot of the hill calmed down, and the tops of the pines by the shore draped themselves in little shawls of white.

Whitehorn lingered uneasily, listening to the mill's hum and watching the slowly creeping winter dusk. At last, a light flickered in the window of the cottage and Whitehorn, his heart going numb, dashed into the cottage in the hope of finding his newly born joy.

In the cottage, the worried midwife met Whitehorn with a screaming newborn in her arms. By Marcelė's bed a wax candle was burning. Shuddering, Whitehorn glanced at the baby and dashed to his wife, not understanding what had happened.

"Marcelė, joy of mine..." he fell to his knees by the bed with his heart going numb.

Marcelė lay there without a word, as pale as a sheet, her bright eyes closed.

"It's God's will," answered the midwife, soothing the newborn. "A daughter was born, a mother died."

Whitehorn didn't hear her words or the baby's cries; he went speechless and numb, hugging his wife's dead body, and felt as if he had lost everything in the world.

After a happy summer and a beautiful fall, a grim winter dusk fell outside the windows.

XII

That sad winter evening Whitehorn's mill stopped turning. With its wings, the wheel of life had turned, and in Whitehorn's cottage, a cradle and a coffin appeared.

The neighbors who had gathered for the wake laid Marcelė out on the table, crossed her arms on her breast, and lit wax candles by her head. The sputtering candles lit up Marcelė's pale face and her lips frozen in their last smile. Even in her coffin she looked like a sleeping bride.

Whitehorn, overcome by unbearable grief, knelt by the coffin and wailed as if he had gone completely mad, begging through his tears that Marcelė would laugh just one last time and give him hope to go on living.

But the frozen Marcelė lay silent and wordless. The only answer was a sorrowful cry from the cradle of the little orphan. Then Whitehorn shuddered and seemed to awake from his grief. He went over to the cradle and stopped. The baby screamed ever louder, as if calling for her mother but failing to get a response. The women gathered for the wake wiped the corners of their eyes with their kerchiefs and rushed over to soothe the baby, while Whitehorn stood as if turned to stone, not taking his eyes off the cradle and thinking very hard about something.

At last, the baby quieted down, as if she had sensed the enormous misfortune, but Whitehorn still didn't move away from the cradle. Huge tears rolled down his cheeks, and he silently pulled the gray hair from his head. It was then he realized what he had so carelessly promised Pinčukas in exchange for the short moment of happiness in his life, and he completely lost his head.

The mourning hymns filled the cottage as the neighbors closed Marcelė into the coffin and prepared to carry her to her place of eternal rest. Rising from the cradle, Whitehorn rushed to the coffin, trying to prevent them from carrying it out of the cottage, as if he wanted it to stay with him forever.

The neighbors carried the coffin out of the cottage by force, dragging Whitehorn behind them. The frozen mill stood on the precipice, and in the glow of sunset the snowy caps of the pines around the lake smoldered like funeral candles.

The sad funeral procession descended from the bluff of the mill and, accompanied by sorrowful mourning hymns, turned down the beaten path by the lake leading to the village cemetery on a small hill. Whitehorn, his head bowed in grief, followed behind the coffin as if in a fog, seeing and hearing nothing, feeling that he was escorting all of his life's happiness to the grave, and that all that was left for him was a hopeless heartache.

The sunset shone dimly through crooked crosses as they lowered Marcelė's coffin into the grave. The first clods of earth thumped on the coffin's lid. As if the dull thud had brought him to his senses, Whitehorn leapt for the grave so he could be buried there, too.

"Brother, have you completely lost your head?" Blackpool restrained him, grabbing him by the shoulders and holding him back. "No one lives forever. When the time comes, you'll lie alongside her, but now you still have a daughter to raise."

Whitehorn shuddered and quieted down, held back by the blacksmith's strong arms, but with each handful of dirt he felt as if his heart were falling into the grave and he himself collapsing along with it. Blackpool, barely holding him back, wondered not so much at his grief as at the force that pulled him to the earth. Only when the hole was filled did Blackpool let his friend go, giving him free rein to his sorrow. Whitehorn, staggering, fell to the earth, hugging the grave and wailing like a woman.

"That's enough now, enough!" Blackpool scolded him, though he himself was deeply touched and wiped away an escaped tear. "Be a man, get hold of yourself! You'll have to live and bear it, let those who have died rest in peace."

In the end, forcefully tearing Whitehorn away from the grave, Blackpool led him back home through the dusk, Whitehorn walking as if he were dreaming and unaware of where he was going. Everything got muddled in the evening shadows. The mill stood on the hill as if floating in the air. But even the mill seemed somehow distant, as though the wings, raised up high into the sky, were communing with the twinkling stars and eternity. Whitehorn clearly heard them talking; he just couldn't understand what they were saying. In his head and heart everything swirled around in a mist.

It was only when he went inside the cottage that he came to his senses somewhat. The midwife sat by the cradle in the darkness, humming and crooning a sorrowful lullaby.

"Hush, little orphan, poor little one,
how is it now that you've begun,
a weaver of fine white homespun..."

The cradle rocked slowly, and inside the newborn slept peacefully. Only the hooks on the ceiling sometimes creaked in unison with the crooning. This mournful creaking and crooning awoke Whitehorn, and again he rushed to the cradle, forgetting the funeral and seized by a new worry, which buried everything else in an impenetrable fog.

"You poor thing!" said the midwife, rising from the cradle. "I've no idea what to do now. I've been waiting for you to return from the funeral, and they're already calling me to see another newborn. But how can I go and leave the two of you here by yourselves?"

"If they've asked you, then go," the blacksmith answered her, groping around in the dark and lighting a wick lamp above the table, which dimly lit up the cottage.

Whitehorn remained standing by the cradle as if he had turned to stone; uneasy shadows crossed his face, and his drooping arm slowly rocked the cradle.

Worried, Blackpool sat down at the table at a loss as to what to do next, so, looking around, he stuffed his pipe full of tobacco leaf and puffed on the bitter smoke.

The midwife, preparing to leave, crept about the cottage as quietly as a mouse. But neither Whitehorn, rocking the cradle whose mournful creaking matched his own sad thoughts, nor Blackpool, inhaling the bitter smoke and not knowing what to do to help his friend, took any notice of her.

At last the midwife, wrapped up in her Sunday shawl, went over to the cradle, tucked the baby in, showed Whitehorn what to do with a newborn, and stroked Whitehorn's bent head.

"It's God's will!" she said, taking her leave. "There's nothing to be done. Tomorrow, if I can, I'll run by to take a look. Goodbye and good luck."

Whitehorn looked at her beseechingly, desperately seeking help. The midwife sighed, nodded her head in sympathy, and quietly left. Whitehorn couldn't grasp what was happening to him. He saw his entire life in front of him—murky, muddled, foggy. It hummed nearby like the mill on the shore of the troubled lake. But was it really humming? He raised his head and listened—silence, not a sound. Just the creaking of the cradle hanging from the ceiling. Suddenly Pinčukas flashed by in the dimness, grinning treacherously. But was it really Pinčukas, or did he just dream it? Something indistinct swept by with the shadow of the mill's wings. Wasn't that Marcelė swinging on them? His heart skipped a beat, and he rejoiced at having heard her shrieking and laughing.

Whitehorn shuddered, and again the deathly silence fell upon him. Where did Marcelė go? But was it really her, or was it just his wishful dream, which dissolved like the morning mists with the mill's wings? Whitehorn bent over the cradle: his dreams and his visions vanished as if they had never been, for a new life was sleeping in the cradle. Whitehorn gazed at it as if bewitched, unable to tear his eyes away.

Blackpool continued to sit at the table where not so long ago he had celebrated at the wedding and from where he had this day carried out the young bride's coffin. Oppressed by somber thoughts, he inhaled the smoke, which rose in puffs to the ceiling and spread through the cottage. Dreary shadows hung in the dark corners like useless worry. The heavy quiet was oppressive. At last, the blacksmith couldn't endure it any longer and gave himself a shake. He looked through the smoke at Whitehorn bent over the cradle and realized that from that cradle a new life would arise, one that would blow away the dreary shadows in the smoky cottage. It would comfort his friend, battered by misfortune, and give him the strength to live again.

Understanding this, the blacksmith rose from the table, walked over to Whitehorn with a heavy step and put a hand on his stooped shoulder.

"Don't worry," he said, "You'll bear this misfortune and be twice as strong for it. You'll raise a little daughter, and she will be all your life's comfort and joy. So don't lose your head. Misfortune will pass like the night, and the sun will rise again."

Whitehorn looked at his friend with bleary eyes, as if he neither understood a word, nor expected to see the morning. A terrible emptiness oppressed him, and nothing made sense to him, except what he felt with all his heart—that as long as he had life in him, he wouldn't budge from that cradle, where all of his hopes lay.

XIII

Crushed with grief, Whitehorn spent the first night after the funeral next to the cradle, never taking his eyes off of it. The blacksmith stayed a bit longer and then went home before midnight. Whitehorn never even noticed he had been left alone with his newborn.

The winter night crept by quietly. The wick lamp on the table went out, but Whitehorn didn't miss its light. Outside, white hoarfrost fell on the mill's motionless wings, and through the window the pale moon gazed at Whitehorn bent over the cradle.

Towards morning, the door creaked, and the baby woke up and cried. Whitehorn glanced at the door, thinking the midwife had returned, but saw that Uršulė had entered. Wrapped in a shawl, she stopped by the door as if she didn't dare go any farther. Whitehorn looked at her for a moment in surprise, wondering how she came to be there, and then turned back to the cradle, rocking and soothing the crying baby.

Uršulė, hearing of Whitehorn's misfortune, had come for the very purpose of offering comfort and assistance, forgetting all her own injuries and misfortunes, and wanting to help him with all her heart, as she still loved him with the old unquenchable passion, jumbled as it was with the bitterness of disappointment and newly found hope. But, stepping over the threshold she herself had put a curse on, she lost her nerve and froze to the spot.

Suddenly Uršulė was seized by a mixture of grief and fright, crushing her anew with despair and renewing her old frustration. She wanted to jump back immediately and run, but she couldn't move from the spot; her feet froze like stumps and she stood rooted to the ground.

Uršulė pulled free from the threshold only when the newborn in the cradle started to cry again and the befuddled Whitehorn, at a loss, looked about. Then, wiping away an escaped tear with the corner of her shawl, she resolutely approached the cradle and put her hand on Whitehorn's shoulder.

"Let me," she said. "I'll stay by the cradle; you go to your mill."

"You go yourself, to wherever you want," answered Whitehorn, swaying after the sleepless night and all of his heartbreak.

However, Uršulė, once her mind was made up, didn't back down.

"What will you do, you silly fool, with a child?" she objected. "How will you raise it? Thank me for coming to help, instead."

The determined Uršulė pushed Whitehorn away from the cradle, changed the baby's diaper, and the newborn quieted down. Whitehorn stood by the cradle a while until the child fell asleep, and, engrossed in thought, went out to the mill, not knowing what else to do.

Little by little, the wings of the mill began turning again, along with Whitehorn's new worries. And Uršulė stayed by the cradle, forgetting her disappointments and making peace with her fate.

"If only God had been willing," she just sighed, "I'd be rocking my own daughter. But now…"

However, the bitterness that smoldered in her heart was extinguished by a new hope:

"But God might still be willing… Whitey will come around… What will he do with a child and no wife?"

With that hope, Uršulė began housekeeping anew in Whitehorn's house, taking everything into her hands and rocking a stranger's cradle.

Whitehorn, as if he had forgotten all about it, hovered about the house quietly and engrossed in thought, paying no attention to Uršulė; but wherever he happened to be, he kept stopping by the cradle, and couldn't pull himself away for a long time. All by himself he pondered over something, never reaching a decision, and all the while grew sadder still.

"What's this now, why are you always next to that cradle," Uršulė, glaring, would reproach him. "Have you gone completely out of your head, that you see nothing but that cradle?"

Whitehorn, to Uršulė's even greater frustration, wouldn't say anything in reply, and out he would go to the mill again.

Meanwhile, time didn't stand still. Winter with its frosts and thaws crept by, and glimmers of spring shone through the mill's wings more and more often. The tops of the pine trees surveyed the surroundings through the greenish mist and a lively soughing came from them.

That winter Whitehorn went completely gray and bent from worry and grief. Closed up in the mill alone with his sorrow, he didn't notice the budding spring. It was only when the baby in the cradle, her tiny hands catching at the sun's rays, started laughing, that White-horn smiled for the first time after his long mourning. The baby's laughter evoked her mother, as if Marcelė had left her cheerfulness behind with her daughter. Whitehorn, with an awakened joy in his heart, took the infant into his arms and smiled happily, forgetting his worries and sorrows.

It surprised Uršulė to see Whitehorn smiling with the baby in his arms. She stopped pushing the pots around by the hearth, fixed her scarf, and, smiling herself, approached the happy father.

"You see, Whitey," she said sweetly, "The little one's laughing. I'll raise you a daughter... If you'd only catch on… You'd have yourself a wife, and a mother for the baby…"

But this sweetness of Uršulė's didn't please White-horn. He just looked askance at her and was sad again. Laying the child down in the cradle, he went out, engrossed in thought, to the mill.

Uršulė was despondent again too.

"He'll never catch on," she said to herself, and brushed away a tear with the corner of her scarf. "It would be possible to raise even a stranger's child, if only he'd catch on… But how is a fool like that going to get it?"

The disappointed Uršulė lost her patience and angrily shoved the cradle with her foot. The baby inside cried.

"Like I'll rock you all the time," she muttered angrily, and turned back to the pots. "Scream if you want, you'll croak faster."

But the baby, jostled in her cradle, quieted down, as if she sensed neither her mother was standing by the cradle with love, nor her father stooped with worries.

Whitehorn, returning to the mill, considered how he could shake off Uršulė once and for all, since apparently she wasn't going to give him any peace again. But how are you going to raise a child without a mother? So, unable to find an alternative, he endured it. Besides, Uršulė was the least of his worries, even if she annoyed him with her carping.

In front of Whitehorn's eyes, wherever he looked, he seemed to see Marcelė like a soaring little bird, and the babbling of the brooks in spring reminded him of her ringing laughter. These memories of his lost happiness drove Whitehorn out of his mind. Only his worries about his daughter blocked them out. Night and day he tried but failed to think up a way to save his child from the promise he had so carelessly given to Pinčukas, and to buy back that too-brief and too-deceptive good fortune of his.

The truth of it was that Whitehorn tormented himself needlessly. There was still plenty of time left before he would need to fulfill his promise, and sometimes happenstance shows a person a good way out. You just need to see it when it comes.

In the end, Whitehorn, quite unexpectedly, found a solution with the help of the annoying Uršulė, and for the first time he was grateful to her with all his heart.

XIV

The twelfth year was coming to an end, but Whitehorn, still at a loss to find a way out of his dilemma, couldn't regain his peace of mind. He looked at his daughter as though he just couldn't get enough of her, and day after day he grew more and more despondent. This despondency wasn't dispelled even by the laughter of his daughter, who steadily grew merrier and prettier, thereby saddening her father even more.

Because of this despondency and regret, Whitehorn grew more and more frail. And the worst of it was, he had no one to share his heartache with. All alone, he had tormented and tortured himself until he had turned into the shadow of a man, on whose head the wind tousled the grey hairs the way the wind in autumn tousles the last yellowed leaves left on the trees.

Wherever he went, whatever he did, the promise he had made to Pinčukas was never far from his thoughts. He would have accepted eternal torment with pleasure, if only he could save the sole comfort of his widow-hood—his daughter Jurga. Because his daughter had never seen him other than worried and remorseful, she didn't know her father was grieving. She only sensed his boundless love, and that was quite enough for her to grow up cheerful and happy.

Whitehorn, in his worry and remorse, forgot and neglected everything in the world—except his daughter. He even failed to look after the mill, so the winds were on the verge of picking it apart. Uršulė alone took care of everything. She became a truly enviable housekeeper, and scolded Whitehorn on account of his carelessness. Seeing that Whitehorn completely ignored both her and her scolding, her patience at an end, she would start swearing to high heaven that with such a fool—who had first lost his head because of the mill, then because of his wife, and now because of his daughter (why did God ever give someone like that a brain?)—she couldn't live this way any more. She would marry whomever she fancied, even if it turned out to be the devil himself, since, living with such a blockhead, she would all the same be damned and go to hell for all eternity through no fault of her own.

With Uršulė going on in this manner, Whitehorn suddenly laughed and cheered up about something. Surprised, Uršulė gaped at him, dumbfounded. What did he find to be so happy about? Had he completely lost his mind? So, making the sign of the cross over herself and then doing the same for him, she went off, saying her rosary and repenting for the sins she'd committed.

The thought had just then entered Whitehorn's head—why couldn't he deceive Pinčukas, who had deceived him, and give that old maid, that sanctimonious old biddy Uršulė, who annoyed him to the bone, to the devil to marry in place of his daughter? The more so since she wanted it herself. So, let her go, get her off his poor back. Why envy someone's good fortune? It was only because he hadn't believed he could deceive both the devil and the sanctimonious old biddy at the same time that he had procrastinated, worrying, and here twelve years had gone by.

But even then it was far from certain that Whitehorn, what with all his vacillations and doubts, would have extricated himself from his own blunder by dumping it on someone else's shoulders, if Uršulė herself hadn't helped things along. That afternoon, as if sensing something, she went completely off her rocker, slamming around the cottage, banging around the yard, unable to settle down and making life miserable for the others as well. Whitehorn's daughter, unable to bear it, ran off to visit her grandparents on the other side of the lake, while Whitehorn, his patience at an end, hid himself in the mill and resolved to shake off Uršulė for once and for all.

At dusk the matchmakers with the bay steeds and the golden carriage arrived. Uršulė was stupefied by this unexpected good fortune, and then Whitehorn unloaded her on Pinčukas and took back the promissory note.

The night was so stormy, with all the lightning and thunder, that it could have dashed the mill from the cliff, but Whitehorn, after seeing the newlyweds off and burning the deceitful note, was happier than he had ever been in his life. It was as if an enormous rock, one that had weighed on him for a full twelve years, had rolled off his chest.

The next day Jurga, running home before dinner from her visit to her grandparents, found the spiteful Uršulė gone and her father unrecognizable—he was so drastically changed and so thoroughly cheerful.

"Now the two of us will live together without any troubles, worries or eternal scolding... Uršulė's gone to the old biddies' sanctuary..." he said to his daughter on her return, and his tired eyes emitted a heretofore unseen happiness.

"Why did she do that?" wondered Jurga.

"Who pays heed to a sanctimonious old biddy?" Whitehorn waved it off. "She soured herself and the entire house too. Lord willing, maybe she won't come back. You straighten up the cottage, I'm going out to the mill."

Jurga didn't know what had happened that night; she believed her father had cheered up merely because he had shaken off Uršulė. So she was no less cheerful herself, since that grumpy old maid had curdled her entire youth and turned her father's house into hell. It seemed that with last night's lightning and thunder all their misfortunes had passed. It was a fine day, without a single cloud.

But that very morning at dawn Whitehorn saw Pinčukas running home from the bogs and was terribly discouraged that his efforts had come to naught. But he recovered himself quickly. The little devil looked so unhappy, muddy, crushed, and crumpled, with one horn twisted off, that Whitehorn, although frightened, immediately understood that he had the devil in his hands, rather than the other way around.

"What's the matter?" asked Whitehorn, brightening up. "It must have been quite a wedding, if even the bridegroom got it."

"What wedding?" muttered Pinčukas, completely despondent. "We hadn't gotten to the wedding yet, and I barely made it out alive. I don't want a wife anymore. Take back that daughter of yours."

Whitehorn understood that Uršulė had made it hot for the devil, and thought he needed to tighten the screws even more, so Pinčukas wouldn't dare complain if at some point he should understand he'd been deceived.

"No, that won't do," Whitehorn answered. "You've seduced my daughter, now what will I do with her? You have to marry her."

"No, no way," Pinčukas even retreated. "Demand whatever you want for the seduction, but I'll not take her for a wife."

Whitehorn thought for a bit and said:

"Well, what's to be done with you now? If you'd agree to work for me for seven years as a hired hand, to turn the mill's wings in place of the wind, and to do any other tasks I may order, then maybe I'll release you from your responsibility to marry my daughter."

Pinčukas immediately brightened up:

"Fine," he said. "I'll work for you for seven years as a hired hand, and I'll serve you most faithfully."

"Fine," Whitehorn agreed. "Afterwards you can go look for another wife."

"Oh, no," the little devil shuddered. "I'll never go looking for a wife again. I don't even want to think about it."

"As you wish," Whitehorn shrugged his shoulders. "It's your business. And now, see, it's dawn already. It's time to start working."

"What do you want done?" the little devil jumped up as if he hadn't at all been worn to a frazzle that night.

"I have a great deal of milling," answered Whitehorn, "and there's no wind. Turn the mill's sails in place of the wind."

"Fine," agreed Pinčukas, and that very instant flew up onto the mill's wings like a top.

The sails immediately began turning, and the longer they turned, the faster they went. Whitehorn was even obliged to restrain his hired hand, so he wouldn't go too fast. And Pinčukas enjoyed turning on the mill's wings so much that he even forgot all the previous night's mortifications, and on the whole this was much more pleasant than stagnating and moldering in the quagmire. Pinčukas was even surprised he hadn't thought of this earlier and hadn't come to Whitehorn to offer his help.

But Pinčukas' satisfaction was premature. As day began breaking, he saw Uršulė returning from the bogs, cursing Whitehorn as well as him, Pinčukas, in an inhuman voice, and determined to light a fire under them both. Pinčukas was so frightened he didn't notice himself jumping from the wing straight through the little window into the mill and, trembling all over, falling at Whitehorn's feet.

"What happened?" asked Whitehorn in surprise.

"Help, your daughter's coming home," the little devil whimpered pathetically.

"What did you say?" Frightened, Whitehorn gave a start and looked through the little window.

It really was Uršulė, huffing and puffing, returning from the bogs all muddy and dreadfully furious.

"Now this, my boy, is no joke. It looks like you really crossed her. We could both get it. You crawl under the millstones for the time being and hide there, and I'll go barricade the door to the mill."

In a flash Pinčukas crawled under the millstones and hid there, trembling, while Whitehorn went downstairs, barricaded the door from inside and watched through a crack to see what would happen. Uršulė came home, raged about, ran to the mill but couldn't force her way inside. For a moment Whitehorn feared the bar on the door was too weak, but then she suddenly went back to the house, ran out with a bundle, and left, but kept turning back, menacing with her clenched fist and cursing.

When Uršulė had run so far away that she could no longer be seen and her curses could no longer be heard, Whitehorn sighed and said to Pinčukas:

"Come out from under the millstones. This time the storm has passed. But take care! Women, like you devils, can make themselves look like anything. When you see a creature like that with a skirt, crawl under the millstones

and hide, for when they come across you, and especially
that witch, even I won't be able to save you."

Pinčukas, still trembling, crawled out from under the
millstones all covered with flour and listened to Whitehorn's advice as if listening to his own father, without
missing a single word. Later he held this advice sacred: if
he so much as glimpsed a woman, he would immediately
flee under the millstones and hide, afraid to so much as
sneeze.

Such was the fear Uršulė had provoked in him, poor
thing. And this time Whitehorn was thoroughly pleased
with Uršulė, even thankful to her. It had thundered like
a swelling storm, and now the day had become brighter.

XV

But what was really going on was anyone's guess. All
sorts of rumors spread around, and people made all
manner of conjectures. Some were even inclined to believe Uršulė: unable to bear her any longer, Whitehorn
really had attempted to marry her off to Pinčukas, and
had dumped her at night into Paudruvė's bog.

Other people shook their heads and didn't want to
believe an old maid's ranting and raving. Everyone knew
very well that Uršulė had annoyed Whitehorn to the
bone, and he just couldn't shake her off, as he was so
slow. So how could he be in cahoots with the devil now?

However, his nearest neighbor, matchmaker, and
godfather, Blackpool the smith, was a clever man, one
who loved pranks and jokes even in his old age. Just let

an opportunity arise and he would at once think of the craziest things. Would Whitehorn really have milled for him for free all this time just for his wit? Earlier, understandably, he had milled for him because of the successful match (it was anyone's guess how Blackpool had married off an old geezer to a young girl; surely he hadn't gotten by then without the devil), but what did he mill for now?

Shrewder people figured it might have been Blackpool who was responsible for it all. When Uršulė had completely exasperated Whitehorn, Blackpool, dressed as a matchmaker with a glued-on beard made from a tow of flax that hung to his knees, and taking along his boy Jurgutis as the bridegroom, after scrubbing him up good and decking him out, drove over to Whitehorn's mill in the evening, and that night dumped Uršulė out with the trough into the bogs.

Then there were some who had heard Whitehorn and Blackpool plotting when the despondent Whitehorn had stopped by the smithy.

"Do what you will, neighbor," declared the despairing Whitehorn. "I've done your milling for free and I'll keep doing it, but just save me from Uršulė. On her account neither I nor my daughter have a life."

"No big deal," answered Blackpool, laughing. "If you want, I'll not only get her out of your mill, but I'll marry her off to the devil of Paudruvė's bogs, Pinčukas, too."

"How will you do that?" Whitehorn was pleased, but doubtful.

"Now that's my affair," answered Blackpool, squinting slyly. "And you, if you'll continue to do my milling

79

for free, then I'll do it next Saturday night. Jurgutis, do you still want to go match-making?"

"I do," Jurgutis jumped out of the corner by the bellows and blew his nose a fathom.

"All right, then stop blowing your nose, work the bellows!" the smith scolded. "And you," he declared to Whitehorn, "can go home quietly and expect matchmakers. I'll finish outfitting that highfalutin phaeton for Cockend's tavern keeper Shaddon, and arrange everything just fine."

Maybe that's the way it was, or maybe not. On Saturday night Blackpool really did finish outfitting Shaddon's highfalutin phaeton, but Shaddon didn't take it that evening. And it appeared Blackpool hadn't gone anywhere to try the new carriage out. As it happened, that night it was very dark and there was thunder, and in the morning there was a heavy fog.

Be that as it may, but at dawn Jurgutis ran home all muddy from the village. Fearing to blow his nose, he sniffled into his fist like a cat, and down by the lagoon he cleaned off the new phaeton, which had gotten muddy somewhere, with a handful of straw. But where he had gotten himself splattered with mud (perhaps he had tried to get into a strange larder with the girls, and the boys had caught him and smeared him with mud), and where the phaeton had gotten dirty, wasn't in the least bit clear. Just as he finished cleaning it, a hungover Shaddon rode up and took the phaeton home, and Jurgutis crawled into the smithy behind the forge to sleep it off.

But even while sleeping he constantly sniffled and blew his nose, and when he awoke he no longer wanted, God forbid, to either go matchmaking, or to marry.

"That's fine," the smith said to him, "Just watch out, don't tell anyone what happened last night, because then you'll have to marry Uršulė and live with her."

"Oh, no," Jurgutis answered, shuddering. "I'd rather pump the bellows my whole life and sometimes blow my nose a fathom through one nostril."

"Well, that you can do," agreed the smith. "And don't you dare breathe a word to anyone about what happened during the night."

But how can you expect a mere boy not to go bragging about a prank like that! That very evening he ran around half the village and, rolling with laughter, blowing his nose and sniggering into his fist, related how at dusk the day before he had ridden out matchmaking to Whitehorn's Uršulė with Blackpool, the smith, in Shaddon's new phaeton and how, later that night, with the thunder growling, they had dumped her together with the cracked trough into Paudruvė's bogs. There he got it good, when he accidentally tangled himself in Uršulė's pleated skirt, but fortunately he had escaped, and the very devil himself, Pinčukas, had got it into his head to marry Uršulė. How Uršulė got out of that trouble, Jurgutis didn't know, he just heard that she had, that very morning, cursed Whitehorn's mill and run off to Švendubrė's almshouse.

But Jurgutis didn't tell the story so much as he sniggered into his fist like a cat and blew his nose a fathom through one and the other nostril, so it was impossible to take anything at face value, and everything had to be held as a boy's—and a dimwit's at that—nonsense. Consequently no one believed him any more than they did Uršulė.

Uršulė, when asked if it wasn't Blackpool with Jurgutis who had called on her matchmaking and had dumped her out with the trough into the bogs, was infuriated, and crossing herself said:

"Am I blind, or what? I saw him with my own eyes. What did Jurgutis have to do with it? Wouldn't I recognize that dolt? He had horns! It was Pinčukas for sure!"

Jurgutis, whenever he saw Uršulė, would run sniggering off to the side, so he wouldn't fall into her hands and have to marry her. It's pure conjencture as to what really happened that night. Jurgutis told it one way, Uršulė another. Everything got confused and it wasn't at all clear whom to believe. And if you asked Whitehorn and Blackpool—the one was quiet, and the other jeered through his mustache:

"You believe a boy's and an old maid's ravings?… Maybe they dreamed it all up?"

A dream is a dream, but the next day, right next to the biggest quagmire in Paudruvė's bogs, a shepherd boy found a cracked trough and Uršulė's pleated skirt caught on a juniper. He left the trough (what can you do with a thing full of holes?) and took the skirt to Whitehorn. In memory of Uršulė Whitehorn hung it in the mill to use as a dust cloth. Later Blackpool tore off half of it and took it home to his smithy, both to clean soot with and to intimidate Jurgutis, so he wouldn't play the fool anymore, and wouldn't get a hankering to go matchmaking.

One way or another, strange rumors started spreading about Whitehorn's mill, and what happened afterwards is anyone's guess.

XVI

Whatever the true story was of that fateful night, from that morning on Pinčukas became Whitehorn's hired hand and served him faithfully for almost seven years.

With pleasure he turned the mill's wings in place of the wind, looked after the millstones and did all the other work that Whitehorn entrusted him with. And he would have become an altogether decent miller, if it hadn't been for all sorts of devilish weaknesses. But what do you expect from a devil, when people are well acquainted with them, and after all, it's said the devil is the embodiment of all evil.

Pinčukas had his good points, too, and what Whitehorn most appreciated that he was conscientious, kept his word, and was afraid of women's skirts. If he so much as saw a woman's skirt from a distance, he would crawl under the millstones, and in his fear whine like a puppy until Whitehorn calmed him down.

Sometimes Pinčukas would be overcome with his old laziness and complete indifference, but it sufficed merely to go out and turn the mill's wings and his head would immediately clear. Pinčukas liked to spin with the mill's wings more than anything. Then, looking out over the wide surroundings, the rippling lakes and the green hills, he would start daydreaming about a great and beautiful life and extraordinary deeds to carry out. But for the time being they were just that, daydreams, that he had neither the time nor a great inclination to fulfill, so Pinčukas became a hopeless dreamer.

The years went by, one after another, and Pinčukas became more and more accustomed to Whitehorn's mill.

He didn't even want to remember his quagmire. Occasionally he would even be clutched by fear: where would he go, if Whitehorn would up and drive him out of the mill? How would he live then, and what would he do? Surely he wouldn't stagnate day and night in the swamp and slumber away meaninglessly. At this thought shivers would actually go down the little devil's spine. He started to thoroughly resemble a human being in all of his weaknesses.

But Whitehorn was a good master, completely satisfied with Pinčukas' work and behavior, and never even thought of driving him out of the mill. If occasionally he would frighten Pinčukas with a woman's skirt—for which purpose he intentionally kept that torn skirt of Uršulė's in the mill, the one the shepherds had brought home that time from the bogs—or with that 'daughter' of his—worse than a witch—he would do this only for Pinčukas' own greater good. Pinčukas understood this and was downright grateful to Whitehorn.

At last Pinčukas grew so accustomed to Whitehorn's mill that he changed completely, and actually started to lose his devilish nature. Even his looks altered: he turned white instead of black, so that the prince of devils himself wouldn't have recognized him if it weren't for the horns on his forehead, one of which remained as it was, half twisted off by Uršulė, and his threadbare tail, which was beginning to disappear altogether. Anyone who had known him earlier in the quagmire would never have suspected that this nimble and hard-working little devil was the same completely worthless lazy devil of Paudruvė's morass.

Perhaps Pinčukas would have transformed himself completely and stayed in Whitehorn's mill forever, if not for a chance event. The seven years were already coming to an end—what are years to a devil, really—like a single day for a human—when suddenly he became interested in who on earth it was laughing so merrily, running around the mill. One time, unable to restrain himself, he looked out through a crack and saw an unusually pretty girl running up to the mill.

The girl ran up to Whitehorn, lovingly threw her arms around his neck, and started whispering something in his ear, still laughing. That laugh was so merry that it tugged at Pinčukas' heart.

At first Pinčukas was dreadfully frightened and wanted to hide under the millstones, but that merry laugh and the girl's bright eyes held him back, and he stood there staring with his mouth open.

Later, hidden behind a corner, Pinčukas overheard the girl telling Whitehorn:

"I don't know, father dear, the matchmakers want to come calling on me too, but I'll fix up such a good match that no one will even want to mention it a second time."

"Oh, you, my naughty little girl," answered Whitehorn, worried. "Is that the proper way for girls to behave? A suitor you fancy will come to make a match, and away you'll go, and leave me on my own."

"Never," the girl shook herself. "Not even for a prince with a golden carriage."

Then the girl hugged Whitehorn and went into the cottage, while Pinčukas followed her with his eyes and wondered who she could be. He didn't want to believe she was that same daughter of Whitehorn's, meaner than a witch, who had nearly torn out his eyes and twisted one of his horns. But if it wasn't his daughter, then who could she be?

Pinčukas was so baffled by this riddle that he racked his brains, but he had become entirely unaccustomed to thinking, formerly, slumbering in the bogs, and afterwards turning Whitehorn's mill, so he had a hard time figuring anything out. It probably didn't help that every time the girl showed up in the yard or the mill he completely lost his head, and, in a daze, would devour her with his eyes, unable to think at all. She was so pretty that he couldn't get enough of looking at her. She was exactly what he used to fantasize about and dream of while slumbering. Could she really be like that?

Love, or something like it, seized the little devil's heart, so that he actually grew thin, following the girl with his eyes and guessing at this unsolvable riddle. Whitehorn, completely unaware of this, worried that perhaps his hand was ill, since he had become so sad and puny. Perhaps he was longing for his quagmire, or hell.

"Don't be sad," he comforted him once, "The seven years are coming to an end, you'll be able to go wherever you want."

"I'm never going to leave your mill," the sad little devil answered, "I'll stay here forever."

"As you wish." Whitehorn shrugged his shoulders, suspecting nothing. "Stay, if you like."

Another time, out of nowhere, Pinčukas said to Whitehorn:

"Who's that girl running around the yard?"

"What girl?" Whitehorn understood, but let on as if he didn't, not knowing what it was that the devil was worried about.

"You know, the one that laughs so merrily and is waiting for someone," Pinčukas explained.

"Oh, that one!" Whitehorn's face clouded over as he understood, and he wanted to frighten Pinčukas into thinking she was even nastier than the other one he had given him to marry, but he looked at Pinčukas and felt sorry for him, as he had become so puny. So he only said:

"Just a passerby. She's waiting for her people to arrive with bells. When they arrive, she'll leave. You have nothing to fear."

But Pinčukas wouldn't let up.

"And who are those people of hers?"

"How do I know?" answered Whitehorn, disgruntled. "But you're getting annoying. Better turn the mill's wings: there's no wind, we need to grind."

For the first time Pinčukas unwillingly turned the mill's wings, thinking all the while about what it was that the miller was hiding from him. He turned and turned, and then stopped to think. At last Whitehorn lost his patience and stuck his head out the window:

"Are you turning or not?" he shouted.

"I'm turning, I'm turning," answered Pinčukas angrily, and stuck out his tongue.

Alas, Whitehorn, absorbed in his work, didn't notice his help had become so impudent and rude.

But this time Pinčukas had due cause.

XVII

At that same time, Jurgutis, having faithfully served Blackpool as an assistant, grew from mostly boy to something of a man, but still the same halfwit, and then he went completely berserk.

He never did learn the smith's trade, since it was quite enough for him to pump the bellows, to listen as they hummed, to watch how the fire glowed in the forge and the sparks flew up to the ceiling and out the vent... And when the smith, grabbing the hot iron from the forge with tongs and placing it on the anvil, started hammering, he would join in, too, beating to the rhythm with a small hammer, and be entirely content. Then, when the smith finished hammering the object and would throw it into a bucket of water that hissed, Jurgutis would merrily blow his nose through a single nostril and the smith would wipe the beaded sweat from his forehead.

"Is it all right?" the smith would ask.

"It's all right," Jurgutis would concur.

"You don't want to go matchmaking?"

"No, I don't."

"Well then, you watch out!" the smith would say, and squinting, he would glance at the torn half of Uršulė's skirt hanging on the wall. "There's never a woman without a skirt, and you know what happens with skirts..."

It was only these unpleasant memories that tormented Jurgutis, other than the fact that the smith, as if on purpose, would order him to wipe up the soot in the smithy with the half of Uršulė's skirt. What could

Jurgutis do—he would wipe up, but after so much time all that was left of Uršulė's skirt was a sooty rag and unpleasant memories, which were also slowly fading away.

Perhaps Jurgutis would have grown old and stayed on forever at the smithy as an apprentice, except that once, sent by the smith to the mill, he saw Whitehorn's daughter Jurga, already a pretty teenaged girl, and that moment changed him forever. And when he heard her merry laugh he lost his head completely.

He returned to the smithy flustered and irritated, blew his nose through one and then the other nostril, and couldn't seem to stand still at the bellows. The forge would flame up one minute, go out the next. The smith, waiting for the iron to heat up, lost his patience:

"Are you pumping or not?" he snarled at Jurgutis.

"I'm pumping, I'm pumping…" answered Jurgutis, blowing his nose through both nostrils as if he were crying.

"What's the matter with you?" the smith pricked up his ears.

Jurgutis blew his nose even harder and lay on the bellows full tilt without answering.

The forge flared up so high that not just sparks, but the flame as well flew through the vent.

"Have you lost your mind? You'll set fire to the smithy!" The smith dampened Jurgutis' excitement. "What's come over you? Blow it out, it'll pass…"

Jurgutis blew his nose and disappeared from the smithy. For the time being the smith didn't miss him, and so Jurgutis loitered around Whitehorn's hill and the mill, wanting to see Jurga again and to hear her merry laugh.

He met Jurga flying with the seagulls by the lake, and stood there staring.

"You're so beautiful!" the captivated Jurgutis said. "I could look at you all my life and I'd never have enough of looking at you."

"What are you dreaming of now, Jurgutis?" Jurga paused running by. "Better blow your nose and everything will be fine."

This time Jurgutis didn't blow his nose, he only sighed and looked at her so mournfully that Jurga felt uncomfortable, and she flew off all the faster to the mill.

Still Jurgutis stood there for a long time, gazing at where she had run off to, and returned to the smithy only late in the evening. In the dark, blowing his nose, he crept into his corner behind the forge and couldn't fall asleep. He kept sighing and blowing his nose as if he were crying. And in the morning he didn't want to get up and pump the bellows.

"Why did you take me matchmaking to that witch Uršulė?" he reproached the smith. "You've just made an eternal joke out of me…"

"Well, you wanted to go yourself!" the smith snarled.

"There are lots of things I've wanted!" Jurgutis reproached him. "So now take me matchmaking to Whitehorn's Jurga."

"Oho, so that's what he's gotten a hankering for!" said the smith, surprised. "There's grey on your head and the devil in your bed… Why, you're an old bachelor already, and she's just a girl…"

"But when Whitehorn was an old bachelor you fixed him up with Marcelė," Jurgutis objected.

"It makes no difference what's happened before, it won't happen a second time," the smith answered sternly and began working. "Pump the bellows!"

"Well, if it won't happen, it won't happen." Jurgutis, discontented though he was, blew his nose and took up the bellows. But he didn't so much as pump as he would think about something. More and more often, he would vanish from the smithy and circle about Whitehorn's mill.

At last the smith lost his patience and went to the mill to look for Jurgutis, who loitered there constantly, as if he was under a spell.

"Well, neighbor," he reproached Whitehorn, "it wasn't part of our bargain that you would steal my assistant."

Whitehorn was merely surprised:

"Who's stealing him?" he answered, shrugging his shoulders. "I have no use for him. He's just going to blow his nose in the flour with his endless snorting."

At that very moment Jurgutis was upstairs by the millstones, wanting to help Whitehorn move some bags. But overhearing the smith and the miller scoffing, he got insulted and, throwing the sack of flour aside, he fled the mill.

"Wait, wait, let's talk, what's there to be done with you?" The smith tried to stop him. "You've deserted the smithy and don't fit in at the mill. Maybe you want to go somewhere matchmaking?"

Jurgutis didn't answer; he only gave the smith a reproachful look and went down to the lake, terribly dejected. He would have gone as far as his feet could carry him, as far away as possible from his unhappiness, but he couldn't tear his gaze away from the mill, where Jurga, who had conquered his heart and all of his thoughts, flew about like a seagull.

But, since he couldn't think of anything to do, he merely circled around the mill as if enchanted, from time to time glancing at the mill's wings from afar and sighing. And when he would meet Jurga, he would stare at her like an owlet, unable to utter a single word. It was hard for Jurga to bear Jurgutis' despairing gaze and she avoided meeting him.

Despondent, Jurgutis would return to the smithy, but he couldn't settle down there, either. Pumping the bellows, he felt as if it wasn't the forge that flamed, but his heart flinging sparks. And it seemed as if the smith's hammer wasn't striking the anvil, but his head. Unable to bear it, Jurgutis would again flee the smithy for the lakeshore.

"He's gone completely berserk!" the smith worried. "But what can you do? He'll be a fool for a while, it'll pass, if he doesn't drown himself first."

Jurgutis perhaps would have drowned himself a long time ago, but the depths of the lake wouldn't have cooled his heart. He wandered the shores of the lake and waited for a chance to see Jurga one more time, then to leave, if for nowhere else then to the ends of the earth. But he didn't go anywhere; he merely went around in a vicious circle, fearing to lose sight of Jurga, wanting to see her, if only from a distance.

And on Saturday nights, when the matchmakers' bells could be heard on the roads along the lake, Jurgutis would be at his wit's end. He would flee the smithy and run around like a madman, with no idea what to do, and fearing just one thing: that the matchmakers with their suitors would arrive at the mill and take Jurga away. He couldn't live without seeing her, any more than he could live without the sun. And to him Jurga was brighter than the sun.

Then Jurgutis in his anguish invented things that you would never suspect him to be capable of. But he wasn't acting alone in this; he had an accomplice, who was also going out of his mind because of Jurga. It's anyone's guess how it was they never met and never noticed one another. Probably one was to the other like his own shadow.

XVIII

It was already getting on towards fall when Pinčukas, turning the mill's wings, heard a bell off in the distance. This bell, barely audible at first, kept getting louder and louder, through the hills and by the shores of the lake— coming closer all the time.

"What could this be?" Pinčukas worried, and tried to rise up even higher, so he could see what was jingling there.

At last he saw it. From the tavern at Cockend's cross-roads, a wagon with a bell turned in the direction of the mill. In the wagon sat two men: one young, the other old.

"It's probably that girl's people coming to take her away," Pinčukas realized, and he became terribly vexed.

In his vexation he spun the mill's wings so hard that the mill jumped in place, and he himself flew off up to the clouds and vanished, the deuce only knows where.

"Have you gone out of your mind?" shouted White-horn, angered, and stuck his head out of the window.

But not so much as a scent of Pinčukas remained on the mill's wings, even though they still spun, howling, from that furious shove.

At that same moment Jurgutis, hearing the match-maker's bell, suddenly disappeared from the smithy too.

"Where on earth has he gotten to?" the smith won-dered, but, unable to wait for him, he made do by him-self: with one hand he pumped the bellows and with the other heated the iron in the forge.

Jurgutis, bolting out of the smithy in the nick of time, stuck a stake into the wheel of the matchmaker's wagon as it drove by. The suitor and the matchmaker didn't notice this malicious trick and clattered off to Cockend's tavern, scattering the wheel's spokes along the road.

Pinčukas had already flown in across from Cockend's tavern, and when the matchmaker with the suitor rode downhill from the crossroads, he clung to the rear wheels with all his might and hung on, so that the wagon actually came to a stop. The matchmaker waved the whip above the horses, the horses, straining, yanked as they pulled, and then the rear wheels cracked and fell apart. Pinčukas fled into the ditch behind the bushes and watched to see what would happen next.

The horses got spooked and the matchmaker and the suitor rolled out the end of the wagon, and it's a good thing that in falling they didn't let go of the reins. They stopped the horses, and then they looked and couldn't believe their eyes.

Then the matchmaker said:

"Was it the devil who broke those wheels? There was nary a rock, nor a pothole, nor anything else; it surely was the evil one himself."

"Come on now, uncle," the suitor answered, shaking the dust from his coattails. "Why would he meddle in here now? The sun is only just now setting."

"You can't tell me, I'm an old man, I've seen everything and I know: this can't be anything else but that one's work," the matchmaker insisted, fearing to mention the devil's name at an inappropriate time as he looked over the broken wheels.

"That's enough, enough already," the suitor disagreed, feeling disconcerted that his first matchmaking excursion should end this way.

"You just look," the matchmaker persisted, and he showed the suitor the collapsed wheels. "It's not like the wheels were broken, but more like they've been ripped out. I told you, better not go calling on that daughter of Whitehorn's. The father's a sorcerer, so you know there's devils hanging around the daughter. They're surely the ones who broke our wheels."

Hearing this, Pinčukas grinned in satisfaction. Apparently, his devilish nature had returned, and he was pleased to have played a prank on a human.

"Come on now, uncle," the suitor objected. "You're prattling nonsense in full daylight."

"You can see for yourself what sort of nonsense this is." The matchmaker shook his head. "At least the front wheels are left. We'll fix the problem and go home."

"How can we go home, now, uncle? That wouldn't be nice." The suitor was dejected, but he realized at the same time that there was no other option.

"Thank God, my child," said the matchmaker, "or thank the devil who broke our wheels and stopped you from getting together with that sorcerer's daughter. What would you have done if you'd gotten a wife like that? You'd be cursing for the rest of your life."

Overhearing this, Pinčukas remembered his misfortune with Uršulė, which ended happily, and grinned again. But right then he smacked himself on the forehead, and put two and two together:

"What a fool I've been!" he said to himself. "Whitehorn swindled me like the very stupidest of devils. And here I spun his mill for him for seven years, too! It's as clear as day that he wanted to stick me with some witch and keep his daughter for himself, to marry off to someone else. No, that won't happen. No suitor with his matchmaker will make it to Whitehorn's daughter. He'll learn, the old geezer, that he can't deceive and swindle devils."

Pinčukas waited until the matchmaker with the suitor fixed their problem with the broken wheel and drove off home, having removed the bell.

"It'll be the same for them all, if not worse," Pinčukas threatened, listening to the receding clatter. "Whitehorn, you won't live to see any matchmakers, even if you'll hear their bells."

So resolved, Pinčukas didn't return to Whitehorn's mill, even though the seven years weren't up yet. After all, he had been used so treacherously as it was!

Whitehorn waited in vain for his help to return. As if on purpose the days were calm and the mill stood with its wings folded. Whitehorn was angry. Where could that devil have gotten to? The mill was full of grain to be ground, and now such a delay. At last he understood why Pinčukas didn't return. Apparently, even if he was a fool, he had nevertheless finally realized he had been had and took umbrage at it.

Whitehorn racked his brains looking for a way to avoid the devil's revenge. The problem was, he couldn't come up with anything because he didn't know what form the revenge would take, and how he was going to need to defend himself from it.

In the meantime, Pinčukas returned to his bogs, and he spent a great deal of time racking his brains too. He constantly thought up new obstructions for White-horn's daughter's matchmakers and rushed about setting them up. Meanwhile, the matchmakers, as if in agreement, drove to the mill one after the other, some-times even several of them from all four directions. It was a great deal of trouble for Pinčukas to keep them all at bay; the most determined ones he would lead astray into the bogs between the lakes, or shove off a cliff somewhere, destroying the wagon and breaking their necks. Pinčukas got completely worn out chasing the matchmakers; he didn't have the time to either lie in the duckweed nor daydream, but for all that, he re-covered all of his diabolic power and dexterity.

That fall Jurgutis got into unusually good shape too; he couldn't stand still in the smithy and was constantly disappearing somewhere.

"Where on God's green earth have you been?" The smith scolded him on more than one occasion, but Jurgutis just blew his nose and said nothing.

Blackpool suspected that Jurgutis was still crazy for Whitehorn's daughter. But what was there to be done? He didn't know that Jurgutis was working hand in hand with the devil Pinčukas, so he didn't do anything. There's no fool like an old fool, but this too would pass. In the meantime, perhaps Whitehorn's daughter would get married and the temptation would be eliminated.

But throughout the entire fall not a single suitor with a matchmaker succeeded in paying a call on Whitehorn's daughter. Something always happened on the road and the matchmakers with the suitors would go astray somewhere. No one suspected Jurgutis. They kept blaming everything on the devil of Paudruvė's bogs, Pinčukas.

At last even Whitehorn came to believe that this was his assistant's revenge, but he didn't know how to defeat him, and once more Whitehorn grew gray and stooped from worry, even if he sometimes was pleased that since the matchmakers and suitors couldn't get there, they couldn't take away his daughter, whom he loved so very much.

In the meantime, more and more rumors and gossip about Whitehorn's mill and the misfortunes of the suitors and their matchmakers spread around, so that in the end no one dared to pay a matchmaking call on his beautiful daughter Jurga.

XIX

At last Whitehorn, unable to endure people's gossip, decided to edify his devil a bit and, if he succeeded, to set Pinčukas to work again. He had fooled about a bit that fall, enough was enough. Surely he wasn't going to run about all the surrounding roads like that, with his tongue hanging out, forever? If he didn't want to work as a hand in the mill, then so be it, Whitehorn could do without him. He could doze in the duckweed again, what was stopping him? So Whitehorn resolved to have a friendly chat with Pinčukas, neighbor to neighbor, and if that didn't help, to at least give him a good hiding and intimidate him so he'd stop fooling around.

Accordingly, one evening, having cut a good ashberry rod, and just in case taking along the dusty old half of Uršulė's skirt left over from earlier times, he headed out to Paudruvė's bogs just as dusk was falling to look for Pinčukas.

Jurga, seeing her father going out, asked in surprise:

"Where are you going so late, father?"

Flustered, Whitehorn turned around, sticking the skirt under his apron, and didn't know what to say.

"Oh, me?" he asked. "Nowhere in particular. To the village. I have business."

Jurga was even more surprised. What sort of business could this be? Father never went to the village on foot and never had business there, and here he was going somewhere, and at nightfall, too.

"Don't be late," Jurga cautioned him, "The nights are dark now."

Whitehorn, hurriedly going downhill, was already a ways off when he answered his daughter:

"It's nothing. I won't be late. Don't wait up for me, go to bed. I might take a while."

And off he went. Jurga followed her father with her eyes, baffled as to where he could be going. When he got to the foot of the hill, he didn't turn towards the village, but in the opposite direction, towards Paudruvė's bogs. Jurga, neither knowing nor suspecting anything, shrugged her shoulders and went off to the cottage.

Whitehorn reached the edge of Paudruvė's bogs when it was already completely dark. He waited a bit, looked around, and started quietly calling Pinčukas. But only the ducks and drakes and other water birds that breed there answered. Then even the birds quieted down. It got rather eerie. But Whitehorn didn't want to return home empty-handed, so he resolved to summon Pinčukas without fail and to have a chat with him. All the same he was afraid to go any farther into the bogs in the dark, as he might sink somewhere into the mire, so he waited patiently on the edge and called from time to time. At last his patience wore out.

"Where on earth have you gotten to?" he said angrily. "I call and call and can't summon you."

"So, what is it you want?" a voice from the bogs suddenly answered.

"I don't want anything," Whitehorn answered, recognizing Pinčukas by his voice. "You're the one who is missing something. You ran out, who knows why, without taking your wages or taking leave. It seems we got along nicely for seven years, we could part nicely as well."

100

"But you deceived me," Pinčukas retorted angrily.

"Now, how did I deceive you?" Whitehorn pretended he was innocent. "We did as we had agreed. And I didn't, it seems, treat you badly. I got used to you, I treated you like one of the family. You yourself never complained, either."

"What of it?" Pinčukas still wouldn't relent. "You just pulled the wool over my eyes."

"How on earth did I pull the wool over your eyes?" Whitehorn didn't understand.

"What else could you call it? You stuck me with some witch, and kept your daughter for yourself. Now you can't deceive me any more, I know everything. If you want to come to terms, give me your daughter of your own free will, and we can live together nicely from now on, like neighbors and relatives."

"See what his heart's set on!" thought Whitehorn to himself, and aloud he said:

"No, no way. You got one and led her astray, a second one you won't get."

But Pinčukas dug in his heels, too:

"If you won't give her to me," he said, "you'll be sorry. I'll wreak my vengeance on you until life becomes unbearable for both you and your daughter."

"Oh, I see, an avenger has appeared," Whitehorn answered contemptuously. "Do you see this skirt? In a minute I'll pull it over your head and give you to that witch. That's what will come of your revenge."

"I'm not afraid of you or your skirt," answered Pinčukas. "And I'm not afraid of that witch of yours any more, because with her rumors and gossip she'll be working in cahoots with me against you, and will help me, and ruin you."

"Oho, so that's what sort of villains you are!" said Whitehorn, seeing their friendly chat was going nowhere. "When I gave her to you, you fought, and now the two of you are ganging up on me. Well, fine. There's no gratitude to be expected from a devil and a sanctimonious old biddy! If you fall into my hands again, you'll be sorry. I'll tie your tails together so you'll be tugging and fighting each other for eternity, and you'll forget everything else in the world."

But Pinčukas just laughed at this threat of Whitehorn's.

"So, you don't want to make peace?" Whitehorn was thoroughly angry.

"I don't," Pinčukas answered.

"It makes no difference to me. Here I thought I'd talk to you man to man, we'd discuss it, but once a devil, always a devil. So, rot in your bogs and don't show yourself to me again. Pfui!" Whitehorn spat and left.

Pinčukas, seeing how angry Whitehorn was, wanted to follow after him, to offer him if not peace, then at least mountains of gold for his daughter, but Whitehorn spat and went off without looking back, so Pinčukas couldn't catch up to him even if he wanted to. So, abashed and thwarted, he returned to his bogs, contemplating revenge and putting his trust in that.

Meanwhile, Whitehorn, returning to his mill, was also thinking, although not about revenge, but about how to shake off Pinčukas once and for all, since he was getting to be even more tiresome than Uršulė. If only he really could tie them together by the tail like a cat and a dog and set the two of them loose, then they would fight between themselves and leave others in peace. But how could he tie them together, if one had a tail and the other not? Unless perhaps he tied the sanctimonious old biddy's tongue to the devil's tail.

But without capturing either one or the other, there wasn't a thing Whitehorn could do about it, and in the evenings bats started flying and owls started hooting around the mill, so there was no telling what to expect.

XX

Girdvainis' journey to Whitehorn's daughter Jurga wasn't easy either, even with the dapple-grey steeds. All week he kept waiting for Saturday, and then for the evening, so that he could set off with his matchmaker Anupras.

At last the happy hour arrived. He led the eager dapple-grays out of the stable and wanted to harness them this time not to the dung-cart, but to the carriage, beautifully outfitted and painted, still left from his father's father, but Anupras advised against it:

"What do we need it for?" he said. "We'll drive over to pay a call on this one the same way we drove to all the others. We're not going to some estate, just to a mill."

"But just in case, uncle," Girdvainis hesitated, "Maybe this time it would be better if we went with the carriage."

"Don't worry," Anupras dismissed it with a wave of his hand. "What we drive with isn't important, just as long as we get there."

"And why wouldn't we get there?" wondered Gird-vainis.

"You've heard what people say?" answered Anupras.

"Rumors and gossip," Girdvainis waved it off scorn-fully.

"We'll see," replied Anupras, fussing about more and more, as if he was preparing for a long and dangerous journey.

But all the same, Girdvainis heeded the match-maker's advice and harnessed the dapple-grays to the same dung-cart he had paid calls on the other girls with. However, this time the suitor didn't have the same boldness and confidence he had had those other times, and the matchmaker was not only worried, but some-how enigmatic, too.

Before driving off, Hearall went around the wagon and the horses, muttering something under his breath as if he were casting spells, and then he made the sign of the cross over himself and the suitor.

"Sit," he declared at last. "With the Lord God's help perhaps we'll get there."

Anupras' superstitiousness seemed strange to Gird-vainis, but then who pays attention to an old man? Girdvainis was impatient as it was, so he jumped into the wagon, whistled, and off they thundered.

The dapple-grays took off like whirlwinds and flew as never before—hill or dale, their hooves barely touched the ground. Anupras restrained Girdvainis so that he wouldn't wear out the horses, since the road was a long one—seven miles—and they would need their nimbleness yet, but Girdvainis just shrugged his shoulders: what an unheard of thing, that his dapple-grays would lack for nimbleness! And he let them go full speed. They scarcely noticed how the long road flew by and they arrived in the land of Paudruvė. Lakes large and small sprawled between the hills; the road twisted around the bends of the lakes, spanned little bridges over the peninsulas and creeks, rose up the hills, descended to their feet, and meandered through endless curves. In those curves of the road, the horses suddenly started to snort, to perk up their ears, to flash their eyes, and to fly so fast that even Girdvainis started to slow his dapple-grays down.

"Never mind," Anupras advised him then, "Now let them run as fast as they can."

Girdvainis looked at Anupras in astonishment but said nothing. It just seemed strange to him that Anupras didn't want to slow the horses, when usually he would avoid so much as a fast trot.

The horses went bounding ever faster. It seemed they weren't going to gallop there this time, but fly there, if only they didn't destroy the cart and the reins held out. Even though Girdvainis wanted to get to Whitehorn's as quickly as possible, he found the unusual speed of the horses, Anupras's serious concentration, and the mysterious signs he cast all around them rather curious.

'Could the road really be enchanted?' Girdvainis thought to himself, and he let the horses go faster still, giving them free rein, so that their speedy pace nearly took the riders' breath away.

And then what's more, driving by Paudruvė's smithy, some nitwit jumped out of the ditch and threw himself at the horses, as if he wanted to hold them back or make an end of himself, but the excited dapple-grays knocked him to the side into the quagmire like a straw, and flew onwards.

With the horses careening along, suddenly some sort of squealing and screeching started up, now from the wheel on one side, now from the other, or else falling behind the back of the cart. Girdvainis looked around—there was nothing to be seen, only Anupras still making some sort of signs. When they made the turn by Blind Lake's bend, the squealing screeched off straight through the quagmire towards an isthmus of the lake, where there was a small bridge.

The speeding horses didn't have time to kick off the little bridge with their forelegs when snap! The bridge collapsed, but the excited horses jumped over the collapsing bridge, taking the cart through the air with them.

Then something under the wheels squealed and screeched even louder, as if someone had been run over. The horses got even more furious and ran so fast that Girdvainis didn't have time to look around to see what had happened.

Anupras didn't turn around either; he merely made some sort of sign with his hand turned backwards and said to Girdvainis:

"Don't look back. We've driven over only one bridge, and there are seven of them. Fly straight onwards, don't look at anything."

Girdvainis couldn't have done otherwise even if he had wanted to, since the horses were so agitated they were ungovernable. In an instant they drove over the second little bridge—the same thing happened. Only this time the horses managed to set all four legs down on it. The third bridge they got halfway over when it collapsed. The fourth they didn't even notice how they flew over. The fifth crumbled as they finished driving over it. The sixth crashed down after they crossed it, and the seventh they themselves didn't know whether they had driven over it, or whether it had vanished somewhere.

Whitehorn's mill was already visible atop the hill when suddenly an impenetrable fog arose from Paudruvė's bog and flowed over everything—the roads, the lakes, the hills—you couldn't see so much as a hand in front of your face. Fortunately, Girdvainis had noticed the direction of Whitehorn's mill and let the horses head straight for it.

The horses even wheezed as they flew; there was no telling whether they were going up hill or down. That's how dark and foggy it was. The wheels no longer squealed; instead something simply roared and howled, trailing from behind and unable to catch its breath. The faster the horses flew, the further that breathless roaring got left behind.

At last the horses stopped on their own and neighed so loudly that the fog suddenly cleared, and Girdvainis saw they had arrived in Whitehorn's yard. It was apparent that they hadn't come by the road, but rather by the steepest cliff on the side by the lake, which was hard to climb even on foot. Neither Girdvainis nor Anupras noticed this; only Whitehorn saw it from the threshold of the mill and therefore didn't venture to approach the arrivals, since it wasn't clear who they could be if they had flown up such a steep hill.

Girdvainis and Anupras, on their arrival in Whitehorn's yard, looked around and were astonished: they had driven through an impenetrable fog, but here it was the clearest evening, as pure as the waters of the lake. In the light of the sunset, the mill stood with its wings folded as if it was slumbering, and above it shone the evening star. Only below Lake Udruvė was misted over and the fog spread itself through the fields and bogs.

It was so quiet it seemed there wasn't a living soul about, and, standing still, Girdvainis and Anupras looked at each other, hearing only their own breathing and the worn horses' panting.

"You see, with God's help we've arrived," Anupras finally said, and started looking around to see if he couldn't see someone.

Hearing God mentioned, Whitehorn got up from the threshold of the mill and went over to the arrivals.

"Good evening," he said. "Have you traveled far?"

"Yes, so far, that you couldn't see it from here, even from the top of the hill," answered Anupras. "But we drove and drove and we lost our way. Only your mill saved us. Will you take in some travelers to rest awhile and catch their breath?"

"You're very welcome," Whitehorn bowed, and his white hair gleamed in the twilight.

Girdvainis, his regards given to Whitehorn, kept looking around to see if he could spot the one he had come here for. His eyes wandered to the parlor windows, but only the last rays of sunset quivered there.

"Hitch your horses and we'll go inside." Girdvainis heard Whitehorn's voice as if in a dream: he couldn't pull his eyes from the parlor window, where, at last, a light twinkled like the evening star.

Girdvainis gave a start and quickly threw his inside-out sheepskin coat on the wagon, set the horses by the mill, and they all went into the parlor. There Jurga met them with a broom in her hand, as if she meant to drive them out.

"Have you been expecting guests, my dear?" Hearall addressed her.

"What sort?" laughed Jurga.

"That sort," answered Hearall, looking askance at the broom.

"I thought," said the flustered Jurga, hiding the broom, "that you would circle seven miles around and keep on going. Are you sure you haven't gotten lost?"

"No," Girdvainis answered, looking Jurga straight in the eye. "Earlier I circled a hundred miles around, but this time I flew straight here and destroyed all the bridges on the way."

"So what will you do now?" Jurga laughed. "How will you get home?"

"I'll build new ones," Girdvainis retorted, not giving in.

"We'll see," said Jurga doubtfully. "Where did you put your inside-out sheepskin?"

109

"I'll find it where I put it," said Girdvainis, getting flustered.

"Maybe you drank it away?" Jurga teased. "And your dapple-grays, too?"

"No," Girdvainis shot back, recovering his pride. "I'll lose my head first, before I give up my dapple-grays."

"Maybe you'll give up your dapple-grays and lose your head, too?" Jurga kept it up, but the mocking light in her eyes kept fading, and without realizing it she pushed the broom under the bench.

With Jurga and Girdvainis trading barbs, Whitehorn invited the guests to the table.

"Thank you," answered Anupras and from his pocket he pulled a bottle decorated with a twig of rue and a handkerchief. He spread the handkerchief on the table and set the bottle on it. "Perhaps a glass can be found?" he asked. "It would be nice to warm up after the journey."

"Perhaps it will," answered Whitehorn. "Jurga, dear, would you find one?" he addressed his daughter.

Jurga spread a cloth over the table, set down a glass and bread with salt.

"Help yourself," she said, and turned away.

"Wait, my dear," Anupras wouldn't let her go. "Who's going to take the rue off for us?"

"You put it there yourself, sir, you can take it off yourself," answered Jurga, glancing at her father as if she couldn't bring herself to do it.

Her father smiled sadly in assent. Something flashed by the window, perhaps a bat, or perhaps Jurgutis had peeped in with his despairing eyes. Jurga gave a start and

looked at Girdvainis—their eyes met and she hung her
head, while her hand of its own accord took the rue off
the bottle. Girdvainis, pleased, took the rue and thrust it
behind Jurga's braids.

"Well, then, all's well," said Anupras, looking at the
young ones. "We'll drink to the father, that he raised a
beautiful daughter, and then maybe you two will bend
an elbow and come to an understanding of the heart."

"Who knows?" Jurga wavered, and turned as red as
a poppy, glancing at Girdvainis. "It will be as father
says."

"Well, what can a father say, surely he wouldn't be-
grudge his child's happiness. A heart presses to a heart
like a blossom to a blossom." Anupras was bandying
words so, that even Girdvainis wondered where this
eloquence of his had come from. "And we need a
housekeeper, a homemaker, a hearth keeper and a
weaver of fine linens. We've looked everywhere for one,
and only here did we find one. So, to your health, father-in-law!"

Hearall drank with Whitehorn, Girdvainis drank with
Jurga, and they all sat down at the table. The matchmaker's bottle wasn't finished yet when a pitcher of ale
and something to eat appeared on the table. The talk
began, urged on by the foam of the ale.

Anupras related their difficult journey to the mill to
Whitehorn. Whitehorn listened and smiled as if he
didn't believe it, but the young people didn't hear a thing
of what the elders were saying, because they were speaking to each other with their eyes. And that speech told
them a great deal, as they felt they had found one an-

other and would travel together throughout their entire lives.

Thus Saturday night went on until the third crow of the cock, as there was plenty of talk and no shortage of ale. The barrel of ale in the pantry, brewing all week, never stopped foaming.

XXI

At that moment, in a separate larder-room at Cockend's tavern, hidden from people's eyes for three days now, shut away alone with a bottle of vodka, sat the old horse thief Tatergall, with his long brown beard and one leg shorter than the other.

The farmers had caught Tatergall stealing horses more than once, and in retaliation they sometimes shortened one leg, sometimes the other, but never both the same. So it fell to the horse thief to be lame now in one leg, now in the other, so that not only other people, but he himself didn't know which leg it was he was lame in. But this didn't hurt the horse thief in the least. On the contrary, it even helped, since people couldn't recognize him right away, not knowing which leg he was lame in.

But that wasn't the reason Tatergall was in a stew, even if thievery had consumed no small part of his health. He drank vodka and chewed on his brown beard because he hadn't, as yet, been able to steal Girdvainis' dapple-grays and ride them to Prussia. No matter what he did or how much he tried, he merely agonized over it in vain. Night and day he couldn't get those horses out of his head—they flew in his thoughts, they neighed in his ears—night and day he dreamt of them.

Those horses wouldn't give him any peace even now. That was why he cursed and tormented himself with the thought that he had gotten to be an old geezer and had become a worthless horse thief. Oh, he'd stolen his fair share of horses, and fine ones at that! But if Tatergall hoped to console himself with the assertion that Girdvainis' horses were mere kittens in comparison with those he had ridden to Prussia, it was in vain.

Tatergall seethed in rage and dismissed Girdvainis' dapple-grays because he hadn't been able to steal them. It was impossible to even get near them, because Girdvainis guarded them like the apple of his eye. He got up with them, went to bed with them, and never let the dapple-grays out of his sight. So how could you steal horses from someone like that, if not with the devil's help?

At the very moment the devil crossed Tatergall's mind, the warped door to the tavern opened, the rusty hinges creaked, and in came, from wherever he'd been, the very devil of Paudruvė's bogs, Pinčukas. However, this time he didn't come dressed as a little gentleman with a cane in his hand, a little green hat on his head and a dove feather in his hat, the way he usually showed up at Cockend's tavern. This time, with twilight falling, Pinčukas came into the tavern not only without a cane or hat, but so crumpled and mashed, so trampled and tattered, that it was dreadful to see, and so miserable it was impossible to even recognize him.

Pinčukas' old friend, the tavern keeper Shaddon, that flea-bitten remnant of aristocracy, who was on the point of drinking away the roadside tavern, which was all that was left of the entire estate his parent's parents had owned and squandered—that honor of nobility, whom tavern-keeping suited like a fifth leg suited a dog—even that flea bag didn't at first recognize Pinčukas now, and took him for a piddling boy whose master had given him a good thrashing, catching him crawling through the window into the pantry with the girls.

Pinčukas, opening the tavern door, glanced in apprehensively, as if he was afraid to go inside and was on the lookout for something. Then, cringing, he turned around to see if something wasn't following (those horses of Girdvainis kept haunting him!), and only after carefully listening (the hooves of Girdvainis' horses kept clattering in his ears!), did he calm down a bit and come inside the tavern.

"Good evening," he said timidly, and glanced at Shaddon as if he was looking for sympathy.

Shaddon didn't even take a good look at Pinčukas; he just cast one eye in his direction and turned away. Pinčukas was so bedraggled and abused that it was revolting to look at. On his face there was nothing but bruises and bumps, and on his right jaw the impression of a horse's hoof still showed. There was nothing left of his clothes but rags; his jacket was trampled and dirty, his pants tattered; one foot in a clog, the other entirely bare, so that a horse's hoof stuck out for all the world to see. Apparently, it was Pinčukas' first encounter with such misfortune and disgrace, that he should have even lost his awareness of how to appear in public.

So it wasn't surprising that Shaddon, that proud blue-blooded mutt, didn't recognize Pinčukas and didn't answer his greeting, just glanced over his shoulder like someone greeting an unwelcome guest and muttered disapprovingly:

"You can go back to wherever you came from, I'm closing the tavern soon."

"I won't be long, Shaddon," mumbled Pinčukas pitifully. "I've got important business."

When he heard this, the tavern keeper drew himself up and got completely riled. Some half-pint urchin, and he's calling him Shaddon! Outrageous! What would he think up next!?

"For some it's Shaddon, but for some it's Master Shaddonshire," retorted the angry tavern keeper. "I haven't herded hogs with you, you piglet. You should know how to speak to a nobleman."

This completely deflated Pinčukas. Were all of his partners going to turn away from him in his misfortune?

"Don't you recognize me, Master Shaddonshire?" Pinčukas said with pitiful reproach. "It's me, Pinčukas."

"Master Pinčuky?" said Shaddon, shocked. "It can't be!"

Unable to believe it could be him, he came closer to Pinčukas, and when he recognized him, his eyes popped out of his head:

"Where did you come from in that condition? Don't tell me your brothers in hell would have beaten you up like that for working for that peasant Whitehorn as a hand? Was it Whitehorn who committed this outrage upon you? I told you, Master, don't start with that worthless peasant. It's not a nobleman's place to work for a boor."

"No, Shaddon, it wasn't Whitehorn who committed this outrage on me," sighed Pinčukas. "He just deceived me."

"Deceived you?" Shaddon's eyes widened in surprise. "That's just what I thought. What else can you expect from those boors?"

"That's how it turned out, Shaddon," sighed Pinčukas. "There's nothing to be done now! But I'll pay him back for it in spades."

"Pay him back, Master Pinčuky, pay him back," Shaddon concurred. "If you let those boors have their way, there'll be no life left for us noblemen."

Noblemen's business was of no import to Pinčukas (even in hell they didn't value them much: you could buy ten noblemen's souls for a penny), so he looked around the empty tavern and asked:

"You wouldn't know where Tatergall is at the moment?"

"Of course I do." Shaddon was patting himself on the back, on account of knowing more than the devil himself. "He's been drinking in my larder for the last three days. The sooner you carry him off to hell and get him off my hands the better. That boor's stunk up the entire tavern."

"Fine," Pinčukas agreed. "Let me talk to him for a bit."

"You're very welcome, Master Pinčuky," Shaddon bowed and opened the door to the larder.

But he hadn't quite opened the larder door when a sullen growling was heard from inside and an empty bottle flew whistling through the door, nearly hitting Pinčukas on the head. He ducked his head in time and the bottle crashed into the wall.

"I told you, you aristocratic piece of trash, not to let anyone into the larder," they heard Tatergall's churlish voice. "How many times do I have to tell you, you swine? I have troubles, I need to think things out by myself."

"Tatergally, don't be a fool," Shaddon was furious with the horse thief for deriding him in front of Pinčukas. "Master Pinčuky's here to see you on business."

"What Master Pig and with what business? There's nothing I want to know about or listen to," Tatergall kicked the door from inside and slammed it shut, and then shouted, "Bring me another bottle."

"You'll get one, just don't slam around," Shaddon gave in and turned to Pinčukas. "There's nothing for it. You won't be able to talk to him today. He's as drunk as a skunk. A real boor."

"No," Pinčukas replied. "I need to make arrangements with him today, whether he likes it or not. If he won't let me in through the door then I'll go in through the keyhole."

Pinčukas did just as he said. Shaddon didn't have time to see it; the devil just shook himself and went in through the keyhole, leaving behind his clog and his rags.

"So what's this urgent matter?" Shaddon wondered, and his curiosity got the better of him. He stuck his ear to the keyhole to listen to what the devil and the horse thief were talking about.

117

However, he didn't succeed in overhearing any of it. At that moment, the smith's apprentice Jurgutis came into the tavern all muddy and, sniffling a bit, stuck two new pairs of horseshoes under Shaddon's nose as he bent over by the door.

"What do you want?" the angry Shaddon sprang away from the door.

"The dapple-grays trampled everything under their feet…" said Jurgutis, snuffling again as if he were crying. "Here, take the horseshoes. Give me some vodka."

"You stole them?" Shaddon pounced on him mistrustfully.

"They're mine, not yours," Jurgutis retorted.

But Shaddon didn't have the time to argue or to bargain, so, taking the horse shoes, stolen or not, he gave Jurgutis a half-pint of vodka and pushed him out into the front room, and then rushed back to the keyhole to the larder, where negotiations of some sort were going on between the devil and the horse thief.

XXII

In the larder, when Pinčukas showed up in all of his devilish nakedness, Tatergall not only sobered up, but the hair on his drunken head stood on end. In his fright, his mouth flew open and he couldn't utter a word. At last he collected himself and said, his eyes popping out in fear:

"You haven't come for my soul, have you?"

"No," Pinčukas answered calmly. "I'm here on a different matter. If you help me out, you can have your soul, I've absolutely no use for it."

Tatergall calmed down then, sat himself down, and asked Pinčukas to sit.

"I don't have time," answered Pinčukas. "It's an extremely urgent matter."

Tatergall became still more anxious about what this urgent matter was that had driven Pinčukas here, so he wanted to delay a while, in order to better sober up and not make a mistake through haste.

"Let's have a drink while we weigh this matter," Tatergall suggested, and shouted through the door, "Shaddon, bring some vodka and something to eat."

"Don't bother," answered Pinčukas. "I don't, as you know, drink vodka. The business is this: steal Girdvainis' dapple-grays for me."

"If only I could!" Tatergall sighed. "That's been on my mind for a long time and I can't do a thing about it."

"I've already thought about it, you just have to do it," Pinčukas said, and leaning over, started whispering in Tatergall's ear.

So Shaddon didn't hear what the devil and the horse thief were discussing. That smith's half-wit Jurgutis, nine poxes on him, interrupted him with his horseshoes. Then, after shooing him out into the front hall, Shaddon ran to the larder door again, but all he managed to hear was something about some dapple-grays. What on earth was this about? Jurgutis had mumbled something about dapple-grays too, and now here they were conspiring against them. But then Tatergall shouted for more vodka. Shaddon jumped back and then stuck his ear to the door again, but he couldn't hear a thing, because Pinčukas was saying something in a whisper.

"You understand," Pinčukas finally said aloud. "When you drive off, I'll start neighing from the opposite direction and throw him off the scent."

"Very good," rejoiced Tatergall. "And when will we do this?"

"When they go for the banns," answered Pinčukas.

"Excellent," Tatergall concurred. "And you'll return my soul, too?"

"I'll return your soul," Pinčukas agreed. "Just don't you go crawling with it into Girdvainis' dapple-grays through the hind end. That'll be the end of you and that soul of yours, too."

"What kind of idiot would I be to crawl into a horse's rear end?" answered Tatergall, and he was as pleased as could be. "As soon as I snatch them, that minute I'm off for the border and Prussia."

"That's your business," answered Pinčukas. "You can put them wherever you want. Just as long Girdvainis never sees them again."

Then Shaddon, standing on the other side of the door, hearing that they had already finished their deal, came in with a bottle and, putting on an air that he knew everything, said with a tavern-keeper's greed:

"And what will I get out of this?" He grinned at Pinčukas and Tatergall.

Tatergall understood that Shaddon had been listening at the door, so he answered angrily:

"Whatever's left of the horses."

"Boor," retorted Shaddon angrily and wanted to slam the door, but he thought better of it and put the bottle on the table, as he had come up with a better plan: "There, lap it up."

But Shaddon made a mistake this time, too. Tatergall guessed his intention, that is, to get him to drink so he could worm out his secret.

"No," Tatergall answered merrily; even his brown beard lit up. "This time I'm not drinking, I'm sobering up. I have important work to do."

"What's this work of yours?" Shaddon got even angrier. "Stealing horses!"

"Yours is even more crass," the cheerful Tatergall wouldn't back down. "Cutting the tails off stolen horses."

"Have you caught me out, that you said that?" Shaddon got insulted.

"And have you caught me out, that you said that?" Tatergall retorted.

"Boor!" Shaddon cursed.

"Blue-blooded mutt!" shouted Tatergall.

"Don't fight, brothers," Pinčukas cautioned them. "What's good for one won't be bad for the other, either. Better we sniff some tobacco."

He felt around his waistcoat for his tobacco tin, but it was gone. He realized that he had lost it somewhere on the road or by a bridge while he was racing with Girdvainis.

"I'm going to look for my tobacco tin," said Pinčukas and took his leave. "Maybe I'll find it before the third crow of the cock."

And out he went. Tatergall was left alone to drink his vodka, so he'd sober up, and an angry Shaddon went to lie down in the front hall, where the drunken Jurgutis had crashed under the bench and fallen fast asleep. However, Shaddon didn't notice him, or he would have thrown him out. He collapsed onto the couch, but he couldn't fall asleep. His honor had been slighted. Besides, he couldn't get Girdvainis' horses out of his head.

"Those horses, sir," he rolled onto his other side, "aren't for horse thieves to steal, nor for boors to have. Such horses are only for real nobility to ride."

But no matter how much Shaddon tormented himself over Girdvainis' horses, he couldn't think of any way to get them into his hands. He was angry with himself that he hadn't heard Pinčukas and Tatergall's secret, how they were going to steal those horses; he intended to go and tell Girdvainis all about it, only he was afraid of the horse thief's and the devil's revenge, so he did nothing and kept his mouth shut. In the end he reassured himself with the thought that he would get something, at least, out of Girdvainis' horses.

XXIII

The first cock had crowed, but Girdvainis and his matchmaker Anupras were still sitting in Whitehorn's parlor, not at all prepared to leave the table.

The barrel of ale in the larder hadn't run out; full pitchers still foamed on the table, loosening the matchmaker's and the father-in-law's tongues, and even though they didn't entirely understand one another on account of Anupras's one deaf ear—often each spoke to himself—they sat hugging each other like the best of friends, unable to get enough of the conversation.

Whitehorn scolded Anupras, half in sincerity and half as a joke, that he, old man—what a crook—pretended that he was a passerby in order to steal Whitehorn's most precious possession, the daughter who was the sole comfort of his old age; while Anupras, although he wasn't hearing everything the future father-in-law said, maintained that he was the most generous person, having brought Whitehorn such a son-in-law, the likes of which couldn't be found anywhere else in the world.

"Oh, you lying matchmaker," Whitehorn wouldn't give in. "Aren't you ashamed to lie so?"

"I'm not lying," Hearall asserted. "Next to a daughter like a reed I'll give you a son like an oak, the comfort and support of your old age."

At last the matchmaker and the father-in-law settled their differences. They shook hands and each drank yet another pitcher of ale. But seeing that they weren't going to conquer the entire barrel in one sitting, they leaned on one another and dozed off, so that after a bit of a snooze they could start anew on another pitcher.

In the meantime, Girdvainis and Jurga still couldn't get enough of looking at one another. They didn't really dare look at each other; they were only sneaking glances, afraid to say the words and reveal the feelings they were both brimming over with. It was as if those glances, which spoke more than words, had taken away their tongues, and they watched each other in silence, unable to say a word.

Girdvainis didn't understand what had happened to him—all of his smartness had evaporated. Jurga, too, forgot her promise to invert Girdvainis' inside-out sheepskin (Girdvainis, alas, having left it on the wagon where he had thrown it on entering the parlor, forgot all about it), and to laugh in his face.

Oh, she laughed in his face all right, but with a laugh entirely different than the one she had promised. That laugh came from the depths of her heart, and beguiled him like happiness met with for the first time.

It was only when the elders dozed off (finding themselves unable to drink the entire barrel of ale and to say all they had to say) that the young ones spoke.

"Jurga," Girdvainis said, and didn't recognize his own voice—it was so uncertain and seemed hoarse. "Marry me. With my dapple-grays we'll fly through life."

"I don't know," Jurga answered, but her traitorous eyes laughed. "Where would we fly off to?"

"There, where we'll find our fortune!" Girdvainis stretched out his arms, wanting to embrace the girl in his happiness.

"Hardly," Jurga slipped away, and in provocation glanced in his eyes. "You'll seduce me and throw me away."

"No," answered Girdvainis, following Jurga. "I'd rather lose my dapple-grays and my head, too, than throw you away."

"Maybe," laughed Jurga, "you'll lose your dapple-grays, misplace your head, and throw me away as well."

"Never!" Girdvainis got riled. "With you and my dapple-grays I'll fly like the wind to my fortune."

"Or maybe misfortune?" doubted Jurga, and enticed him by slipping out of his embrace.

Girdvainis chased Jurga through the entire parlor and couldn't catch her. She slipped away like the wind and laughed.

"You'll be mine, anyway," the boy fumed. "Even if the earth should split."

"If it splits apart, then how will we meet?" the girl laughed.

Only at the third crow of the cock, with Girdvainis starting to get discouraged that he couldn't catch Jurga, did she catch Girdvainis herself.

"Whatever will be, will be, I'll marry you, I'll fly with your dapple-grays even to the ends of the earth!" she said in one breath; her arms like a rambling vine encircled the boy's neck, and she kissed him so that Girdvainis' night suddenly lit up.

Girdvainis took Jurga into his embrace, spun about the parlor three times and said:

"Let's go for the banns!"

Then the matchmaker, dozing by the table, woke up, opened his eyes, and looked about:

"Already?" he asked.

"Already!" answered Girdvainis, and flew through the door, carrying Jurga in his arms.

Dawn was breaking, and the dapple-grays, who had been waiting impatiently for their master a long time, neighed when they saw him.

"We'll fly, my little steeds, like we've never flown before," declared Girdvainis, jumping straight up on the bottom of the cart (the sides had gotten lost somewhere along the way) and pulling Jurga up.

"Now hold on!" he hugged Jurga and let the horses go with all their might. As if they had merely been waiting for a sign, they started up like whirlwinds, so fast even the mill's wings began to turn, and they flew down the hill, carrying off Girdvainis and Jurga.

Anupras, who wasn't completely sober after all his boozing and snoozing, heard the wagon's thundering and ran out of the parlor into the yard, but all he saw in the dimness of dawn was the suitor and his bride, already far off down the slope, flying as though with wings.

"Wait!" he shouted, but he heard only his own voice. "Wait! You won't get there by yourself without me!"

Anupras worried, remembering how difficult the journey was, but worry alone wasn't going to help a bit. Girdvainis was completely unconcerned about either the road or its dangers. He would drive to announce the banns with his bride whether there was a road or not, even if he had to fly through the heavens.

"God help you both," said Anupras when Girdvainis and Jurga disappeared in the twists of the road, and he returned to the parlor.

Whitehorn was still dozing, leaning on the table, and didn't hear his daughter being taken away. A heavy sleep had fallen over him, like that before death.

"Wake up," Anupras shook him. "We've overslept, us old ones, and the youngsters have driven off."

"Who drove off?" Whitehorn didn't understand at first.

"Well, the suitor with his bride," Anupras waved his arm, "For the banns. And they left me behind."

Whitehorn sobered up, and suddenly he was sad. He felt lonelier than he had ever felt in his life. With his palm he brushed a tear from his eyelashes and leaned over on the table.

Anupras understood the father's sadness, and, so he wouldn't break down himself, said:

"Well, let's have a drink, eh, father-in-law?"

"Let's have a drink," Whitehorn agreed.

The elders drank and were silent. Each one was thinking his own thoughts.

So they drank in silence.

XXIV

Girdvainis and Jurga drove straight to Švendubrė for the banns the same way they had begun, neither hills nor bridges stopping them. The first bridges they flew over without noticing whether they were standing or not, and seeing the last ones, Girdvainis was quite astonished: they were completely untouched, as if they hadn't collapsed the night before.

He didn't have time to think about how this had happened. The dapple-grays bounded, his heart beat joyfully, and he couldn't take his eyes off Jurga, holding her tightly by the waist with his right arm.

He didn't see how they flew into Švendubrė and stopped across from the churchyard by the parsonage gate. The steeds neighed and woke up Švendubrė's parson, who was still sleeping sweetly in his warm bed.

"Who could have come here so early?" Boniface Bobbin thought through his sleep. "Perhaps some blue-blooded mutt has come to finish a game of whist?"

But sweet sleep weighed heavily on his eyes, so the parson turned over on his other side.

"Let them drive to hell if they must, they can finish with the devils," he thought and fell asleep again.

Girdvainis hitched the horses to the churchyard fence, took Jurga by the hand, and they went together into the empty church. They stopped by the altar and waited for the parson to appear.

But only the sexton Benjamin, as tall as a pole, appeared. Girdvainis tugged at his coattails as he went past him kneeling at the big altar, and said:

"Get the parson up! I have very urgent business."

The sexton looked at the suitor with his bride and understood what the matter was, so he answered indifferently:

"You have time. There's no fire."

"How do you know, maybe I am on fire?" Girdvainis got peeved, and pressed a banknote into the sexton's palm. The church's servant calmed down at once and said:

"Immediately. I'll just dust off the altar and then go."

The sexton left and came back, but the pastor still didn't show up. The newlyweds waited an hour, and then another, before the pastor could be aroused and appeared. He called them into the vestry.

"What do you want?" he asked, irritated.

128

Girdvainis, without a greeting, without even kissing the pastor's hand, said straight off:

"Pastor, marry us now or after three weeks."

Then the vexed pastor took a good look at them and the last sleep fell from his eyes. He made the sign of the cross over this ardent suitor and stepped back:

"Are you under a spell, or what?" he asked. "Let the spells pass first, and then talk about marriage."

"It won't pass," Girdvainis smiled. "I'm under a spell for life."

"I'll not marry you and I won't take your banns," answered the pastor. "You've had dealings with evil spirits—let them marry the two of you."

Girdvainis saw that there would be no wedding if he couldn't get the pastor to agree, so, not wasting any time, he pulled a tenner out of his pocket and put it on the table.

The pastor took a good look at the tenner, yawned, and said:

"Well, well, now, what's to be done with you two? Say prayers, or what?"

They said prayers then, the pastor in Latin, slowly, yawning; Girdvainis and Jurga, in Lithuanian, hurriedly, letting parts go by, glancing at one another.

After the prayer the pastor scolded the newlyweds again and said:

"You're entering the sacred vocation of marriage, and you don't know your prayers. I can't take the banns."

"Too little," thought Girdvainis, and put yet another tenner on the table.

The pastor squinted at the new tenner and said:

"What's your first and last name and where are you from?"

"Jurgis Girdvainis from Manywish village," answered Girdvainis, pleased he had finally overcome the pastor's stubbornness.

"I've heard of you," said the pastor, writing. "Your father was a good farmer and you, I heard, are a great squanderer. You should straighten up, entering the sacred vocation of marriage."

"I'll straighten up," Girdvainis promised.

"And where is the bride from?" asked the pastor.

"From the village of Paudruvė," Girdvainis answered for the bride. "The miller Whitehorn's daughter Jurga."

"What did you say?!" the pastor stopped writing. "What Whitehorn? Not that sorcerer who wanted to marry one old biddy of ours to the devil?"

"The same," Jurga answered merrily.

"That's just what I thought," the pastor gave up. "He's bewitched you, you simpleton, and you've lost your head."

"Even if I had two heads, I wouldn't regret it," answered Girdvainis.

"I see, I see," the pastor agreed. "I'll take the banns, but you think about it while there's still time."

"I don't have anything to think about," Girdvainis answered and glanced at Jurga. "Isn't that so?"

Jurga answered with a smile.

At that moment, the horses neighed resoundingly, rattling even the church windows. Girdvainis gave a start and listened.

A shriveled little woman suddenly ran in the vestry door and, hardly catching her breath, shouted:

"Horse thieves! Horse thieves!"

That was Uršulė.

"What horses?" the pastor was confused.

Girdvainis jumped up like a shot and ran out the door.

Outside the horses neighed even louder. But Girdvainis couldn't make out what direction they were neighing from. It seemed that the neighing came from whatever direction he turned.

He ran first in one direction, then another, but the dapple-grays kept neighing from the opposite side. Girdvainis' head got turned around as he spun himself about, and off he ran straight through the fields, left his bride behind, and forgot the entire world.

And still the horses neighed.

XXV

That Sunday the people gathered in Švendubrė didn't know what to be more amazed at: Girdvainis' unexpected banns with Whitehorn's Jurga, which the pastor nevertheless announced after the sermon (and a very stern sermon he delivered, too, about all sorts of spells and witchcraft, which inevitably sank the soul to the depths of hell), or that Girdvainis' horses had been so mysteriously and unexpectedly stolen.

If it hadn't been for the theft of the horses, perhaps no one would have been surprised at the banns of Girdvainis and Whitehorn's Jurga, since, after thinking about it calmly, this was just as it should be. The two of them fit each other like a hand fits a glove, or maybe even better. Now people understood why Girdvainis spent so much time paying calls on young ladies without finding one to suit him, and why not a single suitor could call on Whitehorn's Jurga with a matchmaker. The two of them were obviously made for one another, and that was the way things were meant to be.

But why did they steal Girdvainis' horses just exactly when the two of them had arrived for the banns? There was something odd here. Girdvainis' horses could have been stolen earlier—after all, more than one horse thief circled around them, looking for a chance to snatch them. Well then, some horse thief saw his chance just exactly when Girdvainis had gone for the banns. But where did that unearthly neighing come from, the neighing so many had heard but no one could say which direction it was coming from? It was so dreadfully confusing and deceitful. That's why Girdvainis got so befuddled that instead of following the horses by the road, he ran straight out into the fields and hadn't returned since.

Many people had come across the fiancée—Whitehorn's Jurga—on the road from Švendubrė to Paudruvė. It seemed strange, so early in the morning, that she wasn't going to church, but in the opposite direction. It didn't occur to anyone then that she was Girdvainis' betrothed and was returning from the banns. They didn't dare ask—she looked so proud, and if someone tried to joke with her, she gave no response, as if she hadn't heard it.

It was only when they arrived in Švendubrė and heard about the unusual events that had happened early that morning did they realize, even if they didn't know the whole story, why Jurga went home alone. After the horses neighed and the bridegroom ran out of the vestry, she turned as pale as a sheet and nearly collapsed in Uršulė's arms. But she got control of herself, raised her head, and left the vestry, holding herself strangely stiff all over.

She walked through the village that way. In vain Uršulė followed her for a good quarter mile, urging her the entire time to make a vow of chastity or else she would be damned, but Jurga didn't turn around. However, Uršulė was a determined sort. She didn't give in until the bells for early mass started ringing, and only then, after giving Jurga a thorough scolding, did she run back to church. But she couldn't calm down there, either.

Even in church people couldn't help whispering about these extraordinary events. They traded news and rumors but couldn't make head nor tail of it. Uršulė alone knew everything and understood it all. But she was silent, as if she had been infected with Jurga's pride, merely from time to time throwing dirty looks at those who were whispering and disturbing the pious gravity of a holy place.

At last even Uršulė couldn't bear it any longer. After the sermon, when the unsettled crowd left the church and started speculating about the details of what had happened, Uršulė couldn't resist the temptation and snuck out into the churchyard, which she never used to do. On holy days she would sit around in the church from early morning, when the sexton would light the first candles, until early evening, when all the candles would be snuffed and they started sweeping the church. Only then would Uršulė rise from the altar rail and go out. But this time the temptation was too much.

Outside the church, she stood next to one group, then another, listened and listened, tilted her head to one side and finally said:

"You didn't see anything and you don't know anything; that's not at all what really happened."

What had really happened was not, however, that easy to get out of Uršulė. She minced around for quite some time yet, arousing people's curiosity, until she spoke:

"It was like this," she finally said, when people's patience had worn thin and they were nearly ready to kill her for her affectations, "I'm going to church early in the morning, I look—someone's horses are tied to the churchyard's hitching post. Who's this here so early, there's no telling. And what horses, more like dragons, hardly standing in place, and hitched to just wheels, neither a seat nor sides, only the bottom left between the wheels. Who could have driven here like that, I couldn't make head nor tail of it. Judging by the horses—some fine gentleman, but by the cart—the worst scum. I meet Bernard the organist, he's going to ring for the early mass, so I ask him: 'Who could have driven here like that?' He answers: 'Why, you don't know? Girdvainis with Whitehorn's Jurga, for the banns.' Oh, Lordy-dee, I think, someone's turned up after all, who's torn her away from her sorcerer father's plans and the devil's claws. I sighed and looked up to heaven. Why, I look—high up in the sky, it's like a giant hawk is carrying a giant chicken. I simply don't want to believe my eyes. But then, don't all the dogs in the village howl, don't all the roosters crow! Well, I said, the Day of Judgement has come. I didn't manage to finish crossing myself, when I look, and the evil one himself is coming down with a bag on his back, right by the church. When he lands, why, I look—the devil shakes a horse thief out of a bedsheet. They raised a cloud of dust, but I recognized both of them anyway. It was Pinčukas and Tatergall. 'What are they going to do here?' I think. They landed right by Girdvainis' horses. I didn't figure out what was going on nor yell for the organist. Tatergall looks around, grabs the reins and flies straight off through the fields—the ground even shook. Then the devil lifted up, turned into a bat, and started to neigh like a hundred horses. I ran into the vestry to tell Girdvainis that his horses had been stolen, and he ran out like he'd lost his head, he didn't even ask me who stole them and how, that's how the devil befuddled him, and that's the end of his horses. Where are you going to find them now? With horses like that, Tatergall's a hundred miles away by now. If he'd asked me, I'd have said to him: 'Look for a way to save your soul, not your horses, because you can't do a thing now, not when the devil and a horse thief are in cahoots, and there's a sorcerer behind them too. So either give up the bride, whose father, the sorcerer, promised her to the devil, or lose your horses. And if you want both the horses and the bride, then you won't get either one, and only make an end of yourself.' "

"An old woman's babbling nonsense, and grown men listen," someone in the crowd answered.

"When the devil snatches you, you'll see what kind of nonsense it is." Uršulė threw them a dirty look and turned away, raising the dust with her skirt. "If you don't want to know what happened, then I could care less."

Peeved, Uršulė went inside the church, since the bells had started ringing for vespers. Some tried to ask the bell-ringer Bernard if Uršulė had told the truth, but he could only vouch that when he had met Uršulė while going to ring for early mass, she had asked whose horses those were, and he had answered, but then he went into the bell tower and didn't see anything more, he only heard the cart thundering and the horses' neighing. When he came out of the bell tower, the horse thief was flying with the horses down the road to the west, the neighing was to be heard right around here and then moved off to the east. Girdvainis had run through the fields to the south. That's how confused he was, poor thing.

People didn't know what to think or what to believe. They parted making all sorts of conjectures. Whatever had happened, they'd probably never know for sure, and rumors about Whitehorn's mill had been going around for quite some time. So it wasn't surprising that this had happened with the match, too.

XXVI

In any event, Uršulė wasn't babbling complete nonsense this time, although what had really happened she didn't know herself. Jurgutis could have confirmed her story and supplemented her knowledge and wisdom, but he had disappeared, no one knew where, without saying anything to anyone about what he had seen and what he had been through.

Pinčukas wasn't the only one who had raced with Girdvainis' dapple-grays, but Jurgutis, too—like the devil's shadow. When he heard the extraordinary thundering of a cart and hooves above the hum of the bellows, he leapt out of the smithy and saw the dapple-grays flying like mad straight at him. In fright, he dashed into the ditch so they wouldn't trample him, but then, realizing this was quite likely the true suitor paying a call on Jurga, he jumped out in front of them, wanting to spook them. But the dapple-grays, flying like whirlwinds, knocked him into the quagmire, which he only just managed to clamber out of.

Afterwards an impenetrable fog suddenly rose out of the bogs. Only the cart rumbled somewhere and the dapple-grays neighed not far from Whitehorn's mill. Then Jurgutis, too, ran like a fool through the fog straight to the mill, where he hadn't been since Whitehorn had made fun of him for that sniffling of his.

Up atop the mill's hill it was a clear evening; the fog, like the sea, billowed and drifted into swirls only at the foot of the hill. The cart with the dapple-gray steeds stood by the mill and a light shimmered in the parlor

137

window. Disheartened, Jurgutis went up to the window and jumped back in shock—the suitor took the rue from Jurga's hands and tucked it behind her braids.

"Jurga's ruined," said Jurgutis. "Those no-good dapple-grays have trampled everything under their feet."

And such heartache came over him then, that he didn't know what to do with himself, unless simply to up and sink straight into the ground. He wanted to untie the dapple-grays from the mill's hitching post and spook them so they would fly down the slope (oh, those dapple-grays had trampled his heart!), but as soon as he got close to them they snorted and neighed so, that in his alarm Jurgutis didn't know himself how he rolled down the hill.

Then he returned to the smithy, but there was no peace for him there either. Jurga, her head bent, constantly appeared before his eyes, and the suitor was taking the rue from her hands. Why didn't he jump through the window then and take the rue away? Jurga would have escaped like a seagull and flown off along the lakes. Now everything was over, everything ruined. The strange suitor would take her off to some corner of the world, and he would never see her and never hear her ringing, silver laughter. The despondent Jurgutis grabbed a rope and wanted to hang himself under the vent, but the rope broke and he fell down on the dirt floor in front of a heap of horseshoes.

Stunned and completely stupefied, Jurgutis arranged the horseshoes from one pile to another in the dark, pondering what on earth to do, where to disappear to, because it was so dreary and awful that it seemed as if all the corners had come alive and started rustling, and his hair stood on end. Around him the ground shook from the horses' hooves and the dapple-grays neighed so resoundingly that it split the darkness like thunder. But the moon shone calmly through the smithy's vent. This storm raged only in Jurgutis' heart.

At last, unable to bear it, he, for some reason, took two pairs of horseshoes from the pile and went outside with no idea of what to do next. An infinite number of stars were twinkling in the glorious night, but they all, it seemed, were falling on Jurgutis' head, their rays piercing his heart like swords. In his uneasiness, he himself didn't know how it happened that he staggered to Cockend's tavern and traded the horseshoes with Shaddon for a half-pint of vodka.

Jurgutis, driven out into the front hall, knew nothing of what was going on in the tavern. He gulped down the vodka together with his tears that burned like fire, and wanted nothing more than to sink straight down into the earth and forget everything. But he didn't forget anything and he didn't sink into the earth; rather, guzzling the vodka, he felt everything around him spinning—the tavern, the mill, the smithy, Jurga with her suitor, and oh, those dapple-grays, slashing with their hooves, flying straight at him as if they wanted to trample him. Then Jurgutis took his head into his hands and fell down, rolling over right there under the bench.

Jurgutis, out cold, knew nothing of what happened afterwards. He came to only towards morning when Pinčukas noisily burst in through the door. Jurgutis saw him then for the first time in all of his devilish horror, with horns! And cloven hooves! At first glance he looked truly horrifying and frenzied.

But Jurgutis, since he was terribly frightened, didn't have the time to get a good look at him, and Pinčukas was unusually hurried to boot. Rushing into the tavern, Pinčukas dumped the sleeping Shaddon off the bench, snatched the duvet stuffed with straw out from underneath him, shook the straw out right there—upending it on Jurgutis, crawling out from under the bench—and then snatched the drunken Tatergall out of the larder, stuffed him into the sack and flew out like his pants were on fire.

It was the devil's good luck that he had lost his tobacco tin racing with Girdvainis, and had missed it in time to go out looking for it. By the bend of Blind Lake he found his tobacco tin and saw Girdvainis with Jurga flying towards him through the dawn. He barely managed to get out of the road or Girdvainis would have run him over, and that would have been an end to all his plans with the horse thief. He then flew back breathless to the tavern and carried Tatergall out in the duvet cover to Švendubrė to steal Girdvainis' dapple-grays.

Pinčukas nearly got a hernia by the time he had carried that drunk-as-a-skunk horse thief to Švendubrė and landed next to the church. It was a good thing, too, that Tatergall, as he was carried through the skies, sobered up, and, shaken out of the sack, immediately came to his senses and rushed to the dapple-grays. But it's doubtful their plan would have succeeded if Boniface Bobbin hadn't overslept and hadn't delayed accepting the banns with his prayers. Nothing would have come of all the devil and the horse thief's efforts, since Girdvainis with his bride would have had time after the banns to fly out of Švendubrė with his dapple-grays on wings of wind. How could you have caught him and stolen his dapple-grays then?

At the time Jurgutis knew none of this, horribly frightened as he was, floundering in the straw as he crawled out from under the bench and totally mystified about what was going on here: was he dreaming, or hallucinating? Shaddon, seeing him floundering, became even more frightened. In the meantime, Pinčukas with the sack on his shoulder fled out the door, breaking it down in his haste.

"Pfui, pfui, pfui!" Shaddon spat so that the stitch in his side wouldn't seize him in his fright. It wasn't so much Pinčukas carrying out the horse thief in a sack that scared him, as much as the sight of a second devil crawling out of the straw to take him off to hell.

But when he saw Jurgutis, he came to his senses and starting swearing.

"Oh, so it's you, you drunkard, rolling around under the benches!" he yelled at Jurgutis and stamped his feet like he'd been stung in the rear end. "Out of this tavern, the faster the better."

Jurgutis needed no urging, and fled through the toppled door without delay, but Shaddon, coming to his senses, stopped him in the doorway by his coattails.

"Wait!" he said threateningly, "if you say even a single word to anyone about what you saw or heard here, the devil will snatch you too, and carry you off to hell."

Horror-stricken, Jurgutis just stared, gaping, at Shaddon, with his eyes as big as dinner plates, completely dumbstruck. Escaping from the tavern keeper's hands, he took off running blindly through the fields.

Oh, Jurgutis didn't know then that Pinčukas hadn't carried Tatergall off to hell, but to Švendubrė to steal Girdvainis' dapple-grays and to ruin Jurga. If he had known, then nothing would have stopped him—neither fear nor horror—he would have flown to Švendubrė ahead of the devil and the horse thief and saved Jurga, who of all things was the most precious to him.

But at the moment Jurgutis, fleeing the tavern, didn't realize either what had happened or where he should hide from all that horror. So he went through the fields without knowing where he was going. It wasn't so terrible that the devil might snatch him and carry him off to hell (let him carry him off if he wanted to, he didn't have anywhere to go, anyway), as much as he was sorry and terribly ashamed that the evening before he had stolen and drunk up two pairs of horseshoes. Jurgutis had no idea how that had happened. Unless perhaps the devil had meddled in here, too, and tempted him? How could he return home now and look the smith in the eye?

But all of that was a mere trifle when he remembered that he would never again see Jurga flying by the lakes, never again hear her ringing laughter. How was he to live then? The lakeshore would forever be as dark as night, and the mill on the hill would persecute him with its memories like a ghost. What would he do with himself then?

It got so awful, dreary, and sad, that Jurgutis, when he fled the tavern, turned around in the opposite direction and went where his feet led him. Where it was he was going, he didn't know himself, just as far as possible from the place where he was tormented by a terrible disappointment and a guilty conscience.

So Jurgutis went through the fields, avoiding the roads and paths, without telling anyone of what he had seen and knew; as a result of all that horror, heartache, and grief he had lost his tongue completely and couldn't utter a word. He just sniffled and mumbled under his breath, as if sobbing uncontrollable tears.

Meanwhile, the smith didn't miss the horseshoes (he never noticed that two pairs were missing from the pile), as much as he missed Jurgutis himself. He kept asking people if anyone had seen him or run into him, but no one knew anything about him; it was as if he had vanished into thin air. The smith wondered if Jurgutis hadn't drowned himself over that foolhardy love, but the lake's waters didn't give their secrets away.

So it was that Jurgutis disappeared from the land of Paudruvė, and no one knew where. The horror he had experienced drove him farther and farther, until at last in his heartache he wandered to an unknown land, where people took him for a mute little half-wit and felt sorry for him. And still he couldn't find peace.

XXVII

After those unfortunate banns, things became grim and dreary at Whitehorn's mill and in his home, as if the banns had bespoken some unavoidable misfortune that was to be expected any day now.

Whitehorn did indeed expect it, graying and completely stooped over, as though carrying some unbearable burden. His daughter, when she came home that day from Švendubrė, shut herself up in the parlor without saying anything, not even to her father, and wept more bitterly than she had ever wept before. For three weeks she wept her maidenly tears, looking through the window and waiting all the while.

The father felt terribly sorry for his daughter. Her tears fell like stones on his gray head, but he neither knew what to do himself, nor how to reassure her. Not being able to bear her bitter tears, he wanted more than once to confess and tell her his secret, but the words would stick in his throat and he would be crushed by the weight of his secret. His gray head couldn't fathom what was to be done.

The second and third banns went by, his daughter kept weeping and waiting, but the suitor never returned. He roamed through the entire countryside as if his brains had been addled, and he didn't know which way to turn or what to do with himself. Some had seen him on one road, others met him on another road; he kept asking everyone if they had seen some dapple-gray steeds, but never once did he mention his bride. It was as if he had completely forgotten about her.

"Don't cry, daughter dear," Whitehorn tried to comfort his daughter, even though he himself had lost hope, "your suitor will find his horses and come back for you."

Jurga's eyes dried for the first time then, and flashed with a pride that only seizes a person when they have conquered themselves.

"I don't need a suitor like that anymore," she answered her father, "one who throws me over because of his horses."

Her father didn't know whether to rejoice or to grieve on account of this change in his daughter, so he just sighed, and grief pressed at his heart.

"Little daughter of mine, little orphan of mine," he stroked her head, "I'm the one who's to blame."

Whitehorn would have given his secret away to his daughter then, but the burning tears he tried to hide from his daughter took his words away.

"No one is to blame," his daughter answered, comforting her father. "I wasn't destined to be happy, so I'll do without."

"No, my dear daughter, no," her father disagreed, "You must be happy, because otherwise I won't be able to bear my heartache."

Jurga was sorry for her unhappy father; her eyes shone with an endless love, and she hugged his gray head.

"Don't worry, father dear," she said. "With you I will always be happy."

This weighed even more heavily on the father, but he said no more to her, since he was already somewhat comforted that she had at least calmed down a bit.

From then on, they both avoided mentioning Girdvainis and his dapple-gray steeds. It was as though he had only driven by and hadn't left so much as a memory.

So fall passed, rainy and windy; winter came, blowing eddies around the mill and creaking the wings, which hadn't spun for quite some time. At first people stayed away from the mill themselves, avoiding a place of misfortune, and later Whitehorn himself, oppressed by his worries, told people the mill didn't work, and he was old and didn't know when he would be able to fix it.

People believed him and drove to the surrounding mills, more than once regretting the loss of Whitehorn's mill, which stood like a ghost on the frozen lake's precipice and, it seemed, waited for spring, when it could lift up and fly away.

Spring was still a long way off, and it was sad to listen to the piercing wind, which howled through the neglected mill's sails. During the day Whitehorn would be shut up by himself in the mill. Even his daughter didn't know what he was doing there. In reality he wasn't doing anything, just thinking about one and only one thing: how to redeem his guilt and see his daughter happy.

Whitehorn understood that his moment of happiness had been purchased at an exorbitant cost, an unbearable lifelong torment. He didn't know how to erase that shadow from his daughter, whom he loved with all his heart and soul. Sometimes he imagined the neighing of Girdvainis' horses in the howling of the north wind, and he would put all of his hopes in his son-in-law, who would at last arrive and save his daughter. It was this sole hope that Whitehorn lived on.

Jurga waited for Girdvainis' return, too, even though she had renounced him. Frequently at night she would dream of the dapple-gray horses' neighing, which would draw nearer and then suddenly disappear. Then she would see Girdvainis at the crossroads, hatless, tossed by the piercing winds, and she would dream of a spring storm that would waken her with its lightning. But this lightning thundered only in Jurga's heart.

In the fields the winter storms still raged, and the piercing wind howled about the parlor windows. But Jurga's heart heard the coming spring in its howling. She didn't dare admit it even to herself, but she believed with all her heart that a spring storm would soon thunder, in that storm the dapple-gray steeds would neigh, and her suitor, whom she couldn't forget even if she wanted to, would fly to her on wings of wind.

So she waited for Girdvainis with all her heart, and he perhaps sensed this, but he couldn't return to his bride without his dapple-gray steeds, the pride of his youth. So he roamed through the fall downpours and the winter blizzards, along all the highways and byways, looking for his dapple-grays and not finding them anywhere, but constantly hearing the neighing that had deluded him.

So what could a rejected bride do?

XXVIII

At last Anupras took pity on Girdvainis and went out searching for him in the crossroads. There was no finding the dapple-grays anyway; he needed to save what he still could, namely, Girdvainis himself, who had completely lost his head over those horses of his.

Ever since the morning when he had run out of church as if the ground was burning under his feet, he had rushed about, charging in all directions, hearing his dapple-grays' neighing everywhere but never finding them. And where could you find them if Tatergall, when he snatched them, had sped straight off to Prussia without stopping anywhere, not even long enough to catch his breath?

Girdvainis had also more than once gone as far as Prussia and back, asking everywhere if anyone had seen his horses, but people just shrugged their shoulders—they had neither heard nor seen them. When Girdvainis would start to explain in detail how his horses looked—whirlwinds they were, not horses—then people would glance at Girdvainis suspiciously and, turning away, would point a finger at their heads. "Apparently, no one's at home upstairs," they would think and leave him alone.

But Girdvainis was never in one place very long, because right there, even while he was asking about his horses, they would neigh in some direction or another, and he would start, listen, and then set off without saying a word, straight through the fields in the direction where he had heard the neighing. So how could there be

148

any doubt that this wasn't a matter of stolen horses, but rather there was something wrong with the man's head?

No one else heard the dapple-grays neighing, only Girdvainis, because in truth they were neighing only in his ears and thoughts. That was why he turned in a vicious circle, without finding a way out, as if he were bewitched.

Anupras hoped perhaps he could succeed in talking Girdvainis around, in straightening out his addled brains and finally bringing him back home, and maybe back to the bride who was waiting for him in vain.

The banns had long since passed in church, sharpening vicious people's tongues and spreading all sorts of stories. Girdvainis' misfortune didn't raise sympathy in people's hearts, only cruel derision.

There were many who, when meeting the unfortunate suitor on the road, couldn't resist teasing him to his face:

"So, you're still looking for your horses?" they would ask mockingly. "Your bride, I hear, didn't wait for you; she's already planning a wedding with someone else."

"Let her go ahead!" Girdvainis would answer at first, but later, when he understood that they were making fun of him, he would glare at them and go on his way without answering at all.

The longer this went on, the more rude and sullen Girdvainis became. Stunned by his misfortune, he found neither a kind heart, nor understanding, nor compassion among people, just cruel derision and mockery, so he turned away from everyone and looked at them all with mistrust, as though everyone had conspired in the theft of his horses and driven him out to roam the highways and byways.

Then he began to hate everyone and look at them as if they were the thieves' accomplices. Now he no longer asked if anyone had seen his horses, and if someone asked about them, even with sympathy, he would angrily shout back:

"And what business is it of yours?" and off he'd go, looking a fright.

He knew very well by now that people weren't going to help him; they would only waste his time and scoff at him, so he avoided them and didn't get into any conversations. If sometimes when he was hungry he would wander in at someone's house—his own house he had completely forgotten, as if he had never had one—then, whether he had eaten or not, he would immediately leave without so much as saying thank you. Where he would spend the night, hidden from the rain and the frost, no one knew. You could run into him any time— day or night—going somewhere along the road, talking to himself about something or other and not seeing a thing. Unable to talk to other people about his misfortune, he talked to himself, asking himself and answering himself as if he weren't a single person, but two at once.

So it wasn't easy for Anupras, when he met him, to communicate with him. Anupras saw him coming down the road from Forester. He stopped, looked at him, and could hardly recognize him. What had become of this man! He was no longer a man, but merely the shadow of one. Girdvainis would have gone on without even noticing Anupras. How was someone like that going to find his horses? Someone like that was fit only to fly with the crows to paradise.

"Why, hello stranger!" exclaimed Anupras. "You're going by without even looking."

"And why would I look at you?" answered Girdvainis without turning around.

"Don't tell me you really don't recognize me?" asked Anupras.

"And just who are you?" Girdvainis turned back, glancing angrily at Anupras.

"Now that's enough!" Anupras wasn't as much surprised at Girdvainis as sorry for him. "You, my dear fellow, are the one who's hard to recognize. I'm still the same as I ever was. You really don't remember Anupras?"

"I remember," answered Girdvainis sadly, thinking about something else. Then, after a brief pause, as if regretfully, he added, "Anupras, why did we go calling on that accursed girl?"

"What do you mean, why?" Anupras didn't understand at first. "You yourself said that with those horses you'd find your girl, even if it was at the ends of the earth. What do you want—we found her."

"What of it, if we found her, and lost the horses," answered Girdvainis, looking off somewhere into the distance.

"It seems it was the way things were meant to be," interrupted Anupras, looking at Girdvainis. "What can you do now? It's either the horses or the girl. But for a spirited girl like that you can't even regret your dapple-

151

grays. You won't find another one like that anywhere else in the world."

"But the same goes for the horses," Girdvainis broke in.

"What's true is true," Anupras agreed. "But all the same, a person's not a horse. You're not really going to reject the entire world because of some horses?"

"But nothing else in the world means anything to me anymore," answered Girdvainis.

"That's enough nonsense, now!" Anupras scolded him. "I'm old, and whatever I look at, everything catches my eye, everything gladdens my heart, even that rock by the side of the road. Let's sit on it, we'll talk, maybe we'll agree on something."

Anupras sat down on the rock, while Girdvainis looked doubtful and mistrustful.

"Sit down," said Anupras once more. "What are you looking around for now?"

Girdvainis reluctantly sat down on the edge of the rock. Both of them sat there for a while in silence. Anupras looked at Girdvainis and he became so sad that he was all the more at a loss for words to comfort or reassure him, while Girdvainis, clenching his teeth, silently looked at the ground beneath his feet.

"So there," said Anupras at last, but what he wanted to say he didn't know himself. He just looked at Girdvainis' sunken face and met his burning eyes. Girdvainis also looked at Anupras as if he wanted to hear something. But Anupras, after looking a while, said only this: "You've wandered enough. Let's go home, and later we'll go over to see her. She's still waiting for you."

"So what if she's still waiting for me," answered Girdvainis sadly. "I can't go back to see her until I find my dapple-grays. How can I go see her without them?" A note of inhuman heartache, mixed with an endless longing, sounded in his voice. "How will I look her in the face? And what will I say?"

Anupras hadn't managed to get a single word out when Girdvainis suddenly jumped up, listened intently and, nearly breaking into a run, took off down the road as if he was after something.

Oh, there he goes again, after the imaginary neighing of his dapple-grays!

Anupras, in his surprise, didn't manage to either hold him or call him back. Shout or not, you still couldn't call him back. But Anupras didn't even attempt to call him or to stop him. He had seen with his own eyes that Girdvainis had met with a far bigger misfortune than the loss of his dapple-grays. Rising from the rock, he went off slowly, thinking, was there really no help in such a misfortune? And Anupras, with all of an old man's stubbornness, resolved to find that help.

In the meantime, Girdvainis, battered from all sides, continued to roam down unknown highways and byways, because in the moan of the wind he kept hearing his dapple-grays' neighing, and then he'd forget everything else in the world. Even the girl for whom he had searched for seven miles around, and, having found her, abandoned her on account of his horses; the girl whom he had left waiting in vain, crying and cursing, but still unable to renounce her suitor, who with his dapple-grays had won her heart and broken the spell on her road. But Girdvainis couldn't drive to his bride without those dapple-grays of his, even though he missed her passionately.

When will you, Girdvainis, catch your dapple-grays, when will you fly with them to your bride on the wings of the wind?

XXIX

After his unsuccessful encounter with Girdvainis, Anupras didn't return to his village; instead he turned down the road to Paudruvė.

From the longing in Girdvainis' voice, which he had heard when the two of them sat on the rock by the side of the road, Anupras understood where it was possible to find help for the misfortune that had befallen Girdvainis, and what could break the spell he was under, quiet the dapple-grays' neighing, and return him home from his fruitless wandering on the highways and byways.

So, decided, Anupras breathed easier, and even though he was tired from his search for Girdvainis, he determined to immediately go to the land of Paudruvė, without delaying or returning home, to talk to Whitehorn and his daughter.

As it was just before the spring thaw, the road was long and arduous, torn up and full of holes. Anupras wouldn't have dared to attempt it if not urged on by such an important and pressing matter. He was sorry for Girdvainis, that smart young man, who, chasing the wind through the fields, seemed to be completely doomed. Sliding, falling, and getting up again, Anupras finally reached Paudruvė's land and Whitehorn's mill at dusk.

In the evening twilight the mill stood with its wings folded, as gloomy as a phantom. There wasn't a single soul to be seen. Anupras looked at the cottage windows. They were dark as well. There wasn't a light anywhere. Even the stars weren't glinting off the windows.

"Maybe they're no longer alive?" Anupras looked about and sighed.

But then he heard a sound as though someone were coming down the mill's stairs. Heavily, slowly, stopping and groping around in the dark.

The door to the mill opened and Anupras saw Whitehorn's shadow. The wind blew and the shadow moved. Anupras cringed; perhaps Whitehorn's ghost haunted the place?

"Are you still alive, or is it just your shade that's come from the other world?" Anupras asked, looking at Whitehorn, on whose bare head the wind tousled the totally white hair.

"Still alive," said Whitehorn, barely audibly. "Whom has God sent us for a guest?"

"It's me," Anupras was relieved that he had met a live person, not a spirit. "Don't you recognize me? It's me, your matchmaker, Anupras."

Then Whitehorn's shadow moved and, approaching Anupras, hugged him with trembling arms.

"What news do you bring?" he asked in greeting.

"I'm looking for help," answered Anupras.

"I don't know," Whitehorn replied, sighing, "if there's any help to be found here."

"Only here, from you and your daughter," answered Anupras, "If I don't find it here, then Girdvainis will be gone with the wind."

"Then let's go into the cottage, we'll discuss what we can do to help," Whitehorn invited him in.

And the two elders, worried about what help there could be and how to find it, went into the cottage.

In the cottage Jurga sat at the loom by the window and watched Lake Udruvė drowning in the evening twilight as if she were waiting for something. But what she was waiting for she herself didn't know, since she had renounced everything and wanted only one thing—to forget it all. It was just that her heart wouldn't listen. It constantly fretted, thrashed, and kicked like a bird held in a hand. She waited for something fearfully, and was angry with herself for waiting.

Now, hearing her father in the front hall coming in with someone, she got up from the window and looked at the door in suspense, unable to guess who would come through it. Since the time of those unfortunate banns the neighbors avoided coming by, and practically no one had dropped in. So who on earth could have come now? Not Girdvainis? But it was only her father and some elderly man, whom Jurga didn't immediately recognize, who came in the door, and her heart fell in terrible disappointment.

"Good evening, my dear," said Anupras, coming into the cottage. "I've traveled a long way to see you about important business."

Jurga recognized Anupras from his voice, and her heart froze in expectation: surely he came with some sort of news about Girdvainis. But what? She got all upset. Suddenly the disappointment she had experienced as a rejected bride constricted her chest like ice, and she cooled.

"I don't know," she answered, fighting with herself, "what sort of business could be worth such a long trip."

"It's worth it," said Anupras, without hesitation. "You are the only one who can help, and no one else. I'm an old man, I know what I'm doing and what I'm saying. But will you, my dear, have the strength to rise above yourself? If you have the strength, everything will be fine, if not—everything will be ruined."

"Hasn't everything been ruined already?" Jurga questioned. Hope and despair tore at her from all sides.

"No, my dear," said Anupras. "Everything's not ruined. Everything can still be saved. All that's needed is goodwill and determination."

"I don't know what you're talking about, uncle," Jurga said, breaking down, unable to wrestle with herself any longer.

"Wait, my dear, we'll sit down, we'll talk it over, that's what I came for, after all." Anupras unhurriedly looked around for a place to put his hat and a spot to sit himself down.

Seeing this, Whitehorn invited his guest to sit at the table.

"Thank you," Anupras said. "It's an urgent matter, but surely we won't discuss it standing? We'll sit down and think about it."

157

Although Anupras had hurried to get there, now that he had arrived he played for time, as if he was considering his mission and weighing it over anew. So, sitting down in the corner, he spoke of this and that, as if he had completely forgotten what he had come for.

Only later, after supper, when he had stuffed his pipe with tobacco and inhaled the smoke, did he look at Jurga attentively, as though he didn't have faith in her or had second thoughts about his idea, but, gathering all of his resolution—what will be, will be—he at last said:

"So, you see, my dear, what my business is. Girdvainis was the only one who could come to you with his dapple-grays and break the spell on your road. But for this he himself fell into the devil's trap, lost his dapple-grays, and, deluded by sprites, wanders the highways and byways. So now it's your turn, my dear. You are the only one who can scatter those sprites from his path, drown out the enchanted neighing in his ears, and return him from his wanderings to the shelter of humanity. Will you do that?" asked Anupras, looking at Jurga even more attentively.

"How can I do that?" Jurga lowered her eyes.

"It's very simple, my dear," answered Anupras, "Your heart will tell you what to do. You have to find him in his wanderings, you have to drown out the lost dapple-grays' neighing with your laughter, you have to scatter the sprites from his path with your smile, and with your love take the place of the entire world for him, because otherwise—he's doomed, and you won't save yourself, either."

"Never!" Jurga jumped up from her spot and her eyes flashed. "Let him be doomed, but I'll never go looking for him when he left me and ran out to the four winds looking for his steeds. I'll never smile or laugh for him, because he exchanged my smile and laugh for the neighing of his dapple-grays. I'll never let my love take the place of the world for him, because he trampled that love under his horses' hooves. Let him wander his back roads, I don't need him anymore."

Jurga said all of this in one breath, and then, as if her breath had run short, she suddenly stopped, and the tears began to roll down her pale cheeks. Then she ran into the parlor and there, without restraint, released all her heartache and all of her maidenly tears. But how could that help her, when her heart was torn, and love and disappointment were wrestling in her breast?

Left alone together, Whitehorn and Anupras looked at each other and didn't know what there was to be done or how to find a way out.

The slammed door to the parlor clanged forlornly after Jurga and the windows rattled, sending shudders throughout the old cottage.

Oh, youth!

How proud and intractable it is. It has never listened and never will listen to the wisdom of its elders. Instead it will go its own way, wherever its heart leads it.

Whitehorn sighed, hanging his head and looking at the ground, while Anupras scratched around in his pipe and went over to the lamp for a light.

"So," he said, puffing on the smoke, "there's nothing to be done, when one is lost and the other's heart is wounded. How can you bring them back together? Each will go their own way."

"Wait," interrupted Whitehorn, getting up. "Don't lose hope at the first setback. I know my daughter better. I'll try and talk her around. Her heart's not made of stone."

"That's what I thought, too," Anupras agreed, exhaling smoke. "We need to bring them together, otherwise neither one nor the other will find a solution."

Whitehorn went to talk to his daughter in the parlor, but he couldn't get anywhere. He tried one way and another to persuade her and calm her down, but Jurga, leaning on the window sill, was silent; her shoulders just shook and tears rolled down her face.

Whitehorn stroked his daughter's shoulders, kissed her on the forehead, wished her good night, and returned to Anupras, who was sitting thoughtfully with his head hanging, weighed down by serious concern. Whitehorn, sighing, sat down next to him in silence. Anupras lifted his head, looked at him, and understood everything without a word.

The old ones sat for a while, sighed, and then laid down—Whitehorn in the corner by the stove, Hearall on the bench, but neither of them fell asleep; each one was thinking his own thoughts. Sometimes they would sigh heavily, but they didn't say a word, as both of them knew full well that no words could soothe a troubled love, which, when wounded, turns into a dreadful storm. It will heed nothing, go down its own path, smash everything, turn everything upside down, wreak havoc, giving no quarter, until out of its disappointed longing only ruins remain.

Oh, both of the elders knew this very well. So what was there left to say; how could it be helped? And although one was sorry for his daughter and the other for his suitor, what could they do when one of them was sobbing in the parlor, leaning on the window sill, renouncing everything, and the other, oblivious to everything, roamed the highways and byways following the neighing of his dapple-grays?

The elders got up from their hard sleepless beds before dawn and each prepared to go his own way with his own thoughts. What will be, will be—there was nothing to be done. And if an unavoidable misfortune was coming, both of them knew very well that there was no getting around it, all there was left to do was to bear it. So the shoulders of age bowed under the sense of all its weight.

Outside it was still dark; a storm raged, banging the shutters and howling in the chimney.

Whitehorn groped around and lit the lantern. Outside the window something flashed by and screeched like a bat or an owl. Whitehorn flinched and froze. Anupras looked at the window and turned to Whitehorn.

"What's this now?" he asked.

"It's nothing," said Whitehorn, turning pale. "Probably an owl or a bat flew over the light and screeched."

Hearall looked through the window again, wondering if his suspicions were true, tilted his head to the side and fixed his eyes on Whitehorn as if questioning him. Whitehorn stood there looking pale and frightened, with his eyes lowered, as if he'd been caught in the act.

"Well, then," said Hearall, at last understanding it all, "It's just that you'll never get rid of that owl or bat, unless you shoot it with a silver bullet."

"Brother, what sort of nonsense is this," Whitehorn broke in, and was going out to see what had happened.

At that moment something hooted again, as if a blast of wind had rushed by or the spring storm had intensified, and the entire cottage shuddered and shook.

Jurga suddenly ran in through the parlor door, dreadfully frightened and as pale as a sheet.

"Father, there are ghosts!" She cried and rushed to Whitehorn's arms, shaking all over like an aspen leaf.

"What's this you've imagined, daughter dear?" her father admonished her, caressing her shaking shoulders. "A spring storm rattles the shutters, and you get scared."

The daughter partly believed, partly doubted her father's words, but she calmed down, ashamed of her fear, which was produced by neither a gust of wind, nor a bat flying by, but by the uneasiness in her own heart.

"So maybe now, my dear, we'll go look for your lost suitor?" asked Hearall.

"No," Jurga replied firmly, recovering her pride. "I'd rather marry Jurgutis, and I won't go looking for a suitor who left me."

"What Jurgutis?" Hearall wondered.

"Who knows," Whitehorn answered, waving it off with his arm. "There was this half-wit apprentice to the neighboring blacksmith... But he disappeared somewhere, too..."

Whitehorn went outside to see what was going on. But he had barely opened the door when something flew from under the window and dashed away with the gusts of wind to the foot of the hill.

162

A spring storm raged before dawn, and in it nothing could be seen. Whitehorn surmised that this could be no one else but Pinčukas, haunting them in revenge, when in reality it was Jurgutis.

Wandering the highways and byways before spring, Jurgutis had returned from his stay among strangers, and with nowhere to go—he was still ashamed to return to the smithy he had stolen from—he wandered over to Whitehorn's mill. All night long he hid under the parlor window where Jurga, huddled into a ball on the other side, quietly wept. But Jurgutis heard and felt those tears, which fell on his conscience like stones, and he was struck speechless.

It was only before dawn, when a light came on in the cottage, that Jurgutis, startled, leapt up and, with his head in his hands, shrieked as if in unbearable pain. He wanted to run into the cottage and confess what a horrible criminal he was, spooking Girdvainis' dapple-grays and drowning Jurga in tears, but he collapsed right by the entrance under the window. He came to his senses only when the door creaked and, even more frightened, he rolled with the wind and the gusts of snow past the mill to the foot of the hill. It was his good fortune that a large drift had formed under the precipice, so that he fell into a soft bed.

Hearall, taking his leave of Whitehorn, understood in his own way what was going on, and left to look for the true villain and rein him in. But where could he find him in a spring storm?

XXX

Oh, that Girdvainis! What trouble he made for himself with those dapple-grays of his, and what dreadful unhappiness he brought down on the heads of others. It would have been better if he had never had them, than to come to ruin himself and drown his betrothed—for whom he had searched seven miles around—in tears.

But everything had turned out so badly. There was nothing to be done, if even Anupras couldn't do anything to help, and his betrothed, drowning in tears and heartache, had renounced him. Life could have been peaches and cream for Girdvainis; having found his bride, he could have flown with his dapple-grays on wings of the wind, never touching the ground. But that sort of happiness wasn't to be, or maybe Girdvainis hadn't found his true bride, since everything had turned out so differently. Instead he had just ruined the prettiest girl in the land of Paudruvė and gotten himself into terrible trouble.

It seemed there would be no way out of this vicious circle, and Girdvainis would have to roam the highways and byways until the end of his life, chasing after his dapple-grays and hovering about the crossroads like a phantom, watching and waiting for his horses to pass by. No one, it seems, would save him from this misfortune, and the young man would turn into a phantom in the prime of life, frightening late passersby at the crossroads.

Lord spare you from meeting Girdvainis now in a crossroad, especially at night, with his frenzied eyes glittering in the dusk, when he stops everyone and checks

whether they are driving his dapple-grays. By now Girdvainis no longer resembles a human being, he's more
like a phantom come from the other world to look for
his horses. He comes up in the dark, stops the horses,
looks them over with his frenzied eyes and goes on
without uttering a word, like a ghost. Perhaps only a
devil could handle meeting him; any mortal running into
Girdvainis would fall ill, and if he survived, he'd have
fits for the rest of his life.

People started avoiding driving at night so they
wouldn't run into Girdvainis, since it seemed that no
matter when or where, he'd be stopping the horses in
the crossroad.

Wearing himself out running about during the day
pursuing the neighing of his dapple-grays, he would
spend the night sleeping at the crossroads, watching to
see if his horses would drive by, but the only one he met
was his enemy, whom Girdvainis didn't recognize at
first.

This was after he had met up with Anupras. Leaving
Anupras sitting on the rock by the side of the road and
chasing after the imaginary neighing of his dapple-grays,
he wandered all day without finding anything. At dusk
he stopped at the first crossroad and settled in for the
night. It was already almost midnight and Girdvainis had
only just closed his eyes when suddenly there was such a
neighing right in his ears that the clouds split open and
the stars flickered. Stunned, Girdvainis jumped up and
looked—there was nothing to be seen, only something
dark moving in the middle of the crossroads.

"Who's there?" asked Girdvainis.

"Me," answered the dark shape.

"Who are you?" Girdvainis asked again.

"Your deceiver," it answered calmly, without even moving.

"What sort of sprite is this?" wondered Girdvainis. "Am I dreaming?"

He rubbed his eyes. He saw clearly—something was standing in the middle of the crossroad, whether a human or not, a ghost or not, you couldn't tell in the dark.

"What do you want from me?" asked Girdvainis in astonishment.

"Nothing," it said and moved. "Just to teach you a little lesson, so you'll know not to go calling on strange girls, matchmaking."

"What strange girls?" Girdvainis was bewildered at first.

"Wasn't it you who flew to the banns at daybreak with Whitehorn's Jurga?" it answered mockingly.

"What business is it of yours," said Girdvainis, piqued, "with whom I fly or don't fly?"

"It's more of my business than you think," it answered. "She was promised to me a long time ago."

"Then maybe it was you who stole my horses?" Girdvainis leapt up from his spot.

The ghost moved back a bit.

"Maybe I stole them, or maybe I just helped steal them," it answered from a distance. "But you'll never find your dapple-grays if you don't renounce Jurga."

"So it's not enough for you, you dirty dog, that you stole my horses, now you want me to renounce my girl because of you, too? Wait a minute, you'll get what you asked for!" Girdvainis charged, wanting to snatch this insolent fellow by the scruff of the neck; he snatched and it seemed he got him, however when he looked, his hand was empty, as if he had grabbed at a shadow.

"Ha-ha-ho-ha-ha!" someone roared with laughter and neighed right in Girdvainis' face. Retreating he said: "You don't want to come to an agreement, so you'll lose your dapple-grays and your bride, and then, losing everything, you'll come to an end yourself."

"Curses! What's this now?" Girdvainis shuddered, and for the first time he himself was frightened in the crossroads. Was it really going to turn out as that voice said?

Astonished, Girdvainis looked around the crossroad, unable to make out whether he had dreamt it or if he had really met and talked with someone. But there was nothing to be seen; a spring storm rose up, and everything got jumbled.

Girdvainis went on down the sleet-drenched road, still unable to collect himself. Towards morning he met some kind of ragged man, a beggar perhaps, who sniffled as he walked, as if he were crying.

"Are you the one who's been haunting me?" Girdvainis stopped him.

"No," answered Jurgutis (that's who it was), terribly scared and barely able to talk.

As it happened, he was in fact looking for Girdvainis. During the night he had listened to Jurga's tears and understood that only Girdvainis could save her. Getting up from the snowdrift, he had gone out in the dark looking for him, and now, meeting him, he got scared and wanted to run away, but he conquered his fear and confessed:

"No," he said, "I haven't been haunting you, I only spooked your dapple-grays when you were driving with your matchmaker to pay a call on Whitehorn's Jurga. It was the devil Pinčukas who stole your dapple-grays, together with the horse thief Tatergall. I myself saw the devil carrying him out of Cockend's tavern in a duvet cover, after shaking the straw out on me."

"What did you say?" Girdvainis, looking hard at the strange ragged man, didn't believe him.

"The whole truth," he answered sniffling. "What will be, will be, and even if the devil carries me off to hell, like Shaddon said, I'll tell you everything. It's just that I couldn't find you. And you with your dapple-grays have drowned Jurga in tears. Stop looking for them, and go help her, otherwise you'll ruin yourself and the most beautiful girl in the world."

"What on earth is this? Am I dreaming again?" Girdvainis was even more amazed, and didn't believe he was talking to a real person. But even the ragged man was here one minute and gone the next, like an apparition.

By the time Girdvainis collected himself, Jurgutis had gone on his way. He wanted to confess all his sins and return home to the smithy as soon as possible. What joy that would be! Maybe he would see Jurga and hear her laughter? But he couldn't return without having redeemed all his sins or without returning the stolen horseshoes to the smith. So he went straight to Cockend's tavern to take back the horseshoes he had drunk away.

But Girdvainis couldn't return to Jurga without his dapple-grays. Only now did he realize what sort of devilry had converged here, that he had lost his dapple-grays and forfeited his betrothed, and he himself was wandering, caught in a vicious circle, unable to find a way out. Could it be that the same devil who stole the dapple-grays and materialized in the crossroads was leading him astray and deluding him?

Suddenly a light went on in Girdvainis' head, and he understood why it was that he heard his dapple-grays' neighing everywhere but couldn't find them anywhere. So now, when he heard neighing in the distance again (Pinčukas was still annoying him with his deception), Girdvainis plugged up his ears so he wouldn't hear anything and went straight through the fields, paying no attention to where he was going.

Wasn't it all the same to him where he went, if he couldn't find his dapple-grays and drive with them to his betrothed, whom he had drowned in tears? So he went on through the fields, weighed down by a terrible heartache, having understood his errors, as forlorn and despondent as if he had lost everything in the world.

XXXI

Girdvainis' dapple-grays, when Tatergall conspired with the devil to steal them that fateful morning of the banns, had ended up in dire straits. Tatergall had quickly sold them to the dealers who carted grain from Lithuania to Prussia.

Ever since the fall when they were stolen, throughout the entire winter, Girdvainis' dapple-grays had carted heavily loaded grain wagons through horrible, crumbling roads, and had lost all of their nimbleness. They turned into true worn-out work nags.

The cruel carters mercilessly drove the horses night and day, the greedy buyers hurried to haul out the grain before the spring thaw and worked the dapple-grays so hard that even Girdvainis himself would not, on any account, have recognized them, even if he had come across them.

The only one to recognize them was Girdvainis' matchmaker, the shepherd of Manywish village, Anupras Hearall, who, although he couldn't see through one eye and couldn't hear with one ear, understood the language of animals perfectly. It was only through their talk that he recognized Girdvainis' dapple-grays.

In the middle of the spring thaw, returning from Whitehorn's mill, Anupras, lost in thought, was walking down the road that led to the crossroads at Cockend's tavern, and saw a heavily loaded wagon driving up, which was pulled by two horse skeletons—their sides heaving—at the end of their strength.

Anupras had seen many worn-out horses on that road (the road went through the hills and plains from Lithuania to Prussia), but it was the first time he had seen such thoroughly worn-out nags. When the cart came closer, it seemed to Anupras that he had seen those horses somewhere before, but he couldn't remember when or where.

Then, unexpectedly, Anupras, with his nearly deaf ear, heard one horse say to the other:

"No," said the completely done-in horse, "Nothing will come of it. Girdvainis won't free us from slavery. I'm going to drop once we get to Cockend."

"Wait," said the other, barely catching his breath, "Maybe our freedom isn't far off. This is the first time since we fell into slavery that we're driving the roads of our home. Maybe we'll meet Girdvainis and he'll free us."

"What of it?" said the first. "Even if we were to meet him, would he recognize us? The two of us have even forgotten how to neigh."

"This is true," sighed the second.

The dejected horses pulled the heavy wagon on in silence, their heads hanging down and straining with their last strength.

"I'm dreaming!" the first horse stopped. "With wings like the wind I will carry my suitor and his bride."

"And who will carry him now?" the second one sighed and stopped as well.

The wagon stopping, the dozing carter woke up and cracked his whip:

"Oho, you skin-bags! What, are you fixing to die already?"

The whip whistled, bloodying the horses' torn sides. The horses helplessly strained in place, but the wagon didn't budge.

The whip whistled again about the horses' heads and curses fell:

"Oho, you worthless hides! Dreaming of the knacker already? You won't need a knacker, I'll flay you alive."

Humiliated and lashed this way by the whip, the horses pulled with their last strength, but stumbled on

171

the spot. By the time Anupras ran up, the first horse had collapsed in the middle of the road and breathed its last, and the second stopped, its head hanging, panting heavily.

Recognizing Girdvainis' dapple-grays, Hearall ran up, looked at the fallen horse and stroked the second's hanging head. Anupras was so sad that he had to wipe away a tear with the back of his hand.

"What horses you have ruined!" he turned to the carter reproachfully.

The sullen carter climbed off the seat and angrily muttered:

"What horses? Carrion is what they are, not horses. These horses are fit only for a devil to ride in hell, and not to carry grain to Prussia."

"But what horses these were, if you only knew!" sighed Anupras. "Lightning, not horses. The man who owned them is even now looking for them like he's lost his head."

"The only place he'll find them now is in hell," the carter answered indifferently. "I've cursed myself driving with them and cursed them, too. It's a good thing they had the sense to croak in front of Cockend's tavern. Maybe that devil's dregs of nobility Shaddon will have some newly stolen horses to exchange for them."

Swearing, the carter went into the tavern, and Anupras was left alone by the fallen horse and the second dapple-gray, its companion in misfortune, standing next to it with its head hanging.

Anupras once again stroked the horse's hanging head, looked at the fallen one's lifeless eyes, sighed and said:

"That's the way life goes! You raced with the wind and fell in the middle of the road, after falling into strangers' hands. What will I tell Girdvainis now? And what will he do without you?"

Worried, Hearall stood for a moment as if he was at a wake, thinking about life's leaps and bounds, its cross-roads and its end, sighed deeply, and lost in thought, went on slowly, turning around to look several times and considering what to do now.

The carter returned from the tavern shortly after-wards, leading two of Tatergall's freshly stolen horses. Shaddon followed from behind like a raven, rubbing his hands.

Hearall stopped and watched:

"When on earth will there be an end to that accursed den of horse thieves?" he said to himself. "If only light-ning would strike it out of a blue sky!"

It was a foggy morning. At the crossroads the creepy tavern stood there like some sort of nightmare appari-tion. It seemed as though a limping Tatergall ran past the stable, and something flew by the corner, like a bat or the shadow of an owl.

"What's this now?" Hearall, making some conjec-tures, was intrigued. "Before dawn around the mill, and now in the morning; it's the same birds circling about the tavern. Maybe this is where all the trouble is hid-ing?"

Anupras's suspicions grew. He tried to get a better look, hoping to clear everything up, but the spring fog stirred, turning into swirls of mist and hiding the tavern. Then through the thick mist, Hearall saw and understood it all. There was no doubt left in his mind that this was a nest of evil that needed to be overcome, and then all the troubles would slip by like clouds.

Worried, Hearall went down the road slowly, thinking about how to overcome the devil's treachery and save the suitor and his betrothed. The dapple-grays were already done for. He needed to find Girdvainis and explain everything to him. Perhaps then it would be possible to save Whitehorn and his daughter from the danger that threatened them.

Hearall quickened his step and went straight through the fields, taking the shortcut.

The carter, leading up the pair of newly stolen horses, harnessed them to the wagon and drove onwards to Prussia on the crumbling road, driving the horses mercilessly.

One dead dapple-gray and a second one that could barely drag its feet were left for Shaddon on the road by the tavern. So the tavern-keeper, without giving it much thought, called the knacker, strangled the dapple-gray that was still alive, and skinned both horses' hides.

That evening Jurgutis came to Cockend's tavern and firmly demanded the horseshoes he had exchanged for drink, intending to work for them. Shaddon told him he could bury the carrion and remove the horseshoes from their hooves. Jurgutis did so, not realizing he was burying Girdvainis' dapple-grays.

Shaddon was left, like Pinčukas had said, with the hides of the dapple-grays that Tatergall had stolen, which he hung up to dry in the stable.

But he didn't rejoice in them for long.

XXXII

After Anupras's visit, things became still quieter and gloomier at Whitehorn's house and mill. The daughter and the father avoided meeting, as if they feared that talking would re-open an unhealed wound. They both strove to go about their business and avoid getting in each other's way.

The spring winds had already begun whistling around the rafters and through the neglected mill's wings. Whitehorn, unable to bear it, tried to fix the mill, but somehow nothing went right; whatever he picked up slipped out of his hands. He wasn't as young as he used to be, he didn't have the energy, and besides, some kind of hopelessness oppressed him, as if the end of the world were coming. So all his efforts to raise the mill from the dead were fruitless. The mill stood the way it had stood, like a ghost, with its gloominess arousing an awful presentiment.

Jurga, remembering other springs, had set up to weave linen, but somehow it didn't go well for her either: the threads constantly broke, the shuttle escaped as if her hands had been coarsened, and the loom didn't make the same cheerful noise it had during other springs. It clattered a time or two and then went quiet as if it had choked, since the weaver argued with herself and couldn't agree with her own heart. So mostly she would either weep uncontrollably, burying her face on the loom, or, leaning on her hands, she would sit motionless, dreaming, and unaware herself of what it was she was thinking about.

Jurga didn't weave during this spring as much as she wrestled with all of the roaring fury of youth, until at last her strength gave out and she was as tired as if she had carried out some enormous task. In reality she was doing nothing, just creeping from corner to corner, not knowing what to do with herself. Sometimes she imagined she would go to the ends of the earth to find Girdvainis. That she'd forget it all, renounce it all, just so that she could meet him and see him, but immediately such a bitter disappointment would arise and such an icy pride awaken, that it drowned out the rising feeling of love, and Jurga, unable to endure it not just by the loom but anywhere in the cottage, would throw a shawl around her shoulders and run out by the lake to wander alone along the shores.

More and more water gathered every day in Lake Udruvė, sinking, breaking, and raising the ice to the surface, while more and more contrary feelings swelled in Jurga's breast, feelings which couldn't fit in her heart any longer and ruptured it like the spring floods broke the ice. So Jurga, too, couldn't calm down and find her place anywhere.

Even the slopes, shores, and precipices of Lake Udruvė, where she had rambled ever since her earliest childhood, didn't comfort or calm Jurga, although she wandered them every day now. It was as if everything that she had loved and held dear had been ruined. She neither saw nor noticed anything; it was as though she meandered, dreaming with her eyes wide open, not seeing a thing. She was stunned by her experiences, which she fought with, wrestled with, and failed to budge.

Thus she saw nothing and nothing could clear her mind, because this clarity could come only from the depths of her heart, and her heart was muddled to its very bottom. It was useless to search for clarity until her heart settled down.

Jurga, wandering by the lake, couldn't agree with herself, so she wept her unhappiness to the lakeside winds, and they tossed the abandoned bride's words of love, curses, her tears, and her insane laughter along the shore. But neither tears, nor angry words, nor laughter could help, since Jurga didn't have the strength to make peace within her own heart, where equally strong but contrary feelings and passions wrestled. Love and hate, forgiveness and stubbornness, modesty and pride, longing and renunciation: one minute—feeling this, the next minute—feeling that, and Jurga, the cheerful one, the proud Jurga, stumbled, unable to bear the dips and falls of her stormy heart.

And then, after Anupras had come, she would have run in a heartbeat to meet Girdvainis with open arms, if only she had known where to find him. But then immediately a cold, emotionless pride surged up, and she would have driven him out if he had opened the door. Her answer to Anupras was only one of the rising and falling waves that constantly raged in Jurga's heart.

Jurga couldn't live that way any longer, so she waited, waited with all her heart for something to happen, whatever it might be, just so the crazy rampaging would calm down and she wouldn't have to fight so cruelly and hopelessly with herself.

If at least Jurgutis would show up!

It would be so good to look into his despairing eyes, hear his sniffling, and calm herself down.

Maybe if Jurgutis had shown up, Jurga would have kept the promise she gave to Anupras and married him, so that their double despair would turn into hope for a new life.

But Jurgutis didn't show up, either.

So Jurga waited now, not knowing herself what she was waiting for. No longer for Girdvainis (in her heart she sensed she would never see him again), nor for her wedding, which had died with the gales of the preceding winter's storms, but for something dreary and unavoidable, something that had to happen and free her from this unbearable torment.

This waiting for the unknown, it seemed, flew with the spring winds and rushed along with the first creeks. The next evening, after Anupras had left, as the father with his daughter sat down at the table for supper, an owl hooted again in the neglected mill. Father and daughter, as if sensing something, looked at one another and put their spoons down on the table.

"Already," said the daughter, turning as white as a sheet.

"What?" the father went numb, looking at his daughter and listening intently.

The owl hooted again, as if moaning, as if cackling, so you didn't know what to expect—a wedding or a wake. At least that's what people say: if an owl cackles—expect a wedding, if an owl moans—expect a wake. But neither the father nor the daughter expected one or the other. They were both waiting for something else, but what—they didn't know themselves.

So they looked at one another as though wanting to read something in the other's pale face and frozen eyes. A terrible foreboding gripped the chest like horror, and the expectation of something unavoidable froze all their joints.

Unable to bear it, the father got up to go into the yard and take a look at what had happened and where the hooting owl was, but the daughter, overwhelmed by a dreadful fear, grabbed onto her father's sleeve and wouldn't let go.

"Don't go, father dear, don't go," she begged. "Whatever will be—let it be!"

The father stroked the daughter's head in sympathy, and she pressed up to his chest, trembling all over. But she didn't have time to calm down when something, no longer by the mill but right there under the window— whether it was an owl or not—cackled terribly and flew off.

Then Jurga gave a start, jumped away from her father and shrieked in an unnatural voice. She felt as if some-one's cold hands had touched her and torn her away from her father. She fell without a word into her frightened father's arms.

Afterwards Jurga was delirious all night. The father didn't move a step away from her bed nor did he close his eyes. Unconscious, she tossed and turned the entire night, battling fiercely with something.

Only towards morning did she recover consciousness. She jumped up from bed, staring with eyes wide in horror and shaking all over, and grabbed her father by the arm.

"Let's run from here, father," she said mysteriously in a whisper, as if she was afraid that someone would overhear her.

"Where, daughter dear?" her frightened father wondered.

"It doesn't matter where. Just as far as possible from here," she begged, trembling all over.

"Calm down, daughter dear," the father soothed her, even though he himself had the shivers. "You can't run away from your misfortune. It'll come all the same, here or somewhere else."

"But I don't want to die!" Jurga shook all over.

"You're not going to die, daughter dear, what's this?" The father comforted her even though he was shaking himself. "It's just that owl that scared you. Don't be frightened, it'll go away, you'll get better. Everything will be fine, we'll continue as we always have."

But the father knew that owls don't hoot without due cause. And whether that really was an owl hooting or something else—he had his doubts. So at last he decided, whatever happened, to take Anupras' advice and load a rifle with a silver bullet, so that accursed owl would die, and not his daughter.

XXXIII

Late in the evening the worried Whitehorn went to see his neighbor and friend, the smith Blackpool, whom he hadn't visited for quite some time. The smith, as if he had been waiting for Whitehorn, sat on the threshold of

180

the smithy, watching as the twilight spread over Lake Udruvė and night fell.

"Where on earth did you come from?" wondered the smith upon suddenly seeing Whitehorn appear in front of him. "I thought you'd completely forgotten the way to my smithy. I was just getting ready to go see if you were still alive. But I have to go uphill, it's downhill for you. I kept saying you won't hold out, and you'll come over yourself."

"So I've come," Whitehorn replied, glad to see his friend. "You wouldn't by any chance have a shotgun?"

"What do you need that for?" wondered the smith.

"Heaven only knows," Whitehorn answered, wondering whether he should tell his friend the whole truth, but instead he said equivocally, "A devil or an owl has gotten into the mill... At night it hoots... I just can't scare it off..."

"Maybe it really is a devil?" the smith laughed.

"Who knows?" answered Whitehorn, pulling a silver coin out of his pocket. "Maybe we ought to cast a silver bullet... Just to be sure..."

"So you're really serious?" the surprised smith said, peering at Whitehorn in the dusk. What had he thought up now? Maybe something evil really was circling his mill, and had been ever since the time of that unfortunate match with Girdvainis? And there was Jurgutis, too—no one knew where he'd disappeared to around that same time. Maybe he had gone completely berserk and had joined up with the horse thieves out of envy. One way or another, there had to be some connection, but the smith couldn't put his finger on it right away.

"Maybe it's Jurgutis," he said at last, "who's pulling silly tricks around your mill?"

"What does Jurgutis have to do with it?" answered Whitehorn, surprised at the smith's suspicions. "I haven't seen him around the mill for a long time. Isn't he in the smithy?"

"Well, no, that's just it, he vanished into thin air at the same time that Girdvainis' dapple-grays got stolen," the smith worried. "I said, maybe out of craziness he joined up with the horse thieves? Or maybe he got married to someone, without telling anyone about it? You haven't heard anything from people coming to the mill?"

"No, I haven't heard anything," said Whitehorn, even more surprised. "Could Jurgutis really have anything to do with it?"

No, Whitehorn knew very well who was to blame; it was just that he couldn't admit it, even to his closest friend. The smith, because he couldn't figure out what was going on, was inclined to suspect even his lost apprentice. But without good cause.

At just exactly that moment Jurgutis was standing around the corner of the smithy with the horseshoes—true, not the ones he had stolen and drank up, but the ones he had taken off the carcasses of Girdvainis' dapple-grays—unable to gather up his nerve to go in and confess, and he overheard the smith talking with Whitehorn and suspecting him of joining up with the horse thieves.

"Who knows," said the smith at last, "maybe a shotgun loaded with a silver bullet is just what's needed…

Otherwise you'll never get rid of all this devilry… I'll go look for it."

Because he hadn't heard everything, Jurgutis thought they were getting ready to fix up the shotgun with a silver bullet for him, and so, frightened, he ran away from the smithy, without a clue about what to do or where to go with the horseshoes that didn't belong to him. Unless maybe to return to the tavern again and demand his own horseshoes? Then the smith wouldn't have anything to be angry about.

The smith, entirely unaware that his apprentice was lurking about, went to the shed to look for the shotgun left over from the days of the uprising, when he had hammered scythes into swords and fixed up other weapons for his brother farmers. Somewhere in the attic a double-barreled shotgun, left over from those times, was stashed away.

In the meantime, Whitehorn fired up the forge and started heating the silver coin in a ladle. The smith returned shortly with the rusty shotgun, cleaned it off then and there with soot, and then, just at the stroke of midnight with the moon shining, helped cast two silver bullets.

"Well, now, just listen," the smith said at last, after loading both barrels with bullets, "take good aim, just don't hit my Jurgutis." (The smith still thought that Jurgutis, dead or alive, had to be hanging around Whitehorn's mill.) "If it's an owl or a hooter, even if it's the very devil in disguise, then it's no big deal. Pop it once, twice, and you'll scare it off. But you know, the spring lightning could strike your mill. It's standing on such a cliff… Seriously, put up a lightning rod."

"Oh come on, who needs it?" Whitehorn waved it off, pleased that he already had a shotgun loaded with two silver bullets, with which he could defend himself from all enemies, while lightning was no enemy to him, but one of his own, like all of nature. "My family's lived there since time immemorial and it's never been hit, it won't get hit now, either... what grudge could lightning have against me? ... I'll just scare off that damned owl or hooter, and then everything will be fine."

"Well, God help you," said the smith, seeing his neighbor out, and went to bed himself.

The stars were already twinkling in the darkness before dawn, and the lake murmured quietly, as if awakening.

Whitehorn went home along the lakeshore.

Above his hill and the mill the morning stars had gathered. Perhaps they foresaw a clear day and a bright spring? But refusing to believe in them, Whitehorn stuck the shotgun under his coat flaps, stealthily crept into the mill so that no one would see him, and hid the double-barreled shotgun loaded with silver bullets in a corner under the dusty remains of Uršulė's skirt.

"Just you try hooting now!" he said, looking about. "Get off my back, or you'll get what you're asking for."

Morning was already breaking. Whitehorn stood there for a bit, looked at the awakening lake and the slumbering swamp where, through the mist, the tops of the scrawny pines and birches stuck out. He calmed down and went into the cottage. In the entrance he listened—his daughter was sleeping quietly in the parlor. Without waking her up, he went into the smoky cottage, which had brightened up at last with the new hope that had appeared in Whitehorn's heart.

<h1 style="text-align:center">XXXIV</h1>

With Girdvainis' dapple-grays gone, that damned horse thief Tatergall wasn't to avoid his end either. He was the very first to meet the fate he deserved.

It was a beautiful early spring morning. That morning at Cockend's tavern, instead of a rooster, a hen up and crowed. Shaddon, angry at this harbinger of bad luck, threw an axe at the hen, but missed. Chasing after it, he wanted to take another swing at it, but he heard an unusual commotion out in the fields, and, forgetting the hen, went out the gate to take a look at what was going on out there.

Through the fields, straight through the rows, not limping in the least and practically not touching the ground with his feet, Tatergall ran panting, and behind him followed men from Paudruvė and other villages, armed with cudgels and staves.

"Catch that thief!" the fields split with their cries, and more and more men ran out of neighboring yards with cudgels.

The poor horse thief didn't think the men would be satisfied this time by breaking one or the other leg; he was worried about saving his hide, so he dodged like a rabbit driven by greyhounds. "If I could just make it to the tavern," he thought the whole time he was running, "Shaddon will save me somehow."

But Shaddon was thinking just exactly the opposite. "I'd rather that horse thief wouldn't run into the tavern and get me into trouble with the villagers. It'd be better," Shaddon thought, "if they'd catch him somewhere out in the field rows, as long as I don't have to see him anymore."

But it was Tatergall's luck that just as the men with cudgels had surrounded him from all sides, he bolted out of the encirclement like a rabbit and ran, breathless, into the tavern yard. Spotting Shaddon, he fell to his knees in front of him, even though earlier he had treated him with disdain, since Shaddon lived not so much from the tavern as he did from Tatergall's trade.

"Help me, Shaddon!" he cried. "Hide me somewhere, anywhere, just so the men won't find me. I'll bring you ten horses if you save me."

"Where will I hide you?" said Shaddon, frightened. "You can see for yourself that the men have surrounded the yard from all sides."

"Wherever you want, brother, but just hide me," begged the horse thief. "Even a beer barrel would do."

"Wouldn't you know it, all the beer barrels are full." Shaddon, flustered, didn't know what to do. Then, remembering, he cheered up and said: "Run into the stable and climb into the horse's hide that's hung there to dry."

Tatergall didn't need to be told twice. He spun into the stable like a top, and there he crawled into the first horsehide through the precise spot Pinčukas had forbidden him to crawl in.

The hide was the very same one that the knacker had skinned from Girdvainis' strangled dapple-gray the eve-

186

ning before. The second horsehide was hanging right next to it.

Tatergall in his haste and fear completely forgot that the devil, when he made a deal with him to steal Gird-vainis' horses, had warned him not to crawl into those horses through their hind ends. But Tatergall had considered the devil's warning a silly joke and, to his misfortune, completely forgot about it.

There wasn't time to remember anyway, since the men were already gathering around the stable with their cudgels and their shouts:

"Kill the horse thief!"

Even Tatergall's fleas dropped dead on hearing this. He was too frightened to even sneeze, afraid that he might give away where he was hidden. And wouldn't you know it, a sneeze was tickling him unmercifully. The knacker had scattered tobacco dust inside the skinned hide so that flies and worms wouldn't eat it.

The men with the cudgels had already surrounded Shaddon in the yard.

"What did you do with the horse thief?" they said threateningly, and they weren't kidding.

"Come on fellows, I haven't seen any horse thief," Shaddon tried to weasel out of it. "This is a tavern, I have beer and vodka and all sorts of other drinks, please, drink as much as you like. It's on the house today."

"Oho, you see what a fine fellow he is!" The men understood the tavern keeper's ploy. "Give us the horse thief, and if not, then we'll hang you in place of Tatergall and burn down this den of horse thieves, your damned tavern."

"Good people, do what you will," Shaddon crossed himself, "but I'm innocent. I haven't seen either a horse or a horse thief."

"You won't flap your lips here for long," shouted one man, throwing down his cudgel and pulling out a rope. "Say your prayers, we're raising you up to heaven this minute."

Shaddon fell to his knees and begged for mercy, but the agitated man threw the noose around his neck and pulled it so tight that Shaddon couldn't even breathe.

"Wait, fellas, don't strangle me," Shaddon choked out. "Loosen the rope, I'll talk."

But the one who was holding the rope pulled it even tighter, so that Shaddon's eyes started popping out.

"He crawled, he crawled," Shaddon hacked out through foaming lips, and lost his breath entirely.

"What did he crawl in?" The rope was loosened.

"Into Girdvainis' dapple-gray's hide," said Shaddon, gasping for air.

"What kind of nonsense is this?" The men grew angry. "Drag him, that patriarch of horse thieves, under the rafters."

But Shaddon, seeing this was no joke, didn't wait for the rope to tighten around his neck again, and managed to explain to the men in time that the hides, which had been skinned from Girdvainis' steeds the evening before, were drying in his stable, and that they were the very place where the horse thief Tatergall was now hiding.

"Go on, men, go take a look, what's this he's lying about now," offered the one who was holding the rope.

"I'll hold him in the meantime. If he's lied to us, then I'll lift him up under the rafters."

Now Shaddon got scared that the horse thief might escape from the horsehide, so he started begging while still on his knees:

"Hurry up, fellows, just hurry up!"

"You'll hang in time," the one who was holding the rope answered him, and the other men with cudgels went into the stable to take a look.

There really were two horsehides hanging under the rafters; one collapsed, the other bulging. Tatergall, hearing that the men were gathering in the stable, froze in fear, but that damn sneeze started tickling his nose so badly that he couldn't hold out, and he sneezed.

"You see, Shaddon wasn't lying," Tatergall heard someone say, and understood that his old friend the tavern keeper had given him away.

"And he's no better!" Tatergall shouted then, and wanted to crawl out of the hide, but someone smacked him on the forehead with a cudgel, so he just yelped and collapsed back into the hide.

While Tatergall came to his senses, the men discussed what to do with the horse thief. No one wanted to have a murder, even if only of a horse thief, on his conscience, so they decided to sew the horse thief with his soul inside the horse hide, so he wouldn't see the light of day again and wouldn't steal horses anymore.

They did as they had agreed. A needle and thread immediately appeared, and the men went to work. They had already finished sewing the hide—only a small hole under the tail was left—when Tatergall came to and began begging for mercy.

"Don't worry," the men reassured him, "We won't do anything bad to you. We're just going to sew you up in the horse hide and leave you like that forever, so that neither you nor your soul will get out again and be tempted to steal horses."

There was nothing left for Tatergall to do but accept his fate. True, this fate was completely dark, even though the men had left one last little hole unsewn.

"Let's leave him this hole," they said, "so, like the camel, his soul can get out if it's worthy of the kingdom of heaven."

Then the men ordered Shaddon to roll ten barrels of beer into the stable. They drank all day and sang hymns for the horse thief's soul, beating the horse's hide, in which the unfortunate horse thief Tatergall was sewn, like a drum.

Towards evening Jurgutis stuck his head into the stable, looking for Shaddon and wanting to get his horseshoes back, but, seeing what was going on, he ran away, afraid that they might pummel him to death too, for stealing.

But no one even noticed him. Only at dusk a bat flashed by the gable, screeched, and flew away.

"Could that have been the horse thief's soul?" the men got curious and felt over the hide.

After all that pummeling the hide hung limp and Tatergall lay inside it without breathing. The men had gotten so carried away they hadn't even noticed that they had drubbed the poor horse thief to death. What hap-

pened to his soul—whether it flew off with the bat or
not—was never discovered.

XXXV

Immediately after Tatergall's death the tavern keeper
Shaddon saw there would be no life for him any more,
since without stolen horses there wouldn't be their hides,
either. And Shaddon made a living mostly from those
hides. There wasn't any profit in serving booze to peasants. They made more noise than they drank. And what
sort of life was this, anyway, even for a blue-blooded
mutt?

Besides, after the disgraceful murder of Tatergall, the
peasants got really bold and became so insolent that it
would have been best, Baron Shaddon, to leave it all
behind and run to the ends of the earth. They literally
poked him with their fingers and laughed right in his
face:

"Well, how's things going for you, Lord Shaddonshire, without a horse thief? Probably not so good, seeing you're down in the dumps?"

Shaddon tried to shake off these brazen creatures
with both patience and silence, but that didn't help at all;
on the contrary, Shaddon's leniency incited those
shameless creatures to mock him even more.

So Shaddon considered one thing and another, and at
last decided to go discuss it with his friend, the devil of
Paudruvė's bogs, Pinčukas.

He didn't have far to go. He went out just before
midnight, as it was only possible to call Pinčukas at the

stroke of midnight. But the closer he got to the bogs, the greater the fear that gripped Shaddon. He still hadn't got over his fright after Tatergall's murder. And Pinčukas, even if a buddy, was a devil all the same: how could a person know what he might think up? If people had already become so evil, what could you expect from a devil? Shudders ran up and down Shaddon's spine, and then his knees began to quiver, too, so that he nearly turned back when he had already gotten right up to the bogs. But then he reproached himself that here he was, a nobleman, and afraid of the devil, so he gathered up all his nerve, whistled three times, and in a trembling voice called out:

"Pinčuk, don't be a schnook, jump over the brook, and be here so I can take a look!"

He called once—nothing; he called a second time—silence; only the bushes rustled in the dark. He called a third time—even the hair on his head under his hat stood up. Something neighed horribly in the middle of the bogs and then, right next to him, an unseen voice answered:

"What do you want, that you're getting me up in the middle of the night?"

"There's no living for me," spluttered Shaddon, still trembling even though he recognized his buddy by his voice. "Those boors did Tatergall in, they've turned really insolent, what will I do now?"

"And what's it to me?" replied Pinčukas, still grumpy. "I told that drunk not to crawl into Girdvainis' dapple-grays through the hind end, so what did he do that for?"

"But there was no other way out," Shaddon tried to answer for his friend.

"There wasn't, so he isn't," Pinčukas answered indifferently. "And what do you want?"

"Tell me, buddy, how am I supposed to live now?" Shaddon implored. "The peasants will poke me to death. Help me defend myself from them."

"Humph." By now Pinčukas was really angry. "How am I supposed to help you? Manage for yourself, as best as you can. I have my own troubles. Besides, I've run around all winter misleading Girdvainis, I'd like to rest a bit and get some sleep."

"So that's what you're like," Shaddon was indignant. It was entirely unheard of, for a baron to demean himself in front of a mangy devil and not even get anything out of it. "In other words, you're deserting a friend in need? Well, all right, but you'll regret it."

Having said this, Shaddon was shocked at himself: where did he get the nerve to talk to a devil at midnight like that, and on the edge of the bogs, too? One misstep and he'd sink to the bottom of the swamp. But if his nobleman's honor was already insulted, so be it, but a baron doesn't give in. So Shaddon spewed out all of his frustration right in the devil's face.

"Don't be angry," Pinčukas finally said. "If you want it that badly, you can get your revenge for Tatergall's murder. Go into town and complain to the government that the peasants are revolting, and have murdered an innocent man. They'll start dragging them off to jail—they'll even start regretting Tatergall. And if that isn't enough for you, then pick out a horse's tracks, spit three

times and say: 'May you, too, be as dead-beat as Girdvainis' dapple-grays.' The horses whose tracks you've
spat on will fall. You'll ruin more horses than Tatergall
rode off with, and you'll have your revenge on your
enemies. Just don't spit in the wind, so you don't get spit
on your beard. Then you'll bring misfortune down on
yourself. Now, good luck, and don't bother me. Whitehorn is waiting for me with a silver bullet, but he won't
succeed in shooting me. He still doesn't know what I've
fixed up for him," said Pinčukas, who then neighed out
of old habit, and vanished.

Shaddon was pleased that he could get his revenge
on the peasants and said to himself:

"Well, now I'll show those dog-faces what I can do!"

Contented, he returned to the tavern, and without
waiting for morning, decided to take action immediately.
Sleep or no sleep, he got up with the first crow of the
cock, hitched a half-dead mare to the phaeton and drove
off to town.

It was still early morning and had barely started getting light, but the road was a long one. He wanted to get
there early, so that he would have time to go around to
all the government offices and complain about the un-
ruly peasants. He remembered the days of serfdom enviously; back then he wouldn't have needed to go
knocking about in the dark to town; he'd have tanned
half of the peasants' hides himself with a whip, so they'd
rub themselves for a year or two and remember the
lord's kindness. But times had changed. In the dawn he
urged the nag on, poking her with the whip-handle, so
she'd move at least a little faster, but the mare, as if on

purpose, would stop when she was poked with the whip-handle as if wanting to ask, "Why are you, dummy, poking me?"

"A plague on you!" Shaddon swore, unable to bear it. "Such a hack is only fit to haul tar to hell, and not for driving to town on urgent business."

While he was arguing with the mare it started getting light, and Shaddon saw a profusion of horses' hoof prints on the road. He remembered that yesterday had been market day; apparently a lot of people from Paudruvė had driven to town. Shaddon was happy that he had started so early—he could kill two birds with one stone: complain to the government about the peasants, and do in their horses.

So Shaddon, climbing out of the phaeton, started picking out horse tracks, spitting downwind and repeating the spell's words. The abandoned mare with the phaeton kept turning around to look back, as though wondering why he wasn't poking her with the whip handle and why he was spitting at something on the road instead. But Shaddon was so preoccupied that he didn't notice what it was his mare was doing. He only remembered her when he hit his head on the stopped phaeton (apparently he was bent over to put a spell on some new tracks), and, lifting his head, he shouted angrily:

"Well, you carrion, too much for you to pull already?"

But the mare didn't even turn around to see who was yelling at her, she just swayed from side to side, and then collapsed in the middle of the road.

"What's this now?" wondered Shaddon, "Have you taken it into your head to croak?"

The mare was already kicking her last and baring her teeth.

"Don't tell me I've put a spell on my own mare's tracks?" Shaddon caught on. Well, sure enough, the last track he had spat on was indeed his bay mare's. "Blast it, that you should be so careless!"

But Shaddon wasn't upset about the mare, on the contrary, he was actually pleased, because he saw that the spell Pinčukas had told him about really worked. So, leaving the highfalutin phaeton with the dead mare in the middle of the road, he continued to town on foot, spitting into every horse track, so that at last he even ran short of spit and his mouth went completely dry.

Shaddon didn't waste any time after reaching town, either. He rushed about with his tongue practically hanging out, from one country bumpkin lawyer to another, writing complaints and proclaiming to the government that the peasants of Paudruvė were starting a revolt and murdering innocent people.

The government promised to send an entire police platoon to suppress the peasants, so Shaddon, even though he was without his mare or his phaeton, returned to his Cockend tavern very pleased, still spitting into horse tracks along the way, and rejoicing that the land of Paudruvė was to meet with such a dreadful punishment.

Back at his tavern, he didn't do anything but look out the windows and rub his hands in glee, waiting to see what would happen next.

XXXVI

Well, extraordinary things started happening in Paudruvė. First the horses started falling. A plague of some sort simply came over them. It was totally inexplicable (it didn't occur to anyone that this could be Shaddon's terrible revenge): the healthiest of horses fell while going down the road, right in front of your eyes, or else in the mornings they would be found in the padlock as though they'd been strangled. And it was always the very best horses, draft horses or riding horses, as if Girdvainis' dapple-grays had pulled all the other horses after themselves.

Even older people couldn't remember a horse plague like this. If it had been some sort of illness you wouldn't be surprised, but now the healthiest of horses started grunting and turned up their feet. Reluctantly, people started speculating about what this was and where such a plague could have come from so suddenly.

It didn't occur to anyone that Shaddon was to blame. After all, his horse was the first to croak on the road, and the highfalutin phaeton was this very day still dangling there, shoved into the ditch. But people's attention turned to Shaddon's tavern anyway. After all, Girdvainis' dapple-grays fell next to the tavern, and that was where the plague had started. Maybe they had been the ones to bring it?

And then people remembered Tatergall's demise at Cockend's tavern too. Some were even sorry about it, and said that perhaps it wasn't necessary for the men to so unmercifully, although cheerfully, drub the horse thief to death. Let him drive off one horse or another, but now—horses were falling as you watched, and there was nothing you could do.

There were even more observant people who had seen some remarkable things. When a horse suddenly collapsed, what seemed to be Tatergall's shadow would materialize; it was as if he had ridden off on the horse and left just the carcass for the owner. And the longer it went on, the more people turned up who had seen and clearly recognized Tatergall's spirit sneering when a horse croaked. It was as though the horse thief had come from the other world to jeer at people losing their horses. And here spring was coming, what are you going to do in the spring without a horse? So many people, be it reluctantly, condemned Tatergall's tormentors for bringing down such bad luck.

But those who had participated in his killing, and whose horses hadn't yet died, tried to turn the whole thing into a joke: the trouble was, they hadn't sewn up that last hole, you see, that damned horse thief's soul had gotten out through that very hole, and now it was strangling horses in revenge, since it couldn't steal them. But even they stopped joking when their horses died, after all, how could you really know what was going on? Whether they wanted to or not, they gave in; perhaps they had drubbed the horse thief unnecessarily. But then again, events had taken such an unfortunate turn, and it had all worked out so badly. Under other circumstances perhaps they would have whipped his hide some, short- ened one leg or the other, and let him go, but when he crawled into the horse's hide himself, everyone had beat him mercilessly and didn't realize they were driving his soul out of his body.

But what was to be done now? It was over and done with. Maybe they should go to pastor Boniface Bobbin (some even suggested this seriously) and buy a mass for the horse thief's soul. Perhaps then it would forgive them and stop seeking revenge—people kept meaning to do it and never got around to it. Come now, who was going to go and buy mass for a horse thief, as if he were some relative? It was awkward, and somehow even embarrassing, so people, not knowing what to do, suffered, and that was that. Only the tavern keeper Shaddon was truly pleased and even happy about it. At every opportunity he would remind them:

"I told you not to murder an innocent man. (Some innocent!) Now you see what's come of it. And it'll get even worse. Not just the horses will croak, but there will be people rotting in jail, too."

People didn't believe that was possible, why would they start dragging people off to jail because of a horse thief? But after a few days the police platoon, summoned by Shaddon's complaints, up and arrived in the land of Paudruvė to suppress the revolt. Alas, they didn't find any revolt; all they found was a strange horse plague. They hurriedly downed several shots of vodka at Cockend's tavern, and rode home so that their horses wouldn't catch it and start dying as well. Just in case, they wrote up a report on the horse thief Tatergall's murder from Shaddon's testimony, cursed him out, and shoved him around for having lied and misled them.

After the platoon had ridden off, the village men gathered at the tavern to find out why they had come over and what they were planning to do. They couldn't really be going to punish them on account of a horse thief? Shaddon tried to claim that they were just the scouts, that the entire army was going to arrive and wipe the village of Paudruvė from the face of the earth. But the men, seeing Shaddon himself pushed around and not lying very convincingly, didn't believe him. On the contrary, instead of getting scared, they surrounded Shaddon with their cudgels and threatened:

"Now, just you look here, you rat! If you start complaining, it'll be worse for you than it was for Tatergall. By the time the army gets here, we'll have sent you to see Tatergall on foot."

"What do you mean, fellas?" The frightened Shaddon pleaded ignorance. "Why would I complain? The thought never entered my head."

All the same, he had complained; the snake lied, not just about those he had seen in the stable drubbing Tatergall, but also about those he hadn't seen, but simply didn't care for. But the men didn't know this, and they left without doing any harm to Shaddon.

But Shaddon really didn't feel so wonderful after the men had left. What sort of life could this be? The platoon that had arrived to suppress the rebellion had pushed him, Shaddon the nobleman, around, and then the peasants with their cudgels had threatened him as well. No, if things were going to turn out this way, then this was really no life at all.

Thinking it over, Shaddon decided to once more go consult with Pinčukas. Maybe he would come up with a solution. But, on arriving at the bogs, he shouted and shouted and couldn't summon a thing.

He considered whether Pinčukas, too, his last buddy, had deserted him, and was starting for home when here Pinčukas crawled out of the duckweed and asked grumpily:

"So, what do you want now?"

"Oh, Master Pinčuky," Shaddon cheered up despite his earlier dejection. "There's still no life for me. I complained to the government, and the horses are falling, but what use is it to me? The police platoon came, shoved me around instead of the peasants, and then the peasants gathered and started threatening me with their cudgels."

"Oh, it's nothing but trouble with you," the discontented Pinčukas replied. "You're not happy about this and you're not happy about that. You've annoyed me to the bone."

"But what should I do, Master Pinčuky?" Shaddon whined in despair.

"Well, crawl into the duckweed here with me, if you don't have anywhere else to go," Pinčukas retorted angrily.

"Come on, Master Pinčuky," Shaddon got frightened. "Who will keep the tavern, get the peasants drunk, and drive their souls to hell?"

"Well, all right," Pinčukas agreed unwillingly. "I'll give you some advice one more time, but it's the last. You can start healing the horses you've bewitched. Blow on the hoof of the horse whose track you've cursed, and say: 'Feel, peel, I've ordered you to heal.' Just don't get the hooves confused, or else the horse will kick you and knock all your teeth out. Besides that, watch out for Girdvainis. Since his horses have fallen, I can't lead him around any more, and he's on his way back. If you meet up with him, you'll be smoked out. But don't bother me anymore. I have my own worries without you. Why do you keep bothering me all the time now?"

"All right," Shaddon promised, "I won't bother you any more. Somehow I'll get by on my own."

Shaddon returned to his tavern, thinking that now he could manage wonderfully without either Pinčukas or the horse thief, knowing a secret of that sort, of how to protect horses and cure them. So on his way home he decided to take up the horse healing trade.

Only things didn't quite turn out that way. The next day Shaddon started bragging that he could heal ailing horses, if he was well paid for it.

At first people just laughed at this boast of Shaddon's, but later one or another began to wonder, who knows, maybe that offspring of the devil did know how to save horses?

Someone took him to his horse; Shaddon blew on the hoof, muttered something, and the horse recovered. Another took him to his horse, and that one recovered. Both Shaddon and the farmers were pleased, even though the farmers had each thrown away a tenner to Shaddon for the horse's healing. But a good horse is worth more than money! Shaddon had already started calculating how much he could earn and when he would be able to buy back the estates his ancestors had drunk away. But when he went to a third horse, he hadn't managed to either blow on the hoof or say the magic words before the horse kicked Shaddon and drove all his teeth into his throat.

Shaddon returned to the tavern with nothing, just coughing and spitting up teeth. It wasn't, after all, an easy thing, being a horse doctor! So when he got home he thought about how to protect himself from such unfortunate occurrences. It was possible that quite often he wouldn't pick up the same hoof whose print he had bewitched. Then he wouldn't just lose all his teeth, but his head, too.

But Shaddon hadn't managed to think it all through carefully when he met up with a new and much larger misfortune, and Pinčukas couldn't be summoned because he himself was caught up in his own troubles.

XXXVII

Whitehorn was still lying in wait for Pinčukas at night, hiding in the mill behind Uršulė's skirt with the shotgun loaded with silver bullets.

But Pinčukas, engrossed as he was in his evil deeds, didn't show up. Together with Shaddon he was stirring up the dreadful horse plague ravaging all of Paudruvė.

Whitehorn had an idea of who was behind all of this, and he held the shotgun tightly in his hands, waiting for that villain to show up.

But he waited and waited—he spent many anxious sleepless nights and got terribly tired—until at last he up and fell asleep.

Pinčukas was waiting for just such a moment and decided it was high time to give Whitehorn a good fright, settle old accounts, and force him to honor their agreement.

It was a quiet moonlit night.

Fluffy clouds floated in the skies and were reflected in Lake Udruvė. The mill stood sleeping on the shore.

Like a sudden wind, Pinčukas flew onto the mill's wings and started turning them, roaring with laughter and neighing.

The entire mill cracked and creaked, and the wings started howling as if a whirlwind were blowing. Whitehorn awoke in alarm and didn't realize at first what was going on. He thought a whirlwind had struck, and rushed to stop the mill, but Pinčukas answered from the wings:

"Maybe we'll come to terms now?" he grinned. "You see what's going on? It'll get even worse, if you don't keep to our bargain and don't give me your daughter in marriage."

"All right," said Whitehorn, coming to his senses. "Wait… You'll get it…"

Pleased, Pinčukas jumped down from the wing and glanced in the window.

"We should have done this a long time ago," he said, nimbly jumping into the mill.

"True, true," Whitehorn, in the dark, agreed with him, snatching the loaded shotgun out from under the skirt.

Pinčukas jumped back out the window, but not fast enough—his hoof got caught.

Suddenly a shot rang out like thunder, and the silver bullet hit Pinčukas in the heel, but he didn't notice it; he just rolled down the mill's wings and ran headlong down the hill.

Whitehorn followed with another shot to be sure, but the silver bullet ricocheted off something and sparked. Whitehorn thought Pinčukas had sunk straight down into the earth with the second shot, but he was mistaken.

The second bullet hit Jurgutis and ricocheted off the horseshoes he still carried—he still didn't know what to do with himself and was afraid of returning to the smithy. As it happened, that evening he had come for the express purpose of apologizing to Whitehorn for his snorting, and to ask him to intercede for him with the smith. But he didn't dare go into the cottage, and, waiting for nightfall, he fell asleep beneath the mill's wings, and now—like thunder on a clear day—one shot after another. It was a good thing, too, that the shot ricocheted off the horseshoes, or else Jurgutis would have perished for nothing. Jurgutis didn't understand what had happened, he just ran away with the horseshoes, terribly frightened and still not knowing where to go with them.

Whitehorn, unaware of who and what he had hit—he was sure that he had struck Pinčukas dead—looked out the window when the smoke from the shot cleared and saw Jurga in her nightdress out on the porch, apparently very frightened.

Whitehorn quickly stuck the shotgun under Uršulė's skirt and descended the stairs, hurrying to reassure his daughter.

"Father, what happened?" Jurga asked when she saw her father coming out of the mill.

"Nothing, daughter dear," answered the flustered Whitehorn. "I just shot an owl... It won't hoot any-more... It'll be quiet..."

"Really, father?" his daughter said doubtfully, looking at her father with suspicion.

"Yes, yes," said Whitehorn in reassurance. "Let's go into the cottage. The night is cool. You'll catch cold, yet."

Jurga trembled all over, but it wasn't from the cold. She had her misgivings and made her own conjectures about what had just happened; why such strange things were going on in the land of Paudruvė, and why they were centered around her father's mill. Could it really be her fault? She thought of running away, as far as possible from it all, but it was hard to leave her father, whom these misfortunes had apparently oppressed so completely that he had turned into a gloomy shadow.

But Whitehorn now felt as if he had awoken from a horrible dream that had oppressed him all his life, and he shook himself as if throwing it off. What had happened, really? Nothing at all, everything had blown away with the smoke from the powder. The harsh spring moonlight shone through the little clouds floating by.

Whitehorn led his anxious daughter into the cottage and put her to bed. But even in bed Jurga still trembled.

206

She seized her father by the hand and asked, shaking like an aspen leaf:

"Father dear, why don't you tell me the whole truth?"

"The truth about what?" Her father didn't understand, or didn't want to understand.

"What's going on here?" The daughter kept pressing him.

"It's nothing, daughter dear," said Whitehorn, controlling himself. "Forget it, and get some sleep. Tomorrow, you'll see, everything will be fine."

After he caressed his daughter and kissed her on the forehead, covered her up, and tucked her in, Whitehorn himself lay down on the bench by the window, threw a sheepskin over himself and wanted no more than to fall asleep as quickly as possible and to forget everything, like a dream.

But sleep didn't come. The moonlight shone through the window, and his entire life flashed before his eyes. It turned with the mill's wings, grew muddled, drifted about, and swirled around like the fog from Lake Udruvė. With its vapors Uršulė arose, sour and shriveled. Pinčukas flashed by like a phantom, and a dark, hopeless fog settled over the heart. And the days run by, the years slip by. Only the mill hums constantly, as if hearing and rejuvenating itself with its own humming. The sun breaks through the clouds, and through its rays a merry laugh is heard.

Oh, it's Marcelė, driving over the crackling ice. A refreshing spring wind wafts by and clears the fog. The merry and lively Marcelė flies like a swallow through the mill and the house, cheering up his life and bringing back his youth. His heart is overflowing with joy, like a sunny summer. But the clouds of autumn float by and the cranes cry. Their cries grow sadder and sadder, the lake stirs, and dark clouds cloak the skies.

The mill freezes like a ghost on the precipice. Snow-flakes fall on its wings like little white sheets, and a footpath wanders farther and farther through the snowy slopes and fields to a hill where crooked crosses stand. They're carrying a coffin, and inside is all of his life's hope and joy. The earth rumbles hollowly, hiding the coffin, and on a small knoll a new cross arises. The dusk falls, as dark and hopeless as eternal night. In the neglected cottage, in the terrible emptiness and gloom, a baby cries in its swaddling clothes. Despondent, he stands by the cradle, and in his heart a dark despair wrestles with responsibility for a new life, which awakens him from his terrible grief.

A storm rages around the mill and the cottage, howls around the corners, rampages on the precipice and rushes over the frozen lake. Oh, that's not the storm; that's only his restless heart. But the skies grow bright with the first clearings of spring, the mill's wings keep spinning faster, and in the cottage, along with the rays peeking inside, comes laughter from the cradle, a laughter that clears away the gloomy shadows. Oh, those shadows clear from his heart, and the joy of a new life sweeps him along like spring.

But the glowering Uršulė creeps about the cottage, glaring like a disappointed past, and through the mill's wings Pinčukas flashes by like a phantom, biding his time and waiting for his reward. Burdensome difficulties

208

weigh down Whitehorn's shoulders and bend his head, but the new life arisen from the cradle fills his heart with joy and stifles the ghosts of the past. Uršulė disappears from the house and Pinčukas vanishes, too. He bends from the weight of life, but it's not heavy; his consolation is a beautiful daughter who brings her mother to mind. The dapple-grays neigh, and his heart is pressed by the sadness of his coming loneliness, but also by the joy that life turns like the wings of the mill and a new wheel of life is beginning.

But here again the ghosts of the past arise—the disappointed Uršulė with her gossip and the deceived Pinčukas with his treachery. The dapple-grays neigh and neigh away, and his miserable past blocks his daughter's future and drowns her in tears. He must overcome his horrible past for the sake of his daughter's bright future. And he overcame it. Uršulė shriveled up in her biddies' almshouse with her frustrated heart full of spells and superstitions, but she didn't embitter his daughter's youthful joy, and the treacherous Pinčukas finally spun away with the mill's sails, shot by the silver bullet, and sank straight into the earth... But was that really Pinčukas? Perhaps it was all some fantasy of the past he had dreamed up?

No, none of it ever happened. It was just a dream, a horrible dream that will clear up with the light of day. There's the mill and its hum, there's the precipice on the edge of the lake, there's the lake too, as uneasy as a person's heart, and its misty shores with green pine forests. His father's fathers lived here, here he lives and raises a daughter, who is all of his life's hope and joy... The daughter sleeps quietly and laughs in her sleep. Perhaps she is dreaming of the dapple-grays who will carry her through life on wings of wind. So it should be, let them carry her, together with her pure longings and heartaches. And he is already happy that at the end of his life he sees it growing anew in his daughter's life, which will be brighter and more beautiful than his.

Relieved, Whitehorn fell asleep, feeling he had conquered all of his life's heartaches and troubles. But even in sleep he found no peace. Suddenly he dreamt that something like lightning had struck the mill, and with the storm coming up, his daughter had flown off over the lake like a seagull... Whitehorn was covered in a cold sweat. He jumped up from the bench and looked— his daughter was sleeping as before, and through the window, in the morning's first light, the mill stood on the cliff as it had always stood, with its wings folded. No, all of it was simply the horrible dream of an uneasy heart.

A bright and calm moonlight spread through his house and the entire land.

XXXVIII

What sort of tricks were the sprites of the night playing? Or was it the spring moonlight with the little drifting clouds that brought it on?

Perhaps it's so. Who knows?

The wounded Pinčukas, cursing Whitehorn, hobbled back to the bogs and sat down on the first little stump.

"Just you wait," he said, recovering from his fright and examining his injured heel. "You'll remember me yet. You'll perish along with the entire mill."

Pinčukas was contemplating a terrible revenge. In the meantime, unable to stand the pain, he tried to dig the silver bullet out of his heel. But the more he dug, the deeper the bullet lodged, and it stung the bone so, he could hardly bear it with his teeth clenched.

It was there on the stump that Shaddon found him, after searching for him in vain all night long through the bogs. He hadn't shouted for him as much as he lisped with his swollen mouth through his kicked-out teeth.

"So it's you here, Master Pinčuky?" he coughed out, holding his mouth as if he were getting ready to cry. "I've been looking for you everywhere and couldn't find you. Oh, what a dreadful misfortune has befallen me."

"To the blazes with you and your misfortune," Pinčukas angrily cut him off through his clenched teeth.

"What's happened?" Shaddon got alarmed.

"Nothing," Pinčukas answered angrily. "Dig this bullet out of my heel."

"Who shot you?" Shaddon became concerned and leaned over the injured heel.

Pinčukas made no reply, he just stuck out his hoof.

But Shaddon dug and dug at the silver bullet and couldn't dig it out. Unable to bear the pain, Pinčukas just kicked him aside with his hoof.

"Why are you kicking like a horse?" Shaddon, landing next to the edge of the quagmire, got angry. "It'd be better if you'd put my teeth back in."

"How can I put them back, if you didn't listen to me and flung them around?" Pinčukas retorted, shaking his hoof in pain so unbearable that even his own teeth started chattering.

Toothless Shaddon, holding his jaw where Pinčukas had kicked him, couldn't bear the pain either and didn't know what to do. He couldn't believe such ungratefulness from his buddy, and in his heart cursed him roundly. But what could mere curses do?

Pinčukas, shaking his hoof, glared at Shaddon. All he needed here was that old geezer, if only he'd just get lost! Pinčukas was furious with all of humankind, and, if he could have thought of how to do it, he would have sent them all to hell, together with the toothless Shaddon.

This was nothing but angry anger and frustrating frustration, and something needed to be done. But what was there to be done, with one toothless and the other shot in the heel? They glared at one another with intractable bitterness and went their separate ways. Pinčukas, clenching his teeth, hobbled off to his quagmire, intending to think it all over by himself and plan his revenge, while Shaddon, completely despondent, dragged himself back to his tavern, as he didn't even know who to take revenge on.

Pinčukas eventually calmed down and thought up his revenge only just before morning. Whitehorn had promised to tie him together to Uršulė by the tail, like a cat and a dog, so they would fight endlessly between themselves and leave others in peace. But Whitehorn had failed to keep his word.

Well, what if he were to do that, to tie Whitehorn together with Uršulė (there couldn't be a better revenge!), and then with Uršulė as an accomplice (having no other accomplices, since Tatergall had died and Shaddon had lost his teeth, he felt as if he was missing his hands), he'd surely win Jurga over.

Putting all this together, Pinčukas decided to try his luck one more time and get his revenge on Whitehorn. Without giving it any more thought, and despite his painful foot, merely shaking his hoof, he changed into the dress of a traveling beggar and flew off to Švendubrė to meet Uršulė.

Morning was already dawning. The mist was thinning out and drifting about. The village was still asleep. Here and there a dog barked, and roosters crowed. These bad omens intimidated Pinčukas a bit, but he calmed himself and gathered up his nerve: what were a few roosters when he had to meet and discuss business with Uršulė, a sanctimonious old biddy and his old enemy?

Pinčukas sat down by the churchyard fence, waiting and weighing everything all over again. How had it happened that Whitehorn had tricked him? Perhaps because he had never seen either Uršulė or Jurga. Now he knew both one and the other quite well and wouldn't mistake them.

Pinčukas didn't have to wait and think by the fence for long. In the semidarkness, Uršulė, wrapped in a black scarf and counting a rosary in her fingers, was the very first one going to church. Pinčukas, emboldened as he was, pressed up to the fence like a shadow. Uršulė didn't even notice him.

Only when Uršulė had gone by did he pull himself from the churchyard fence and go hobbling after her.

"Wait, friend!" he cried. "We need to talk."

Uršulė paused without interrupting her rosary and only looked back and glared angrily—who was this, shouting after her and calling her friend too? Some strange beggar. Maybe it was that unhinged apprentice of Blackpool's, Jurgutis? What did he want? Uršulė got thoroughly peeved and interrupted her counting.

At that moment, Pinčukas, gathering up all his nerve, hobbled up to Uršulė at that moment and gave a deep bow:

"Good morning," he said. "Why should we be angry with each other, my friend? After all, Whitehorn deceived both you and me. We could make peace and together recover what belongs to us: you—Whitehorn, and me—Jurga."

"Wait, wait," said Uršulė, frightened. "And just who are you, exactly?"

For safety's sake, Uršulė took several steps back. What kind of beggar or crazy Jurgutis was this? It didn't seem right. It couldn't be the evil one himself, could it?

Pinčukas bowed deeply a second time and took a step closer.

"Don't tell me you don't recognize an old friend?" he asked. "I'm the same one you got angry with through a misunderstanding and Whitehorn's deceit... But I'm not angry at all, I only wish you well."

"Begone with you, evil spirit!" Uršulė recognized Pinčukas, and in her fright she crossed herself, clasped her rosary, and retreated backwards.

"Don't make the sign of the cross!" Pinčukas retreated backwards as well. "I'm not going to do anything bad to you... If you want, I'll give you the power to do whatever you want with your spells… You'll seduce Whitehorn and take revenge on all of your enemies."

Uršulė paused, interested. But she quickly controlled herself, started making the sign of the cross and waved her rosary in Pinčukas' direction as if he were an annoying fly.

Pinčukas lost his patience.

"You silly woman!" he said angrily. "If you don't listen to me, you'll get nothing. You'll just perish through those spells of yours."

But Uršulė was no longer listening to him. She retreated backwards into the churchyard, still making the sign of the cross and waving her rosary through the fence.

Pinčukas spat in exasperation: why he had tried to start up with that silly woman? Nothing would come of it, what sort of accomplice would she make? He was going to hobble off, but the bells rang and their sound crashed into him like a hammer to the head. Pinčukas, without finishing his negotiations with Uršulė, took off at a run.

In the meantime, Uršulė, finding herself on the other side of the churchyard fence and somewhat recovered from her fear, was just then inclined to talk to him. Well, what if it was possible, with his help, to fulfill her old dream, whose passion had burned out her entire heart? But Pinčukas, frightened at something, took to his heels, and she was left with nothing but her old frustration.

"Wait, where are you running off to?" she shouted, leaning over the fence, but Pinčukas didn't turn back.

The sound of the bells chased him off.

Other biddies were going by, and they saw Uršulė talking to some beggar who was running away.

"Who's that beggar pestering the devil's bride?" they got curious. "Maybe she's planning to get married? But it looks like the groom ran away."

Laughing into their fists, the biddies went into the church. Uršulė, hidden by the fence, saw and heard all of it. A terrible frustration overwhelmed her.

"Just wait," she said, clutching the rosary in her shriveled fist and shaking it threateningly, "There'll be a devil's bride for you! You'll regret it yet! First I'll get my revenge on you, and then I'll make peace with Whitey… Maybe we'll come to an understanding, and together overcome all our enemies."

With this decision made, Uršulė went on into church, firmly resolved to do everything as promised and to passionately pray that for this, the last time, Švendubrė's miraculous Mother of God would intercede for her. After all, Uršulė had overcome the snake of temptation and trampled it under her feet.

Meanwhile, that snake of temptation, Pinčukas, after running away from Uršulė making the sign of the cross and the bells of Švendubrė, flew home to Paudruvė's bogs. In exasperation, he figured he had gotten overexcited and had unnecessarily bothered Uršulė, his old enemy. What sort of accomplice could she be? She would only complicate matters that were already complicated enough. So, he decided to get rid of her at the first opportunity.

Uršulė, completely dismissing Pinčukas (had that really been him in the morning fog?), decided to settle scores with the spiteful biddies that very day, and then to make peace with Whitehorn and live happily ever after.

But Uršulė, energetic woman though she was, didn't manage to get everything done in time.

XXXIX

Who would have thought that poor Uršulė, who really wasn't to blame, would end up answering for everything that was going on in the land of Paudruvė? Perhaps it was just because everything had started with her, so it had to end with her, too.

Things went according to Uršulė's intentions. That day, in the evening, taking her revenge on the sanctimonious biddies, she cast spells on them, intending to leave the almshouse and make peace with Whitey. And early the next morning—it just happened to be Friday—one little biddy by the name of Leokadija, who competed with Uršulė for the top spot in the almshouse, pulled a jar of honey from under her bed, wanting to fortify herself a bit on fast day. But what did she find in the jar? Of all things, a dried toad.

The entire almshouse was in an uproar. Who had done this? The toad couldn't have gotten into the jar by itself, since it was dried up and the jar was tightly stopped up with a rag. They suspected Uršulė, who was the first to be ready to leave for church, but hadn't left in time. Now, cornered, she defended herself and made the sign of the cross over the biddies. But yet another little biddy turned up, by the name of Cecilija, who had seen Uršulė the evening before at dusk crawling under Leokadija's bed and doing something there.

No doubt remained, and all of the biddies fell upon poor Uršulė. After all, who else could do such a thing if not the devil's bride? Pushed to the wall, Uršulė defended herself to the utmost, but at last she lost patience and confessed.

"So, what of it?" she said. "You'll all dry up like that toad, and I'll return to Whitey and live happily ever after."

This utterance was quite enough to prove the terrible crime. All of the biddies, as one, fell upon poor Uršulė, knocked her to the ground and started pulling her by the braids. And what sort of braids could a shriveled old sanctimonious biddy have? About the same as a scruffy rat's tail. The biddies didn't have to pull Uršulė by the braids for long; they pulled out one hair, then another, and all of Uršulė's braids, the pride of her maidenhood, were pulled out.

Then the frightened biddies rushed to their beds and started checking under them to see if that devil's bride hadn't wanted to put a spell on them, too. Well, of course, one found a packet of some kind of herbs at the head of her bed, another at the foot found a knotted-up mouse, a third—a horse jaw under the side, a fourth—who knows what dead thing's tooth, a fifth—again something resembling neither this nor that, and so forth, and the more they looked the more they found, so that the poor biddies, rocked by terror, saw and convinced themselves they really were living with the devil's bride, a terrible witch. Why after all, the depths of hell could have opened and swallowed them all up.

Uršulė, as terribly plucked and pulled as she was, didn't have the time to recover and escape from her enemies when again the entire pack fell upon her, but this time they were even angrier.

"Burn the witch! Tear out her eyes!" and other similar suggestions were shouted by the entire pack surrounding Uršulė, as they didn't know how else to punish such a villain.

At last the screaming and yelling coming from the almshouse attracted the attention of the organist Bernard and the sexton Benjamin, both of them wise and God-fearing men. They lived at the other end of the almshouse and it was their responsibility, assigned by the pastor, to control the endlessly quarreling biddies.

At first it seemed to both men that this was an ordinary everyday biddy hubbub, but, when they arrived and saw what had happened, they got scared and didn't know what to do themselves.

"Let's tie her up so she won't run away," at last, in a trembling voice, said the organist Bernard, a small, crooked little man with sunken and perpetually frightened eyes and an extremely deep voice.

"Good idea," agreed the sexton Benjamin, as tall and as thin as a pole, with a whiny voice and eyes that protruded from his forehead. "And let's take her to the pastor. Let him decide what to do with her."

The entire pack of women agreed with the wise men's idea. Uršulė didn't object, either.

"Take me," she said, "I'll tell everything to the pastor, just like at confession."

So, without further ado, the two God-fearing men and the entire pack of biddies pushed the trussed-up Uršulė out of the almshouse and, screaming and yelling, dragged her to the parsonage.

The pastor Boniface Bobbin was just preparing to go to church to hold the mourning mass for the dead horse thief's soul, which the village of Paudruvė had gotten together and purchased after all. At first the pastor didn't want to agree to it, but, after hearing about the misfortunes that had occurred, and as he was being well paid for the mass, he finally gave in. Now, on his way to hold the mass, he heard an unusual commotion, and, wondering what was going on, glanced out the window. Apparently some strange procession was on its way to the parsonage.

The pastor went out into the entry to see what had happened. He didn't want a gang like that to disturb the parsonage's gravity.

The entire pack of biddies with both of the church's servants, pushing the tied-up Uršulė in front, arrived in front of the entrance at that very moment. Seeing the pastor come out, with one voice they all shouted:

"We've caught the witch, Father."

"What witch?" the pastor wondered.

"Why, this bride of the devil, who wanted to bewitch our entire almshouse."

"What devil's bride?" the pastor was still bewildered.

"This accursed biddy Uršulė, who ran away from Whitehorn's mill a few years back and came here pretending she was devout, when she really was, and still is, the vilest of witches."

"How do you know she's a witch?" the pastor asked.

Then the entire pack of biddies, shouting over each other, and the two men gravely agreeing, started relating what they had discovered in the almshouse and what evil and devilish things they had seen and experienced from this damned bride of the devil. One little biddy, by the name of Elžbieta, had even seen with her own eyes how one evening Uršulė, straddling a broom, went over to the fireplace and suddenly disappeared, as if she had flown out the chimney. The organist Bernard added to her story. Once, going to ring for early mass in the winter when it was still dark, he saw something flashing sparks above the almshouse and then disappearing into the chimney. He was terribly frightened and didn't know what it could be, but now it was clear that this witch had flown home on a broom from a call on the devil she was betrothed to.

"And yesterday morning," the entire pack of biddies agreed, "with our own eyes we saw her talking to some beggar by the churchyard... No doubt with her suitor devil, and then he ran off, frightened by the church bells... And she was yelling for him to wait, too..."

The pastor listened and listened to the biddies' stories and even forgot the mourning mass. (What kind of prayers could they be, after all, for a horse thief's soul?) Listening, even the hair on his head started to stand up on end, just thinking about what kind of deviltry was going on right next to his church, and he didn't know anything about it.

"And what do you have to say?" The pastor at last addressed Uršulė.

She bowed down to the very ground before the pastor, and made a rude gesture at the biddies through her skirt.

"It's not true, Father dear," she said. "I wasn't the devil's bride, although Whitehorn wanted to marry me to him. Yesterday morning, it's true, Pinčukas, pretending to be a beggar, tried to tempt me, but I didn't give in, I defended myself with the holy cross. I only fixed up spells for these damned biddies so that their tongues would rot, pains would dig at their sides and their arms and legs would break... But my spells didn't help them a bit, they're all as healthy as horses, and they're slandering me. I never was a witch and never flew on a broom. Let me give my last confession of my entire life, and then do with me what you will."

XL

Uršulė's last confession of her entire life was long and complicated.

She began from her very infancy, when she was growing up as an abandoned child at the Whitehorns, where everyone was mean to her and only Whitey took pity on her. God granted it so that everyone left the mill and only the two of them remained. And how that Whitey pleased her more and more, and how she wanted very much to marry him, but he didn't even want to talk about it, as if that had never even come into his head.

It was then, taught by this beggar woman, that she took up spells for the first time. She had gone to the bathhouse and worked up a sweat, but didn't wash up with water; instead she had wiped all her sweat off with a scarf, which she had purchased for that purpose at a church festival, and then took it home. There she had wrung the sweat out of the scarf and poured it into Whitey's tea in an effort to attract him. But he didn't drink it at all, even though it was sweetened; he just slurped a bit and spat it out, asking what kind of stinking swill was she giving him to drink. So it didn't help at all. Although women did say that it was truly medicinal.

Then, under the instruction of another beggar woman, on the first warm spring night she had tied a skein of linen to a pole and carried it out by the mill, so that a bat would get tangled up in the skein. It seemed a perfectly simple thing, but she was so fearful that she shook all over, and that hideous bat just wouldn't get tangled in the skein. She had to do the same thing over again for several nights. Finally one morning she found a bat tangled up in the skein. She grabbed it together with the skein and ran to the woods. There she put it on an anthill and took off running for home with her ears covered, and without turning back, because if she had looked back, then she would have gone blind, and if she had heard the bat screaming, she would have gone deaf. But she didn't hear or see anything. She ran home out of breath and waited.

After three days she went back to the woods and found her skein with the bat's bones on the anthill. From those bones she took a wing bone with a hook

and went home. That same day, at dusk, when Whitehorn wasn't looking, she tugged him by the pants with
that hook, but he pushed her away with the back of his
hand and said, "What are you picking at me for?" And
then he left without turning around, and the hook broke
and didn't help at all.

Then that Whitehorn got a notion to marry Marcelė
Alburn, and she, having put so much work into it and
having taken so much sin upon her conscience, didn't
know what to do. Her heart was truly breaking, so she
sobbed, shut up in the pantry, and that was all. Once
again this beggar woman came by, so she told her the
story, weeping all the while. The beggar was sorry for her,
poor thing, and advised her that when that scoundrel left
for the ceremony with that other creature, she should
scatter sand brought home from the graveyard on their
road, so they wouldn't be happy together. Then she also
told her to take the ashes out of the hearth and scatter
them over the threshold, so the bride wouldn't step over
it, or if she did—she would be carried out in a coffin.
And she told Uršulė herself to clamber on the fences until they came back from the ceremony and say some
magic words. But that was a long time ago, she had forgotten the magic words, and besides at the time she had
sobbed them more than said them, clambering over the
fences. Whether the spells helped, or God granted it that
way, she didn't know, but a year later Whitehorn's young
wife gave birth to a daughter and died. Then she was terribly frightened and never cast any more spells.

Later, as everybody very well knew, Whitehorn
wanted to marry her off to the devil Pinčukas, but she

had already made her vows of chastity to the holiest maiden of Švendubrė, and so, saved, she ran away to Švendubrė's almshouse. Here she hadn't cast any spells, lived in a way that behooved a devout maiden, said her prayers, fasted and made atonement for her sins. Only later, when Whitehorn's daughter was already grown, fearing that her father would marry Jurga to Pinčukas (he was a bigger sorcerer than she, that one was a real wizard!), she tried to convince that simpleton to make a vow of chastity, but Jurga had just laughed at Uršulė and didn't do anything, although Uršulė only wanted, after all, to help the silly thing, and not let her father doom her soul. So she waited for a chance and secretly took Jurga's garland of rue and buried it under a cross at Paudruvė's crossroads, so the suitors and their match-makers couldn't call on her and she wouldn't marry. Whether that helped or not, she really doesn't know, but for a long time no one could visit Whitehorn's daughter with a matchmaker, but eventually Girdvainis with his dapple-grays trampled the garland of rue, buried in the crossroads below the cross, under his feet, drove to call on Whitehorn's daughter with a matchmaker, and at dawn flew to announce the banns. But God punished him for that. He lost his horses.

But she wasn't at all to blame for that. She didn't know anything and didn't do anything. She only saw Pinčukas bring Tatergall in a sack and shake him out by the churchyard's hitching post, and the thief had grabbed the horses and flew off with them, and Pinču-kas had neighed, running around and misleading Gird-vainis. She had even wanted to help Girdvainis, but he ran out of the vestry like his pants were on fire without asking her anything, and she would have advised him what to do and how to save his soul, since he would never get his horses back if the devil in cahoots with a horse thief had stolen them, and behind them there was that sorcerer father as well.

She wasn't to blame for the horse plague now raging and doesn't know anything about it. It was probably the devil Pinčukas' and the tavern-keeper Shaddon's revenge for the murder of the horse thief Tatergall. How to thwart that revenge she didn't know, unless maybe to buy a mourning mass for the horse thief's soul. This she had advised the village of Paudruvė to do.

The pastor gave a start, remembering that he was to hold that mass this very day.

"So, you've taken up sacrilege of that sort as well?" growled the pastor, unable to restrain himself.

"No, Father dear, I haven't," Uršulė replied calmly. "I just advised them to, but whether they did it or not, I don't know."

The cat had the pastor's tongue, and Uršulė continued confessing her sins.

It was true that yesterday, early in the morning, she had met Pinčukas pretending to be a beggar by the churchyard fence, but she had shaken off that temptation with the holy cross, and he had run away, chased off by the bells, and the biddies had slandered her. So she had got even with them by fixing them up with spells, but completely innocent ones. She had thrown a dried-up toad into that worthless Leokadija's honey, so she would dry up like that toad, because she is very

226

mean and nagged her all the time. For the others—those under whose pillows she had put herbs, it was so their heads would hurt and they wouldn't flap their lips so much, and for yet others—where she had put a knotted-up mouse, it was so they would break a leg and wouldn't stick their noses in other people's business and anger them with their gossip, and for those under whose beds she had stuck a dead person's tooth, it was so their teeth would fall out, too, and what was supposed to happen from the horse's jaw, she doesn't know herself, but she thought that something like a horse's jaw should do something. Give them a stitch in the side, or something. But apparently, the spells didn't have any effect on them, they were all as healthy as horses and wanted to kill her too.

She herself has had no business with devils (outside of that time when Whitehorn wanted to marry her off to Pinčukas), and she was never a witch, she never flew through the chimney on a broom and doesn't know how to do it. That whiny biddy Elžbieta is lying shamelessly, and besides, she's altogether half-blind and can't see anything, and that shameless organist Bernard guzzles moonshine, so who could tell what had appeared to his hung-over eyes on the almshouse's roof by the chimney.

There was one more horrible sin that had happened in church, but it was against her will. That was the Sunday that Girdvainis' dapple-grays were stolen. When the pastor had started singing during vespers, she had thought he neighed just like Girdvainis' stallions. She was sorry and beat herself on the chest, but nothing helped, and whenever the pastor sang during vespers, she would keep thinking the same thing. In order to avoid sinning she had stopped going to vespers.

"That's true," all the biddies and the two men—Bernard and Benjamin—agreed, "she never went to church during the ceremonial vespers."

Uršulė, her public confession made, beat herself on the breast and promised to never sin again, to cast no spells, to live in chastity, to make peace with Whitehorn, to save his daughter from the devil, and to do penance for the rest of her life.

"Give me, Father dear, even the most difficult penance, but give me absolution." Uršulė kneeled at the pastor's feet and smacked herself so hard on her old, dried-up sinner's chest that everyone standing around felt a dull thud echo in their chests. It got so quiet they could hear one another breathing.

"You won't get absolution," the angry pastor finally said. "They used to burn witches like you. Now, regretfully, there's no such law. So repent alone, rejected by people and severed from the church."

Uršulė, when she heard this decision, rushed to kiss the pastor's feet, begged for mercy, turned blue all over, fainted on the spot, and stretched out on the ground, unable to catch her breath. But this didn't soften the pastor's heart in the least. He was fed up with all of the devilry going on in his parish. And here under his feet was stretched the very criminal who was most to blame for that devilry. It was no coincidence that she had advised the village to buy a mass for the horse thief's soul, either, which the pastor wouldn't hold now, and he wouldn't give absolution to anyone, alive or dead, who

228

had anything to do with the devil. Let them know, he'd had it up to here with it all. So, crossing himself, the pastor went on like Pilate, after strictly ordering the sexton Benjamin and the organist Bernard:

"Take her outside of my parish boundaries, give it to her good on the calves and send her to the four winds."

XLI

Uršulė was escorted out of Švendubrė's almshouse and parish in an unusually ceremonious manner.

Snipe himself, the marshal of Švendubrė's church, a small man, but with a big knobby stave, made a path through the crush of the crowd like he did during the biggest festivities. Uršulė walked behind him (but the Lord save us, what a walk that was!) all wet (apparently, when she had fainted by the parsonage after her confession, they had revived her by pouring several buckets of water on her), her mouth stuffed with tow so she wouldn't scream, a rag tied over her eyes so she wouldn't give anyone the evil eye, her feet and hands tied so she wouldn't run away (where could she, poor thing, run to?), and with a tether tied around her waist, one end of which was held by the organist Bernard, and the other—tightly, too—by the sexton Benjamin. Poor Uršulė stumbled like a driven horse (rumors went flying that she had brought about the horse plague as well), and she could neither stop nor catch her breath, because from one side the organist Bernard prodded her with an ashberry rod (all of God's enemies fear ashberry!) and from the other side the sexton Benjamin kept brandishing something on her calves and shins—it wasn't clear whether it was a horse tail or some kind of aspergillum.

And what a crush of people there was! What yelling, what a commotion! Such a crowd and so much yelling was unheard of at even the biggest festivals and holy days. It wasn't just the people from the village of Švendubrė who had gathered, but people from the surrounding villages as well. Isn't it amazing? A live witch was being driven out of town!

At last, when they left Švendubrė, the crush of people let up. Well, they had seen the witch, and that was enough. She wasn't as terrible as the way she was being driven was. Some were even sorry for her, and others spat to avoid spells and went off. By the time they drove her to the highway, only her escorts and some gaping fools, who still hadn't gotten bored, remained. Poor Jurgutis, with his horseshoes, had somehow gotten mixed in with them; but scared that they might drive him like that too, he ran off. The sexton Benjamin, waving the horse tail, drove the others away.

"What's this now?" Turning around he looked them over with infuriated eyes. "Aren't you going home? You've gawked long enough!"

Apparently the sexton Benjamin thought they'd lead Uršulė past the first hillock, give it to her good on the calves and send her to the four winds. What was this about leading her past the boundary of the parish? They had driven her enough just getting her out of Švendubrė.

But it didn't turn out the way Benjamin wanted. They had barely dragged her past the first hillock and were intending to carry out their plan when some men with cudgels jumped out from the side of the road and shouted:

"What are you stopping here for? Drive your witch further on!"

And this continued all along the road. They'd stop and start to let her go when immediately a pack of men with cudgels would appear and demand:

"Drive her on! We won't let you release that witch in our fields."

What was to be done now? They were going to have to drive her beyond the boundary of the parish. However, the news about the driving of a witch spread through the villages faster than the men drove poor Uršulė down the road. So they unfettered her and started driving her faster. But how can you outrun a rumor? The church servants were walked off their feet, and that witch Uršulė was played out, too. Drag her, if you please, there was nothing else to do. Don't even try to stop, men with cudgels will immediately show up, and you'll have to drive her on! And where are you going to drive her to?

The escorts even started whining:

"Where will we put her, the witch?" Bernard the organist was completely dejected. His forehead had more beads of sweat on it than it did after the toughest bell concert. "Surely we're not going to have to drive her to the ends of the earth?"

"What do I know?" Benjamin answered, hanging his head. "If I had known we'd have this kind of trouble, I would have never started. I would've let the pastor do whatever he wanted with her himself."

Grumbling on in this manner, the two of them got into serious trouble. They had come to the parish boundary—a little bridge over the swift current of Bygodit Creek, which separated Greathall parish from Švendubrė—and there they stopped, in the middle of the bridge. Jurgutis, who happened to be hiding under the bridge, was terrified—what would happen now? Was he going to be blamed for everything? But the Greathall men blocked the road in front and wouldn't let them pass:

"Drive your witch back! We're not going to let you dump her on us."

And the Švendubrė men with their cudgels blocked the road from behind and threatened:

"Drive the witch on further! We've suffered enough from her."

What was to be done now? There was no going forward, no going back. The exhausted Uršulė fell on her knees in the middle of the bridge and bawled like it was the end. The dejected escorts threw the tether down next to her. Run now witch, if you can! And they looked about, first at one, then at the other end of the bridge.

"Where will we put her now?" in dismay they asked the men blocking the road.

"What's it to us?" one and the other side of the bridge answered indifferently. "For all we care, you could go to hell with her."

Bernard and Benjamin looked around and looked about, and saw there was nothing left to do but wait. Benjamin leaned on the bridge's railing and spat into the flowing water, and Bernard sat down on the little bridge next to Uršulė and started quietly cussing her out, you so-and-so, if only you would drop dead and sink right through the bridge with all of your witchery.

Under the bridge, Jurgutis heard this, got frightened and started running through the fields, ringing the horseshoes as if he were calling for help.

The men who were standing at the ends of the bridge couldn't restrain themselves and started trading barbs. Words followed words, and a fight broke out. The blows began falling and hats flew from the bridge into the water.

How the fight would have ended and which side would have won wasn't at all obvious. But while they were fighting, they noticed some little gentleman meddling in their midst and urging them to fight harder. The men stopped in surprise. The little gentleman stood up in the middle of the bridge, leaned on his cane, and laughed.

"What are you fighting about, fellows?" he asked.

"How can we help it?" answered the Greathall men. "They want to dump their witch on us."

"We don't need her, either," replied the Svendubrians.

"Which one's the witch?" The little gentleman looked around.

"Oh, she's lying over here," Benjamin kicked his foot in the direction of the biddy, angry with the little gentleman for interrupting the fight and not letting him escape unseen and leave the witch on the bridge. Let them deal with her.

"Is she really a witch?" the little gentleman asked again, looking over the collapsed Uršulė from all sides.

"Who knows?" Bernard answered indifferently, because he was tired to the bone of sitting next to her on the bridge and quietly cussing her out.

"Have you tried her?" inquired the little gentleman.

"No," was the answer.

"What nincompoops," said the little gentleman then. "You're ignorant people. You're fighting and you yourselves don't know why. First she needs to be tried, to see if she really is a witch."

"Well, how do we try her?" Neither one side nor the other had any idea.

"It's very simple," said the little gentleman. "If you were educated, then you'd know how to try witches. See here, it's even written down in books."

Then the little gentleman with the little hat pulled this large book, roughly the size of the Book of Mass, out from under his arm, set his head to the side, turned to a page and read:

"Here it's written in Latin, I'll give it to you in Lithuanian: 'If a woman is suspected of being a witch, then you need to tie the thumb of her left hand to the right foot, and the thumb of her right hand to the left foot, attach a tether, and throw her into water. If she swims—she's a witch, if she drowns—she's innocent.' So, you see, it's very easy to try her, you just need to know how."

"A learned man is a learned man," a reply came from one end of the bridge. "And here we idiots stand on the bridge and don't know what to do, so we start fighting."

"Well, what now?" they called from the other end of the bridge. "Are we going to try her like it's written in the book, or not?"

"Let's try her," the first side agreed.

Then one end of the bridge joined with the other and got Uršulė—who was lying nearly unconscious (how was it they didn't trample her while fighting!)—to stand up, tied her thumbs to her toes the way the little gentleman had read from the book, tied the tether to her, and asked one another:

"Now, who's going to lower her into the water?"

"Who else if not the ones that drove her here?" was the answer.

Bernard and Benjamin didn't protest. They took the end of the tether and lifted Uršulė up. Regaining consciousness, she moaned:

"Have mercy," she said. "Let me at least repent my sins and get absolution."

"All right," Bernard answered quickly. "You can repent. It's just that we're going to try you first, like it's written in the books."

They lifted Uršulė up on the bridge's railing, and before she had realized what they were doing, Bernard pushed her from behind. She shrieked and plopped into the water, sinking completely under.

Everyone watched from the bridge.

"You see, an innocent maid!" some said. "She's drowned."

But the words were hardly out of their mouths, and look—the water bubbled and Uršulė came to the surface.

"Witch!" they shouted from all sides.

Benjamin and Bernard panicked that now they really wouldn't know what to do with her, and let go of the end of the tether. Uršulė sank again.

"Hold on to her, hold on to her!" others shouted from the bridge.

But how could you hold on to her if the tether was already bobbing on top of the water and floating off downstream?

Everyone watched to see if maybe Uršulė would come up again, but only a bubble or two rose to the surface of the water.

They waited a bit longer, watched—nothing was to be seen, just the flowing water swirling around, as if Uršulė had never existed.

Then everyone turned on Bernard and Benjamin. "What have the two of you done? Why did you let go of the tether? You've drowned an innocent maid."

"Maybe we can catch her downstream," answered the frightened Bernard.

Everyone rushed to the sides of the bridge to search for the drowned woman, while on the bridge, the little gentleman grinned wickedly.

"Where are you looking?" he shouted. "Look upstream," advised the little gentleman, and cackled so horribly that it would have sent shivers down your spine.

The men, worried about saving Uršulė, didn't pay attention. It was only later, after searching a good mile downstream and upstream and failing to find the drowned woman anywhere—there was no guessing where the swirling waters had carried Uršulė off to, together with her tether—did they look around for the wise guy who taught them to try her that way. At the very least he needed a good hiding for such a lesson, but he was here a minute ago and now there wasn't a trace of him.

Who on earth was he? Some had noticed that he was lame, and others saw a horse's hoof. Was it perhaps the spirit of the horse thief Tatergall haunting them? The men became thoroughly frightened.

Then all of their frustration turned against Bernard and Benjamin:

"It was because of those two idiots that we drowned an innocent person and took a sin on our conscience."

They gave it good on the backside to Bernard and Benjamin and, spitting, went their separate ways. It was already completely dark, and here a horse thief's ghost might be about. Everyone hurried home so that they wouldn't meet with some other, perhaps even larger, misfortune.

Bernard and Benjamin, terribly exhausted and wronged despite their innocence, returned to Švendubrė only towards morning, and went straight to the pastor. They told him of their troubles and asked him to hold a mass for Uršulė's soul.

"What's this poppycock now?" The pastor was livid.

"She was an innocent maid," the two of them sighed and told him what had happened on the Bygodit Bridge.

The pastor was furious at his assistants' foolishness and removed both of them from service in the church. The two friends joined the line of beggars and, while saying the Hail Mary for other souls, they would say one Hail Mary for the innocent maid Uršulė's soul as well.

XLII

That same evening, as the sun was setting, while the men clashing on the Bygodit Bridge drowned poor Uršulė, Hearall was going down the road towards Paudruvė's bogs with an ashberry rod, snares, and netting under his arm.

For a long time he had suspected that the true culprit in all these misfortunes was none other than the devil of Paudruvė's bogs, Pinčukas, who had apparently gone completely berserk and wasn't going to stop making mischief. He needed to be caught and reined in for once, so he would stop materializing.

So Hearall, rallying all of his wisdom and experience, tracked Pinčukas' footprints and set snares on his paths to trap him, but Pinčukas was running around everywhere like mad and Hearall just couldn't catch him.

It was only that evening, as he was going past Cockend's tavern—he was preparing to set snares for Pinčukas there—that he saw someone, perhaps a beggar or just some poor traveler, limping along leaning on a cane. At first, Hearall thought that it just might be Blackpool's apprentice Jurgutis, who had been roving around the roadsides unhinged since last year, and apparently had twisted an ankle and was finally returning home. But coming closer, he saw that it might be the evil one he had been looking for all this time, pretending to be a beggar.

"Have you come from far away?" Hearall asked the stranger.

"From far away and from near by," the stranger answered, stopping with one heel not touching the ground. "And where are you heading yourself?"

"Right here to the bogs, to catch some rabbits," Hearall answered, recognizing Pinčukas, whom he had never seen before, but only heard a great deal about.

Pinčukas recognized Hearall, too, however he didn't know what Hearall had in mind or what he intended to do. He thought perhaps the old shepherd really was hunting rabbits, since he didn't have anything else to do. And suddenly a good idea popped into his head.

"Would you like me," he said, "to catch all the rabbits for you and to shower you in gold?"

"Why would you do that?" wondered Hearall, and he came closer, aiming to throw the crossed snare net on Pinčukas' head, and then thump him mercilessly with the ashberry cane, so that the tar would flow out of him.

But Pinčukas, sensing danger, drew back a bit, limping, and took his tobacco tin out of his vest.

"You see," he said, snuffing tobacco and thinking over how to approach it, "you're clever, and I'm no fool. Why should we disagree? We could come to an agreement. As you know, Girdvainis' dapple-grays have perished, and he's gone out of his head himself. Take me matchmaking in his place to Whitehorn's daughter Jurga; then I'll shower you in mountains of gold."

"Why not?" Hearall agreed, wanting to get Pinčukas to come closer, "I could take you there... But what sort of suitor would you make: you're as old as a stump and as lame as the devil."

"That's true," sighed Pinčukas. "You couldn't make me younger and fix my foot?"

"I could," agreed Hearall, interested. "I just don't know if you can."

"I can do anything!" Pinčukas suddenly burned with the determination to do anything for the match to succeed.

Then, smiling, Hearall took his tobacco horn out of his pocket and pulled out the stopper.

"Here you are," he said, "if you can crawl into my tobacco horn, then you'd crawl out of it young and healthy."

"Fine," Pinčukas merrily agreed and shook himself right there, the rags vanished like fog, and he himself in all of his devilish nakedness up and disappeared into the tobacco horn. Only a bit of the end of his tail was left.

Without delay, Hearall clamped the horn shut with a thwack, squeezing the end of the tail with the stopper, then made the sign of the cross over it so the devil wouldn't crawl out, and tied knots around it too. Then, as if nothing had happened, he calmly put it back in his pocket.

Hearall had owned that miraculous tobacco horn for a long time; he had brought it home from the war with the Turks, but its power could only be used once. He had kept putting off using it, since he was reluctant to stuff a live being, even his worst enemy, in there; but now he was happy he had driven that villainous devil in so easily, and shut him up for good. Pleased, he went in the direction of Cockend's tavern, thinking that now all the troubles were over and things could be patched up.

The only problem was that Pinčukas, shut up in the horn, squeaked and whined in his pocket like a cricket.

"Where should I put this monster?" deliberated Hearall, finding the noise unbearable. "I need to put him away somewhere where he won't get underfoot and make any more mischief."

When he got to Cockend's tavern, he stopped and looked around. At the corner where the logs met he noticed a crack. He looked around to see if anyone was looking. The yard was empty, and apparently there wasn't a soul in the tavern. So he stood on tiptoe and stuck the squealing horn in that crack. Then he stuffed it in still further and drove a wedge in after it.

"Well, now you can squeak there forever and haunt the tavern," said Hearall when he had finished his work. "No one will find you here, and you won't be able to do anything bad to anyone, except maybe scare the drunkards."

Hearall checked once more to see if it was well enclosed, stuffed in some moss so no one would notice it, and went on his way, while the whining rang through all the tavern's walls, merging into some sort of vague and terrifying drone.

It was already dark when Hearall, leaving the droning tavern, headed down the road to his village, hoping to find Girdvainis, get some other dapple-grays somewhere, and at last finish the matchmaking he had begun. Alas, although the matchmaker, with everything settled, hurried on his way, he and the suitor missed each other.

XLIII

After all his wanderings on the highways and byways Gird-vainis at last returned to his homeland. The dapple-grays no longer neighed in his ears. It was terribly quiet and bar-ren, as if the entire world had suddenly emptied out.

After the meeting with Pinčukas in the crossroads, he no longer believed he would find his dapple-grays. It seemed as though in losing them, he had lost everything. Returning home after his wanderings, he felt like he had survived a fire—he had no idea where to start, or what to do.

Unable to bear it, he went to Hearall's to talk it over, but he didn't find him at home, so he took off for the land of Paudruvė all by himself, to visit the Whitehorns and apologize that he had taken so long looking for his dapple-grays.

On the way he met a peculiar poor man carrying some horseshoes. Wasn't he the same one he had met before dawn in the crossroads, the night Pinčukas had appeared to him? Yes, it was poor Jurgutis, who, after all his alarms, still didn't know what to do with those horseshoes that weren't his.

"Where did you get those horseshoes?" Girdvainis asked him.

Jurgutis, sniffling, admitted he had gone to Cockend's tavern to get back the horseshoes he had drunk away, intending to work for them, but Shaddon had made an offer that if he buried some carcasses he could take the horseshoes off their hooves, and now he didn't know what to do with them, and couldn't return home because there were dreadful things going on everywhere.

Girdvainis shuddered as he listened. Could this half-wit have buried his dapple-grays? But Jurgutis didn't know anything more, he just held out the unfortunate horseshoes, which Girdvainis recognized and took in remembrance.

Jurgutis was happy to rid himself of the strange horseshoes that had burned his hands as if they were on fire, and he went straight to the smithy with a clear conscience, figuring he had suffered enough and had done what he could to atone for his crimes.

Girdvainis, taking his dapple-grays' horseshoes, went on to Cockend's tavern. Somewhere on the way he by-passed Hearall—he went straight through the fields, taking the shortcut—and so he didn't find out what had happened at the tavern the day before.

At dusk Shaddon heard some kind of vague buzzing or droning, maybe inside the tavern, or maybe not, spreading through the fields outside and throughout the entire tavern, and he shuddered in fear.

"What on earth is this now?" he looked about uneasily, as he couldn't make out what this was, or where the buzzing was coming from.

The entire tavern was full of that horrible sound.

Shaddon went outside to look around. Maybe something was going on out there? But all he found outside was the sunset fading horribly, bleeding through black clouds. On the shore of Lake Udruvė Whitehorn's mill stood with its arms held aloft. Apparently a storm was gathering before nightfall.

Worried, Shaddon returned to the tavern, but the horrible buzzing still hadn't gone away. He lit a lantern, looked over all the nooks and crannies, but the vague sound seemed to be coming from all the corners, as if the entire tavern had been beset by some curse.

"Don't tell me Tatergall's soul is haunting me?" Shaddon surmised, and he became even more terrified.

Things got dreadfully gloomy and uneasy. He'd flee the tavern himself, but where could he go at night?

"If only someone would drop in," Shaddon wished, glancing at the door uneasily, and he almost ran out it himself.

There wasn't much hope that someone would stumble by on such a night, except perhaps some traveler. But who would be traveling this late? No one from the village had showed their face since Tatergall's drubbing. And now Tatergall was going to start haunting the place! This would be no kind of a life at all.

Shaddon was about to run out to get Pinčukas' advice (for some reason even he hadn't showed up in a long time), when a strange man came in the door, apparently someone from far away.

It was Girdvainis. But Shaddon didn't recognize him, and Girdvainis didn't even wish him good evening, he just looked around the tavern as if he was surprised at the strange buzzing, and sat down, as black as night, at the very corner of the table.

It was probably a stroke of good luck that Shaddon, because he had never seen him before, didn't recognize Girdvainis at once, or else he and his entire tavern would have sunk into the ground out of fear. He just sensed that this late guest boded no good. On this account, Shaddon watched his every move with frightened eyes and tried to guess who he could be.

Meanwhile, Girdvainis sat at the table as though he didn't notice Shaddon at all; he just looked around as if he were surprised at the strange buzzing, then sullenly glanced at the tavern keeper, and as if addressing him—or maybe not—said:

"Vodka!" and slammed the horseshoes on the table, which made a terrible twang and drowned out the strange buzzing. "I've come to drink my troubles away."

The frightened Shaddon leapt from his spot and immediately brought a bottle of the best vodka. He set it on the table in front of Girdvainis and made a deep bow, as he would for a gentleman.

"You're very welcome. Perhaps there's something else you desire?"

Girdvainis didn't answer and didn't even look at the tavern keeper; he took the bottle and drank it down in a single draft. Then he smashed the bottle on the floor. Shaddon simply sat straight down on the ground. Girdvainis, as if nothing special was going on, said again:

"Give me more, you monster!"

"Who could this possibly be?" Shaddon stared at Girdvainis, unable to get up from the ground and keep his teeth from chattering. He had never seen anyone like that in his life, even though all sorts of people—gentlemen, peasants, and others—had passed through his tavern. But Girdvainis didn't have to ask a second time before Shaddon had already brought him another

245

bottle. Girdvainis drank it up the same way he had the first, and asked for a third.

It was only then that Shaddon came to his senses and grasped who this was.

"Could this be Girdvainis?" he thought to himself, freezing in fear.

So, bringing the third bottle—more dead than alive—Shaddon started justifying himself, explaining that he was innocent of all blame, that it was the work of the horse thief Tatergall and that devil Pinčukas who had worked at Whitehorn's. He hadn't had any use out of it; he just had a fit when they had so brutally pummeled Tatergall to death in the dapple-gray's hide in the stable. But that's what he deserved, so he wouldn't steal good horses anymore. Pinčukas wasn't going to avoid paying for it, either, after all he was the one most at fault here.

Shaddon, trembling all over, related everything he knew and everything he didn't know. Girdvainis, although he listened to Shaddon's spiel with one ear, wasn't at all interested, and heard none of it. He was immersed in his own thoughts, which had nothing in common with Shaddon's blathering. And those thoughts weighed like a mountain of rocks. So he drank up the third bottle and stood up from the table, barely able to stand, terribly sullen and drunk. He glanced angrily at the still-explaining Shaddon, who froze and was struck dumb.

"Take your pick," he said, "on which rafter you want to hang. I'm paying the bill."

Shaddon, without uttering a word, collapsed right there on the spot, and then, coming to, he crawled on all fours behind a barrel of beer and started screeching in an inhuman voice, as if he were already being strung up.

Shaddon thought he had little hope of escaping the noose this time, but he got into a tizzy for nothing.

"It's all the same to me," said Girdvainis indifferently, shrugging his shoulders. Then he kicked the door open with his foot and went out, leaving behind the horror he had raised in the tavern.

Outside the spring winds whistled. Girdvainis, sobering up, looked about, saw a cudgel that the village men had used to pummel Tatergall thrown down next to the tavern, took it and blocked the tavern door from the outside.

Then, going around the corner, he checked the direction of the wind, dug around in his pocket, found a match, and striking it, started the tavern's thatched roof on fire. At that moment lightning flashed and lit up the entire sky.

Girdvainis looked about as if he were surprised, waited until the flame had spread over the entire roof, and went off in the light of the fire straight through the hills in the direction of Whitehorn's mill.

A storm with thunder and lightning came up. Lightning flashes tore through the entire sky. The wind caught the flames and the roaring fire spread over the entire tavern and the stable, lighting up a wide swath of the land of Paudruvė.

XLIV

Oh, that Girdvainis, what trouble he bought down on his head again, setting Cockend's tavern on fire! But he was completely unaware that while taking his revenge for his dapple-grays he had freed his enemy Pinčukas, who, trapped in the tobacco horn by Hearall, was stuck in the corner of the tavern.

Shaddon was also unaware of this. At that moment, terribly frightened and more dead than alive, he was hiding behind the barrels and trembling all over in fear, awaiting his end. He only came to his senses when lightning flashed through the window and the tavern shook from the thunder. Witless, he leapt out of the corner, but the tongues of flames were already licking through the ceiling and the entire tavern was full of smoke. He rushed to the door, but the door was blocked from the outside and impossible to open, and the flames were already scorching his eyeballs.

At that moment, with a terrible crash, the corner of the tavern where Pinčukas was stuck in the tobacco horn exploded. The tobacco horn caught fire and blew up; Pinčukas leapt out and flew off like lightning, knocking down the entire corner of the tavern.

The terrified Shaddon, thinking that lightning had struck again, fell backwards into the tavern and, scorched, tumbled out a window with the smoke.

Outside the storm raged and lightning split the sky. The entire tavern was crackling with flames. Shaddon wanted to run to the village for help, but he got confused, and—not knowing how—he beat it, scorched like a pig, to Paudruvė's bogs, screaming:

"Help! Help!"

But in the storm no one heard his screams and no one hurried to save him. Smoking all over, he rolled into the bogs next to the first quagmire and met Pinčukas there, who had managed to get there first and smother his burning pelt.

"What are you yelling about now?" said Pinčukas, irritated to see Shaddon flying towards him smoking all over.

"Help! Girdvainis set the tavern on fire," Shaddon mumbled, "and he's ruined me completely."

"So—it's a good thing that he burned the tavern up," Pinčukas answered angrily. "He saved me. I yelled and screamed in Hearall's tobacco horn, stuck in the corner, and you didn't understand that I needed help."

"I didn't know, friend, I didn't know," the despondent Shaddon fell to his knees, "I thought it was Tatergall's spirit haunting me, or a cricket had crawled in somewhere and was chirping ..."

"You didn't know, so what do you want now?"

"Save me, buddy!" begged Shaddon, crawling on his knees.

"How am I supposed to save you?" Pinčukas pulled back. "Climb into the mire, if you want, and curdle there."

"Have pity on me," Shaddon, crawling up, kissed Pinčukas' hooves. "Such a misfortune has befallen me, and you're offering the mire. It's not enough that Girdvainis burned down the tavern, you want to ruin me completely."

"What's it to me?" said Pinčukas, driven to the end of his patience. "What am I going to do with such a scalded, toothless piece of burned toast? Girdvainis has recovered all of his pride and is going straight through the hills to Whitehorn's mill. I need to get there before he does. So, climb into the mire as fast as you can before I stuff you in there myself."

"What's this now, here I am, a nobleman, and I'm going to wallow in the mud like a pig?" Shaddon got insulted and tried to stand up. Why was he humiliating himself this way in front of a mangy devil, who didn't want to help him and made fun of him so cruelly? But Shaddon didn't manage to stand up before Pinčukas, his patience at an end, made his own move.

"Nobleman or not," he said, "I don't have any more time to waste on you!" He grabbed Shaddon, who was getting to his feet, by the nape of the neck, and pitched him into the middle of the quagmire, where only his legs wriggled in the air, and then disappeared in the mire's duckweed.

Leaving Shaddon to gurgle in the quagmire, Pinčukas hightailed it, his hooves not touching the ground, limping and jumping, to get ahead of Girdvainis before he got to Whitehorn's mill. But it wasn't easy to catch up with him. And not just because he was lame. Lightning flashed constantly, thunder growled, and Pinčukas—who, since the time when Whitehorn had shot him, had suffered from fits of fear—was now afraid the lightning would strike him, so he hid like a rabbit behind every rock or stump.

Meanwhile, Girdvainis went by the light of the fire without turning back, straight through the hills towards Lake Udruvė, where Whitehorn's mill stood on the precipice with its wings upheld, like arms awaiting help. Girdvainis went straight towards it, paying no heed to his surroundings, just wanting to get there as quickly as possible. What would be afterwards would be, if only he could reach it before lightning struck them. Then he would save himself and Jurga too. He gave no thought as to how he would do this, or by what means, he just felt that his entire heart was pulling him there, as if all of his salvation was there, in his heart.

So Pinčukas couldn't catch up with Girdvainis, much less get ahead of him. The lightning blinded him and forced him to kneel and hide behind every rock or stump. But the lightning lit up the road for Girdvainis, who went without taking his eyes off the uplifted wings of the mill. Above it the entire storm collected, lightning bolts crossed and thunder growled. Those lightning bolts tore into Girdvainis' heart and the thunder growled above his head.

But he paid no attention to it, hearing and seeing none of it. He went like a storm himself—spontaneous, blind, unstoppable. So how could Pinčukas catch up with him? And he wouldn't have caught up if doubts hadn't arisen in Girdvainis' heart. So what, if he went through the worst storm to his bride—what would he do without his dapple-grays, how could he charm her, and how could he carry her off to a new life? With his heart on his sleeve? But as the doubts rose, his arms drooped, and Girdvainis stopped at the top of the hill, looking with terrible longing at the wings of White-horn's mill, lit up by the lightning and thunder. Was someone waiting for him there? Was he missed there? And if no one waited for him, no one there missed him, then what would he do, all alone with his longing heart?

Pinčukas put that moment to use. He ran in a circle along the side of the hill ahead of Girdvainis, tore off a piece of bark, knotted a noose, threw it over a branch and, pressing himself on top of it, swung there, waiting for the approaching Girdvainis. Faltering, Girdvainis descended the hill and let the mill's wings out of his sight. The treacherous Pinčukas used the opportunity to throw the noose over his neck. Girdvainis didn't have time to understand what had happened, only that the dapple-grays neighed above the thunder and the mill's wings lit up like crossed lightning.

Perkūnas, the god of lightning, hit the pine tree, but he missed Pinčukas. Instead he knocked the pine down, which in falling crashed onto Girdvainis with the bark noose still around his neck. Pinčukas merely cackled at having overcome his enemy, and flew off to White-horn's mill, leaving Girdvainis under the fallen pine with the noose around his neck.

Oh Girdvainis, why wander when you had already found your betrothed, why falter going through the storm? That was how you lost it all and destroyed your-self, too.

XLV

That night Jurga awoke from a horrible dream and leapt out of bed trembling all over. There was some sort of light shining through the parlor windows, and outside the windows an unusual neighing resounded, which shook the entire parlor.

Jurga had been ill and delirious since the evening when the eerie hooting of the owl had frightened her and her father had shot something. The morning before, she had gotten up, still delirious, dressed herself and was getting ready to go somewhere, but her father, who wouldn't let his ill daughter out of sight, managed to stop her in the doorway.

"Where are you going, my dear daughter?" he asked, surprised.

"To look for Girdvainis," Jurga said without regaining her senses.

"How can you go look for him, daughter dear, when you're ill yourself?" The father didn't immediately understand that his daughter was delirious. "Wait, you'll get well, or maybe he'll find his dapple-grays and come for you."

"No," Jurga replied, "without me he'll never find his dapple-grays and he'll never come for me. I have to find him and do everything Hearall said, or else without me he'll come to ruin and there won't be any life for me, either."

She struggled to get out the door. Her father barely managed to restrain her and lay her back down in bed. He was angry with Hearall, why had he come here and stirred up the memories that Jurga, it seemed, was on the point of forgetting? And why did he induce her to go searching for a crazy suitor too? It would have been better if he had never come, than to have brought such trouble.

Compelled to return and lie down in bed, Jurga calmed down, as if she had forgotten her intention to go look for Girdvainis, and peacefully fell asleep.

She slept until late afternoon, and when she woke up she looked around as if she didn't understand what had happened to make her sleep for so long, immediately leapt out of bed as if she hadn't been ill, and was unusually nice and cheerful with her father.

"Oh, father, dear," she complained, ashamed. "What a sleepyhead I've become! And how I've let everything go. Don't be angry, father dear! I'll tidy everything up in a minute."

The father looked at his daughter in surprise and didn't know what to think. Had she really recovered? What happiness that would be! And in the father's sunken eyes a ray or two of happiness shone.

Jurga, as though she had never been sick and had put everything out of her mind, cheerfully bustled about the cottage, straightening up as if preparing for a big holiday. She didn't say a word about Girdvainis; it seemed she had never met him nor heard of him, nor ever had him in her heart.

After tidying up, Jurga fixed a lovely dinner, like she would if she were expecting guests, spread a white tablecloth on the table and, looking at her father, partly making up to him, partly apologizing, said:

"Come on, father dear, let's have supper. You're so tired and worn out, it hurts just to look at you. Oh, it's all my fault! But I'll be better now, father dear, you'll see how good I'll be."

The father just looked at his daughter and smiled. It was such a relief to him that his daughter had finally recovered. Sitting down at the table, he ate for two, as if he had come home starving, after all it really had been a long time since he had eaten such a nice supper. Jurga, sitting next to her father, didn't eat so much as she fed her father, and looked at him with eyes full of love and pity.

"It's so nice to be with you, father dear," she said, pressing close to him, "I'd live this way forever and never part with you. I don't need anything else, just to see your gray head and your shining eyes."

"Oh, you poor little thing, my little beauty!" The father was as heartened as a man starting a new, bright, and happy life. "How I wish that you would always be so happy and cheerful!"

"And I will be," Jurga beamed.

The two of them sat at the table until late in the evening, unable to part and unable to get over their newfound happiness.

Oh, happiness, how simple it is, when it comes from the heart!

Jurga, going to bed in the parlor, kissed her father, who was dizzy with joy. Whitehorn couldn't even remember when he had been as happy as he was that evening.

"Good night, father dear!" the happy Jurga smiled on the threshold. "Good night, you my bright moon, whose clouds of worry have scattered."

Unable to part from him, she ran up to her father once more to hug and kiss him.

"Now, now, daughter dear, isn't it enough happiness for one day?" The father stroked his daughter's golden braids soothingly. "Go on, have a good night's sleep and get up tomorrow like a bright little sun."

He led his daughter into the parlor, laid her down, tucked her in, and returned to the kitchen. He lay down on the bench, but because of his extraordinary happiness, with his heart and his head cleared, he couldn't fall asleep, so he went into the parlor once more to look at his daughter.

He found Jurga sleeping peacefully, as if she were resting after a long road of trouble and toil, and smiling as she dreamed. He looked at his sleeping daughter, stroked her head, calmed down, and returned to the kitchen beaming all over. He lay down and immediately slept a heavy, sweet sleep, such as he hadn't slept in a long time.

But this time—the last time—fortune's bright smile deceived Whitehorn.

Jurga, barely getting past her first sleep, awoke from a horrible nightmare and leapt out of bed, terribly frightened and trembling all over.

She had dreamed of Girdvainis; it seemed he had come to her with his dapple-grays, but a chasm had opened up and he, together with his steeds, had fallen straight down into the earth.

The last neighing of the dapple-grays had awoken her. It was so resounding that the parlor windows rattled. At least that's how it seemed to Jurga in her sleep and fright.

Trembling all over, Jurga ran to the window to see what had happened. In the distance a fire gleamed, and all about the spring winds howled, raising up a storm. Jurga imagined that Girdvainis, terribly sad, was standing outside the window. And his glance, when their eyes met, was so despondent that it pierced her heart. He seemed to beckon her with his hand, inviting her to come out.

Then Jurga screamed in an inhuman voice and ran out to the yard in her nightdress. But Girdvainis was no longer outside the window. His shadow, buffeted by the wind, receded in the direction of Lake Udruvė.

The wind caught Jurga and carried her off after him.

"Wait!" she shouted to the shadow. "Don't perish a second time. Now I'll never, ever, part from you."

The wind had already carried her to the very precipice of Lake Udruvė.

A seagull soaring by shrieked as if in fright and disappeared in the dark.

Below the lake roared, forcing its way out of its banks. And the wind kept growing stronger. It carried Jurga farther and farther. From the depths of the raging lake Girdvainis rose up with his white-maned dapple-grays and flew to meet her.

But just then, Jurgutis, frightened and out of breath, ran up from the foot of the hill, and Pinčukas rose up like a bat from the mill's sails and jumped in front of her. Frightened, Jurga threw herself to the side and flew from the precipice straight into the lake.

The wind spread Jurga's loose braids; she spread out her arms and fell as if into the embrace of her loved one, into Lake Udruvė's storming, raging waters.

A receding wave caught her and carried her towards the middle of the lake.

Jurga imagined that she was riding to her wedding. It didn't seem to her that it was cold waves caressing her, but rather her lover's arms. And such an unusual and enormous happiness embraced her that her heart could no longer bear it, and it froze from happiness.

Then the skies opened up and the stars, twinkling, rang like bells.

Oh, that spring storm, rampaging on Lake Udruvė, carried off in its embrace the most beautiful girl in the land of Paudruvė—Whitehorn's daughter and Gird-vainis' betrothed.

And the storm, as though rejoicing, raged all the more.

XLVI

Just before dawn Whitehorn heard the resounding neighing of steeds and awoke. He thought perhaps Girdvainis had found his dapple-grays and had come to see them. Whitehorn, as he never left his mill and lived only within his own heartache, didn't know that Gird-vainis' dapple-grays had already died next to Cockend's tavern.

"Am I dreaming?" he was still doubtful, but then he heard the front door slam and realized that Jurga had run out to meet her suitor. Then, rejoicing, he got up, and throwing his sheepskin over his shoulders, ran out into the yard.

He had barely stepped out the door when he saw what seemed to be Jurga's shadow flash by on the precipice of the lake and disappear, and then he heard an even more resounding neighing of steeds drowning out the seething storm.

"Jurga, my little one, where are you?" shouted Whitehorn, frightened, and ran to the precipice of the lake, where he had seen Jurga's shadow.

But there was nothing there. Something looking like a frightened Jurgutis flashed by, but it, too, disappeared under the mill's wings.

Below at the foot of the hill the frenzied lake boiled and churned, and in the horrid moonlight the neighing of steeds resounded eerily. Just exactly the same way it had when Girdvainis had come matchmaking.

"What could this be now?" Whitehorn wondered, and looked around.

But there was nothing to be seen. Neither Jurga, nor Girdvainis, nor his dapple-gray steeds. Surely they couldn't have driven off without saying a word to him? But then where was the neighing coming from?

Whitehorn, completely mystified, looked around as his heart grew cold. On the other side of the lake the glow of a fire shone. That was Cockend's tavern burning. But the fire didn't attract Whitehorn's attention for long. Concentrating, he listened to the inexplicable neighing, sensing misfortune.

With his heart pounding, he rushed back into the cottage and ran into the parlor—it was as he had feared: Jurga wasn't there, and the bed was still warm. Apparently it hadn't been just his imagination, she really had run out when the front door slammed.

Oh, the happiness of the previous evening! How deceitful it was.

Whitehorn ran back into the yard like a madman, and looked around completely bewildered. It was only when he glanced in the direction where the crescent moon, as if driven by the storm clouds, flew low on the horizon, that he understood it all, and nearly died on the spot.

On the crescent moon sat the devil—Whitehorn knew who it was very well; it was his hand Pinčukas— who, in his unwonted joy, swung his horse hooves and neighed as loud as he could, to his very utmost.

"The evil one is rejoicing in his work," thought Whitehorn, and he became entirely disheartened, understanding that a dreadful misfortune had occurred.

Pinčukas also saw Whitehorn standing bareheaded in the middle of the yard. He jumped off the moon's horn straight onto the mill's wings and neighed so loud that the mill shook all over, and Whitehorn turned as white as a sheet.

"Ha-ha-ha, hee-ha-ha," Pinčukas cackled straight in Whitehorn's face. "You wanted to deceive me, now you've not only lost your son-in-law, but your daughter as well."

In his devilish glee, Pinčukas, remembering old times, started spinning the mill's wings. The empty mill groaned in a cacophony of sounds, mixing with the devil's neighing and the storm's howling.

Whitehorn stood on the spot without moving, and he was so heartbroken he seemed to have sunk into the earth. Now he understood everything.

"Jurga mine, dear daughter of mine," Whitehorn's numb lips repeated. "It was I who was your ruin."

Pinčukas, turning the mill's wings, got so carried away that he mocked his former master without restraint. He stuck out his tongue, made rude gestures, jabbed with his horns and sneered at him in every other way imaginable.

The mill hummed, roared even, drowning out Pinču-kas' efforts, and under the wings it looked like Jurgutis' shadow was jumping up and down, trying to grab that villain by the horns. But Pinčukas didn't notice him at all, as if he were his own shadow.

Whitehorn, stunned by his unbearable misfortune, didn't pay attention to what was going on at the mill; he saw none of it. In his pain, he stiffened all over and seemed to turn to stone.

Then out of the raging lake a huge storm arose; the lake roared and hissed, knocking down its banks, the heavens flashed in a cross, and lightning struck straight at Whitehorn's mill.

Old Grandfather Perkūnas, going out for a spring drive through the wide heavens on his wagon, had missed Pinčukas the first time under the pine tree, when the devil had thrown the noose around the unfortunate suitor's neck. And now he again noticed that ill-fated devil, who had not only sunk the father in misfortune, but was mocking his heartache as well. He was dreadfully incensed and, with his arrow of fire, smashed Pinčukas to the very depths of hell.

Pinčukas, carried away by rejoicing in his victory and mocking Whitehorn, didn't even notice that his inexorable enemy had appeared in the sky. Through the thunder it seemed to him as if Girdvainis had risen from the lake with his white-maned dapple-grays and was flying straight at the hill. Pinčukas cringed and froze.

Then Jurgutis grabbed him by the horn.

But Pinčukas didn't have the time to escape before the lightning struck him right between the eyes. Everything suddenly got jumbled; it just flashed in his eyes as he fell from the mill's wing and sank straight into the earth without so much as a squeak. That was how he choked for eternity on his ill-fated neighing.

XLVII

A terrible storm roared through the land of Paudruvė that spring night. But no one imagined that it could have done so much harm.

Many people saw Cockend's tavern burning that evening, but it seemed lightning had struck that den of horse thieves, so no one went to put it out. The tavern burned down to its foundations, but no one knew where the tavern keeper had gotten to, and no one missed him.

"Finally that accursed den of horse thieves has come to an end!" People were pleased that morning when they found the burned remains of the tavern's foundations; but of the tavern keeper himself—not a trace.

It didn't occur to anyone that Girdvainis had burned down the tavern in revenge for his dapple-grays. They found him halfway to Whitehorn's mill, under a fallen pine tree, with bark whipstitching around his neck. It wasn't clear whether he had hung himself or whether the hundred-year-old pine couldn't hold the suitor's heartache and fell down. They buried him there, making a cross out of the pine so he wouldn't haunt them, and later they named that hill after Girdvainis.

People missed Whitehorn's mill more, which had stood through the winter like a ghost with its wings folded on the steep bank of Lake Udruvė.

"Surely it hasn't flown off?" someone tried to joke, but the joke fell flat.

People sensed that something truly evil had happened there. Going to the spot, they found the mill struck by lightning and in ruins, and the miller Whitehorn himself—sunk into the ground up to his knees as if he'd been entirely carbonized or fossilized, and not at all resembling a human—altogether more like a rock.

"I told him to put up a lightning rod," said the despondent Blackpool. "The mill was standing on such a bluff, that's why it got struck."

Under the ruins of the mill, in just exactly the spot where the wings had fallen, they found yet another charred corpse that was impossible to identify. People guessed that this might just be Pinčukas, struck by lightning and charred. Some even saw marks of burned horns on his forehead.

But that wasn't true. Blackpool recognized his apprentice Jurgutis, who had returned the evening before from his wanderings completely crazed. Sniffling and mumbling for a long time, he admitted that he had stolen two pairs of horseshoes and drank them up at Cockend's tavern, and then related such strange things that the blacksmith didn't believe them, and took them for the delirium of a half-witted, and now half-crazy fool.

So, after feeding him, Blackpool locked him up in the smithy where he could sleep it off and not disappear somewhere again. The blacksmith intended to interrogate him thoroughly in the morning and sort out where Jurgutis was telling the truth and where he was hallucinating. But in the morning he found the door to the smithy still locked, as he had left it the night before, but of Jurgutis in his bed behind the forge—not a trace. The smith had no idea where he could have disappeared to again.

"What on earth brought him here?" said the smith, finding him burned under the mill's wings. "Last night I locked him up in the smithy, and now you see he shows up here. How did he get out?"

What the smith didn't know was that Jurgutis, shut up in the smithy, calmed down, slept like a log in his old bed, and awoke only as the tavern was burning. The glow from the fire shone through the cracks in the smithy, and it seemed to Jurgutis as if the smith's house had started on fire. He rushed to the door, but the door was locked from outside. The thunder from the storm roared above the smithy, and Jurgutis got terribly worried.

Then he climbed up on the forge and crawled out through the vent onto the roof of the smithy. The rain was pouring like cats and dogs, and lightning tore through the heavens. Through its blinding light he could see Whitehorn's mill on the hill, with its wings raised like arms shouting for help, and Cockend's tavern burning in the crossroad.

Jurgutis remembered the ill-fated horseshoes he had drunk up, on whose account he had had so much trouble, and then, looking at Whitehorn's mill lit up by the lightning, some sort of grief pressed upon his heart. Not knowing why, but driven by an inhuman strength, he took off running through the rain and lightning to the hill of the mill. He ran in a terrible hurry, and shook all over with the fear that he wouldn't make it in time, and that something would happen. He wanted to see Jurga once more, and then let himself come to an end along with the mill.

It was Jurgutis' sad fortune that his last wish was fulfilled. He ran to the mill's hill just as Jurga flew out of the cottage in her nightdress. The thunder growled and the storm's dapple-grays neighed. Jurga ran with her arms outstretched, as if meeting someone, and he wanted to run to her and catch her in his arms so she wouldn't fall from the precipice. But then Pinčukas jumped off the mill with his claws outspread. The frightened Jurga shied to the side and disappeared like a seagull in the blustering lake.

Pinčukas leapt up on the mill's sails, and he started cackling and neighing like mad and spinning the mill's wings. Jurgutis was gripped by such a fury that he crawled underneath the mill's turning wings, determined to grab Pinčukas, the author of his misfortune, drag him back to the smithy, set him on the forge, and beat him with the big hammer until the tar ran out of him. How Jurgutis could have done that, he didn't know and he didn't think about it, he just felt with all of the hatred in his heart that such a retribution wouldn't be enough for such a villain, who had destroyed Jurga, Paudruvė's most beautiful girl and the purest of his dreams.

At that moment the frightened Whitehorn ran out into the yard, and that damned Pinčukas started mocking the unhappy father too. Jurgutis had already grabbed Pinčukas by the horn, but then Perkūnas appeared right there under the skies as Girdvainis with his dapple-grays, and with a terrible crash lightning struck the mill. Jurgutis had time to see Pinčukas roll down the wing and sink straight into the earth, but he didn't even feel it when he was incinerated under the mill's wings himself, with a great love and a terrible hatred in his heart.

But the people gathered by the ruins of the mill didn't know this, and the charred Jurgutis couldn't tell anyone about it. They buried him there under the ruins of the mill. Whitehorn's rock they simply left atop the hill, because what could you do, after all, with a rock?

But where Whitehorn's daughter had disappeared to, the cheerful beauty Jurga, Girdvainis' unfortunate betrothed, no one ever found out. She had conquered her broken heart and had run out into the storm to meet her lost suitor. But she just hadn't managed to do it in time. However, she had escaped Pinčukas' claws and Jurgutis' embrace of love, and had flown off like a seagull, with the spring storm raging and the dapple-grays of thunder neighing, to be together with her perished suitor.

So that's how everything turned out that stormy spring night when people's fates clashed, and only memories were left, out of which, over time, a wreath of legends was woven.

XLVIII

Many years have passed since all of these unusual events, these goings-on once upon a time in the land of Paudruvė, but people still talk of the unfortunate miller Whitehorn of Paudruvė, his beautiful daughter Jurga, and the proud suitor Girdvainis with his dapple-gray steeds who outran the wind. But it's not just people who remember.

It sometimes seems to me as though I myself, not Girdvainis, had those dapple-gray steeds and flew with them on wings of wind to make a match with White-horn's daughter, and then lost my nimble steeds and wandered around looking for them through the high-ways and byways.

Or then again, at other times, it seems to me as if it wasn't Whitehorn, but I myself, who had a mill on the shore of Lake Udruvė and a beautiful daughter whom I loved so dearly and grieved over so much that I turned gray, and then turned to stone upon losing her.

Oh, after all, it's all a fairy tale that misleads and de-ludes, like the ill-fated Pinčukas misled and deluded Girdvainis.

But sometimes that Pinčukas appears to me too, and it seems he is none other than myself, who was deceived more than once on account of my gullibility, and turned

Kazys Boruta

the mill's wings in place of the wind. Later, when I realized I was being outrageously used, I got angry, sought revenge, and laughed when I overcame my enemy.

But whether there really was a Pinčukas isn't at all a given. Perhaps he appeared in Whitehorn's unconscious, came alive in Uršulė's imagination, and, by covering himself with Jurgutis' shadow, misled the suitors and persecuted the crazed Girdvainis like a phantom.

In the end it's anyone's guess. But sometimes Pinčukas would drown out Blackpool the smith's apprentice Jurgutis, merging with his shadow and almost turning into one character, so that it was hard for me to distinguish them at first. But coming alive, Jurgutis stubbornly demanded his rights and forced his way into the book's pages, even though he had been a forgotten legend, as frequently happens with true heroes.

Perhaps that was how it all was, or perhaps it wasn't, but the writing got as baffling as a fairy tale, and enslaved the heart with its colorfulness and variety.

After all, a fairy tale is told from the heart, which is why it charms so.

And in the twilight of evening, when I don't know myself what I am longing for, all these friends gather as if they were alive: not just Whitehorn with his daughter, Girdvainis with his dapple-grays, and the unhappy Jurgutis with the shadow of the treacherous Pinčukas, but the wise Hearall too, and poor Uršulė, and the villain Shaddon, and the horse thief Tatergall, and all the others that I raised from the dead in the pages of this book.

Then it's very pleasant for me to be with them all, and to chat as if I had met myself or my best friends, whom I haven't seen in a long time, and with whom I have lived through many bright and bitter hours.

What sort of fairy tale is this, then? Why, it's life itself!

And truthfully, a fairy tale gets tangled with reality like happiness and unhappiness in a person's life, and then how can you distinguish what's a fairy tale, and what's real life?

And I don't distinguish them.

Neither do the people of the land of Paudruvė, those with a pure heart and bright eyes.

Even now, they say, every spring in the land of Paudruvė, when the first spring storms bluster, Lake Udruvė rises and forces its way out of its banks, breaking up the bluff where Whitehorn's mill stood, and then extraordinary and wonderful things begin to happen there.

In the raging lake an unspeakably beautiful fairy, the unfortunate miller's daughter Jurga, rises on up a wave, laughs and cries, calls for her suitor and cannot summon him.

At the same time, on the road some have seen and even met the proud and sullen suitor Girdvainis, who still searches for, but cannot find, his stolen dapple-grays.

The storm starts raging even more, the lake starts rampaging, and on the shores of the lake and in the surrounding hills steeds start neighing, and their neighing drowns out the spring storm's blustering.

An even bigger storm comes up then; the invisible stallions start neighing still louder and the earth mixes with the sky—it's Jurga riding as if on wings of wind to marry Girdvainis. And then it rings around the surrounding pinewoods like the organ at a wedding, and the storm laughs like a happy bride.

At that same time other remarkable things happen in other places.

Across from the crossroads where Cockend's tavern once stood, Tatergall materializes, sewn up in a horse-hide and unable to escape from it. So he thrashes around the crossroads and moans, calling for help. But no one dares to go near and free him from the hide.

And under Bygodit's Bridge, people have seen a shackled witch starting a fire and begging for absolution. But that's no witch, it's just poor Uršulė, who never got absolution for her sins, repenting under that bridge, starting a fire and warming herself, waiting until she has finally suffered enough for her spells and gets absolution.

In Paudruvė's bogs, which are still as swampy and treacherous as they ever were, the lazy devil Pinčukas no longer slumbers and dreams of a wife, but with the spring duckweed the spirit of the tavern keeper Shaddon rises up and complains about what sort of life could this be in the mire. But no one has heard his complaints yet, and the bogs haven't been drained.

Every spring, lightning strikes the bluff where Whitehorn's mill, now just a pile of stones, once stood.

It's the devil Pinčukas, throughout the year squirming up from the depths of the earth, wanting to break out of hell; but he barely sticks a horn out of the ground when Jurgutis runs up and snatches him by that horn, and lightning strikes him between the eyes, driving him back to hell's darkness again.

Somewhat further from the mill's heap of stones stands a rock stuck halfway into the ground that looks very much like a person turned to stone. It's the unfortunate miller Whitehorn, frozen from his heartache and turned to stone for eternity. Before dawn, only on the night when the storm blusters, Whitehorn's rock comes alive and huge stone teardrops roll down his face.

But when the storm rages and the organ pipes of the pines plays, Whitehorn's rock beams and freezes up again. From the depths of the lake, the white-maned dapple-gray steeds rise up, and the suitor and his bride fly with them as if on wings of wind.

The dawn spreads still wider over the sky, the storm dies down, and everything disappears. Only pure Lake Udruvė shimmers between the pines like a fairy tale.

Afterword

Kazys Boruta (1905–1965), the author of *White-horn's Windmill* (*Baltaragio malūnas* in the original), was fated to live under an evil star; large stretches of his life were spent either in exile or in prison, beginning as a ten-year-old in 1915, when his parents fled Lithuania to escape the encroachments of World War I. Born during the era of Czarist domination over Lithuania, Boruta fared no better during Lithuania's period of independence between the wars, as his leftist leanings brought him arrest, imprisonment, exile, and a ban on his work. However, the Soviet takeover of Lithuania after the Molotov–Ribbentrop Pact quickly proved a disappointment; when the Soviets returned after driving the Germans out of Lithuania, Boruta was arrested yet again and spent three years in prison. He remained under a cloud for quite some time after his release, and his work for the next ten years consisted mostly of translations published under a pseudonym.

Whitehorn's Windmill, most of it written over a six-week period in early 1942 during the German occupa-

273

tion, has become a classic of Lithuanian literature. It has been adapted into a play (1957), a ballet (1979), and a musical film (1975), as well as printed in numerous editions. On one level it appears to fit into the category of juvenile literature, but like all first-rate literature, its appeal is universal. Written in a lyrical style that gives full rein to the oral folktale tradition Lithuania is famous for, it is by turns romantic, farcical, fantastic, and tragic. Taken in a larger context, the free mixing of fairytale elements with reality, along with the sense of powerlessness in the hands of fate that pervades the work, can easily be interpreted as early magic realism or colonial angst.

The sense of spirituality that permeates the work reflects Lithuania's pagan roots, roots that were overlaid with an occasionally over-zealous Catholicism not so very long ago. That pagan imagery is deeply embedded: it is completely fitting within this cosmology that Whitehorn should turn into a rock; that horses speak; that a devil is Whitehorn's nearest neighbor; and that Anupras Hearall, the prototypical wise old man, or in Lithuanian pagan cosmology, the *raganius*, should own a magic tobacco horn and understand the language of animals. Even Perkūnas, Lithuanian's ancient pagan god of thunder, plays a part. At one point, Anupras expresses a particular oneness with the universe: "I'm old, and whatever I look at, everything catches my eye, everything gladdens my heart, even that rock by the side of the road." Whitehorn, when warned by his neighbor Blackpool that he should put up a lightning rod, protests that it's not needed. Boruta explains: "… lightning was no enemy to him, but one of his own, like all of nature."

The concept of the devil as a prankster who can nevertheless sometimes be out-witted also hearkens back to these pagan beliefs. The name Pinčukas is itself an ancient pagan name for a devil.

Boruta, crafting his tale from the fabric of folktales that every Lithuanian is familiar with, poured his poetic talents into crafting a story that gives us a true taste of the Lithuanian oral tradition, which thrived through its centuries of development as more a spoken than a written language. Although the first Lithuanian grammar was published in 1653, the language wasn't standardized and codified until the end of the nineteenth century, as rising nationalism brought it to the fore. Buttressed by abundant details of folk culture—from Uršulė's spells to the rituals of courtship to the use of juniper as protection against devils—aspects such as the narrator's commentaries on the action and characters that are interjected throughout the text bring this storytelling tradition to the fore. "That Uršulė wasn't such a bad-hearted little woman, in spite of everything," Boruta says, and instantly the storyteller himself comes into view.

In Boruta's novel the movement is away from 20th-century urbanization with its accompanying sense of a loss of values and community and back to a rural community setting in which the parish priest—or perhaps the devil?—is the ultimate authority. Government, that bugbear of Boruta's existence, is banished here, playing a strangely distant role; other than the ineffective police platoon summoned by Shaddon's complaints, there is no mention of it. Even its historical setting is vague—Shaddon's regrets about the passing of serfdom and

Blackpool's recollection of the gun hidden away since the time of the uprising (presumably the 1863 Polish–Lithuanian uprising against Russian rule) provide the only clues to a time frame. The archeologist Marija Gimbutas and the linguist and semiotician Algirdas Greimas both noted this sense of timelessness in their reviews of the work, an aspect which lends the book an epic quality that is furthered by the sense of its resolution being determined more by fate than by the actions of individuals.

The first edition, printed in 1945 in Kaunas, was removed from book store shelves when Boruta was arrested, and republished only in 1952 in Chicago. This translation is based on Boruta's revised version published in 1962 in Soviet-occupied Lithuania. The newer version differs from the earlier mostly by the introduction of two entirely new characters, Jurgutis and the blacksmith Blackpool. Boruta had been heavily criticized for the book's failures to meet the requirements of Soviet realism. Some of the changes could be interpreted as concessions to these requirements: for example, in the earlier version Girdvainis commits suicide, an act heavily frowned upon by the Soviet regime, and in the newer version Blackpool and Jurgutis provide possible alternate explanations for some of the inexplicable events. Jurgutis, however, proved particularly troublesome to Boruta, who complained in his letters and journals about his "creeping into the work." This mostly frightened, ineffectual half-wit, whom Boruta describes in the last chapter as a true hero, can be interpreted as a personification of Homi Bhabha's "cultural bomb," the now well-established effect of colonization, in which the colonized people begin doubting their own history, culture, achievements, and capabilities. It is the clash between fairytale and reality, between Boruta's lyric soaring and sometimes riotous humor, between Boruta's idealism and the crushing sense of an unavoidable fate that was so much a part of Lithuania's history in the twentieth century, that makes for such a uniquely Lithuanian story.

A note on the translation

The reader will forgive me, for in the end I was so charmed by the hidden (or not so hidden) meanings of the names Boruta uses that I found myself unable to resist translating them, despite the convention which bids us preserve at least that nuance from another culture. *Baltaragis* is translated as the calque Whitehorn; Uršulė's last name *Purvinaitė*, whose stem is based on the verb *purvinti*, meaning "to dirty, to muddy," became Muddy. The name of the village where Jurgis Girdvainis lives, *Daugnoriai*, translates as "wants a lot of," thus Manywish, while his deaf matchmaker's name *Visgirda* means "hears everything" or "hears all the time," Hear-all in translation. The blacksmith's last name, *Juodvalkis*, could be translated either as "black pool" or as "black draft"; Blackpool he is. The name of the inn *Gaidžgalės* is from the words for "rooster, cock" and "end," and so it became Cockend. The innkeeper Shaddon's name *Šešelga* derives from the word for "shade" or "shadow." Best of all, *Rauplys* the horse thief is the name of a potato gall. Girdvainis's name seems to contain a reference to *girti*, "to praise," and *vainikas*, "wreath," as Bobbin may contain a reference to *boba*, "an old woman," but both of these I let be. Perhaps fortunately, the remaining names are really just names, or else their origins are now so obscure as to be lost, and so I must ask them to do the work of the rest.

Whitehorn's Windmill has been translated into German, Czech, Latvian, Estonian, Russian, Icelandic, and Polish. This is its first English translation.

I have many people to thank for their help, inspiration, and moral support in translating this work, including Prof. Violeta Kelertas, Prof. Anne Winters and her translation workshop, Dalia Cidžikaitė, Giedrius Subačius, Christine Frey, Aida Novickas, and Egidijus Lisauskas. Most of all I would like to dedicate the translation of this work to Mantas Lisauskas (1977–2002), the gentle and loving soul whose memory comforts and delights me to this day.

Elizabeth Novickas
Beverly Shores, Indiana
July, 2009